THIRST

THIRST

First published January 2016 by JD Shaw Publ.
PO Box 7226 Tathra
NSW 2550
Australia.
sales@jdshaw.com.au
www.jdshaw.com.au

National Library of Australia
Cataloguing in-publication data:

Shaw, J.D.
THIRST

ISBN 978-0-646-94716-7

Photos & graphics – Exocarpus

Printed and supplied by LULU
Order - http://www.lulu.com/shop/

In memory of my father, Dr David D Shaw, a rather short giant who taught me to delve under rocks and bark to find the small wonders of the world, and to take a big swing at those mean-hearted souls who would wilfully destroy them.

He who knows he has enough is rich

– Lao Tzu

Harry

The great orb of the sun had barely crested the eastern horizon, yet already syrupy veils of rising heat had begun to warp the dead woodlands and scrub of the plain.

Harry Sinclair lay sprawled in the crook of a long, looping bend of a river that snaked back and forth across the pan of a shallow valley. In the shifting haze his outstretched body might have easily been mistaken for a carcass in that meagre sandstone country. However, an occasional small movement betrayed a hint of remaining life. Soft, infrequent grunts of exertion came and, at long intervals, thin sprays of sand erupted beside him, creating plumes of dust that rolled out with the searing breeze across the dry gravel and through the clutter of dead trees beyond the riverbank.

Harry had come to the dry riverbed well before dawn in order to beat the rising fire of the sun. But his weakness had slowed him and now, as the sun drew higher, the building heat made physical effort near impossible for the old man. Huffing and snorting, Harry dug into the burning sand with slow, conservative movements, first with a flattened piece of tree root and then, flinging the root aside, he had scooped deeper with his bare hands as the sand became cooler. Digging to the extent of his reach, his eyes screwed tight against the dust, Harry delved for a creeping kiss of dampness. But at the depth of more than an arm's length he still felt nothing—no precious moisture welled up to touch his fingertips.

Grimacing, his face only a centimetre from the burning gravel, he scooped up a final handful. Just one more, he thought, just in case. But, inspecting the grains closely, he watched them cascade through his long dirty fingers in a thin, dry stream.

'Fuck!' he mumbled to himself in despair.

He had guessed there would be nothing for him here, yet he had been driven to dig anyway by the raw nagging of his thirst. The frustration at another in a long litany of failures rose like angry hornets in his ears and he moaned softly, but the sound came out only as a thin, despairing whine.

The sun's rising heat bore down on him, scalding his back where his threadbare cotton shirt touched his skin. His long, thin, grey hair gave no protection as the sun beat down on his head and the heat, searing his lungs, caused his breath to run in short, skittering gasps. He shook his head to clear it, but his thoughts continued to flutter incessantly, taking flight like a startled flock of pigeons, only to wheel and circle and settle once again on the rasp of his burning throat.

Coughing weakly, Harry fought back the sudden urge to shout, to curse aloud and shatter the aching, querulous silence. He crushed the urge to scratch and kick at the dust and red dirt, and curse the yellow orb of the sun. His frustration threatened to swamp him. His left cheek had been scalded by the touch of the scorching sand. Gritting his teeth, he bent his mind to the pain and forced the rising anger away.

The disappointment of another failure in his search for water made him slump for a moment as his fit of anger dissipated and he cursed to himself before rolling to sit up. Gulping air like a beached fish, Harry rubbed his hands on his thighs, extracting a cloud of red dust from the faded grey fabric. A patch sewn on the knee of his pants had developed its own frayed hole and he dug at it with his finger for a moment. Thoughtfully he examined the small red moons of dirt beneath his broken fingernails and the raw skin peeling back in painful cracks from the nail edges. He raised his palm up towards the sky slowly in a useless attempt to ward off the fierce sting of the morning sun.

Squinting across the dry riverbed, he began to scan the trees that lined the riverbanks. One dead red gum then the next, then the next, he searched each ancient leafless tree as they continued in two haphazard rows, following the course of the river off through the flat country to the north. Each tortured tree trunk was split with deep grey fissures, the thick bark having been levered back in long vertical gashes by decades of relentless drought.

The river red gums, like most life on the encroaching fringe of the desert, had now lost the game of survival. The ancient gums relied on the floods that had come to the plains maybe once a decade. Through watercourses and river outflows, travelling hundreds of kilometres from the north, the creeping floodwaters had once slowly inundated the flood plains, filling long-empty drainage lines, lakebeds and billabongs, giving life to these ancient sentinels and their fallen seeds. But now, the unrelenting dry of the Great Drought had lasted far beyond the normal cycle and the twisted giants had slowly, year by year, been brought to their knotted knees–they had borne witness as life slowly spluttered to a standstill on the plains until even they, the longest lived of all, had succumbed.

Harry meticulously searched the skeletal branches for signs of movement. Through his long wispy fringe, his pale, grey eyes sought for something moving–something like him–searching for a source of hidden moisture. A rare animal or bird out here, moving in the early morning, would likely be in dire need of water or, as Harry hoped, would have already found a sign of it. But finding the horizon, his eyes had caught no movement. Among the rippling mirages that hovered above the sand, only Harry was desperate enough to be out there.

His need for a sign of other life rose up and clawed at him. He had seen no hint of wildlife in at least a month. He lifted his sleeve to wipe his face but the threadbare cotton shirt felt like sandpaper against his sunburnt skin. Sighing sullenly, he stood, his knees cracking painfully. Movement, in the heat, made his head chime and he teetered unsteadily. Cursing, he picked up his battered hat and the two empty plastic water drums lying in the sand

and began to retrace his footsteps across the riverbed. Scrambling up the powdery red-dirt bank between the twisted roots, he gained the old cattle track that led back into the scrub.

Wheezing, he quickened his pace through the spindly lignum thicket that dominated beyond the band of river red gums. As he pushed his way along the track, the hollow lignum branches exploded at his touch, the splinters peppering his face and his exposed forearms. The whip crack of breaking branches only served to infuriate him once again and he began furiously batting the branches from his path with the empty water containers.

Winded from the short walk up from the river he stopped to rest for a moment and a dark cicada carapace nestled in a clump of rank grass at his feet snared his gaze as it glistened in the sunlight. His breath stopped at the surprising find and he bent slowly to examine the insect casing, sucking his teeth in curiosity. The shiny black casing looked unusually fresh, almost wet, and a fresh thing, out here, might indicate some life underground and, with it, perhaps the tiniest amount of water. And hope sprang up fresh at the thought of it.

Excited, he picked up a twig and poked gently at the insect casing. But at his first, tentative touch it crumbled and fell in small delicate fragments to the dirt. He snorted, croaking with the renewed disappointment. With a sigh, he stood and, carrying the empty water drums, he resumed following his outgoing footprints back to the dray and the soon-to-be-disappointed camel.

A coarse gurgling greeted him as he approached the dray through the leafless ghost gums and the tangle of lignum. The camel, still harnessed to the dray, smelt the lack of water on Harry and the huge beast grumbled and shifted its shaggy bulk between the shafts as Harry, staggering the final few metres, threw the empty water drums behind the dray's rough wooden seat.

'Fuck off ... I know,' Harry spoke out loud to the huge, shaggy animal.

Harry kicked one of the dray's bald rubber tyres and walked to the rear of the wooden tray to check the ties of the threadbare tarpaulin that covered his cooking and sleeping gear and his meagre store of canned food. Nonplussed, the camel let out a rumbling belch and turned its big mangy head away, shunning him in disgust. Satisfied his gear was undisturbed, Harry snorted with derision in the camel's direction and, with a huge effort, climbed up onto the warped wooden seat and picked up the reins.

'Hup, hup,' he called softly and the camel, struggling against the weight, began to slowly move out, back towards the broken road hidden by the scrub a kilometre away. The dray creaked and squealed in protest as the camel fought to gain momentum over the soft, uneven ground cluttered with a tangle of fallen branches.

* * *

Harry's cursing and the creaking of the small four-wheeled dray slowly died, and the river and valley sank into silence.

Long ago, a few minutes would have elapsed before the quiet, peeping calls of small Gouldian finches and scrub wrens would have begun amongst the bent roots on the riverbank, as the tiny birds began foraging again after the human had disappeared. The loud flutter of spinifex pigeons might have shattered the stillness or huge wheeling flocks of wild budgerigars, bright in yellows and greens, might have circled low across the sand between the lines of river red gums. And, as peace settled on the river, a mob of grey kangaroos or a darker, solitary euro might have quietly come in to drink at one of the small waterholes or billabongs that had dotted the river's meandering course.

Once wedge-tailed eagles, brown falcons and whistling kites had circled in vast intersecting arcs above the plain, searching out the dead and dying in the woodlands and saltbush scrub. But now, long into The Failing, the Great Drought rolled on, the animals of the plain had almost entirely disappeared and the soaring scavengers were now rarely seen against the limitless blue of the sky.

Now, under the glowering eye of the sun, the stillness and silence elongated after Harry's departure. The quiet trickled on, slowly building, immersing the dead woodlands of the valley sometimes for weeks at a time, only broken by the occasional crack of a falling limb from a long mummified tree.

* * *

Harry had come across the dray and the emaciated camel a year earlier in the yard of an abandoned farmhouse two hundred kilometres north of the river. After abandoning his third broken-down car since leaving the coast, he had stumbled on the jerry-rigged dray, built using the wooden tray from a utility and two car axles and their springs and wheels, in a half-collapsed corrugated-iron farm shed. The camel had been simply hanging around in the yard of the deserted farm and had wandered over in curiosity as Harry clattered and banged through the shed scrounging for things of use.

He had found a leather harness cast across the dray's shafts, obviously made to suit the dimensions of the large, one-humped beast that loitered in the dusty yard. Harry peered out through the shed door, sizing up the silhouette of the tall rangy animal. Perhaps, Harry thought to himself, the camel had hung around, bound by the smell of stale water in the half empty drum he had found in the back of the dray.

Later he had found the mummified body of a man lying half covered in drifts of powdery dirt behind the shed. One arm stood elbow up through the dust, a flagstaff for the corpse's tattered shirt. He presumed the body was that of the original owner of the camel and dray. Curious, he had stood at a distance and stared for a long while at the dried skin stretched to breaking point across the bones of the half-buried corpse. The body might only have been there for a month but, in that unrelenting heat, it wouldn't have taken long to shrink and mummify.

Squatting over the body for a few moments, he had tried unsuccessfully to fathom the cause of death—there were no signs of a struggle, bindings or wounds of any kind, not that he could see anyway. And, after a cursory inspection of the corpse's cracked and useless boots, he left it where it lay. He guessed the man had probably died of a sickness or dehydration and the thought made him suspicious of the water drum he had found in the back of the dray.

Wary at first of the big foul-smelling beast but encouraged by the animal's strange docility as he started to handle him, it had taken only a few days for him to work out the mechanics of harnessing the camel and directing its movements by the rein tied to the peg through its large crusted nostril.

He had seen pictures and remembered movies from his childhood about these feral, desert-dwelling beasts. And he had seen them sometimes in his youth travelling the desert. They had been brought here to transport goods two centuries before but, eventually, replaced by train and automobile, they had gone wild to become part of the landscape of the arid country. In groups of five or six, loping across the low ranges, they had bred and flourished, free of the predators and diseases of their original home in the arid regions of Asia and India. But it was rare to see even these hardy animals out here now. The wild camels had moved east like everything else, corralled into an ever-shrinking band of liveable country running up to the mountain divide along the eastern coast.

These vague memories helped Harry work out how he should handle the animal, and the rest he construed through tentative trial and error over a few days, a year or more ago. In the first weeks, perched up on the dray's hard wooden seat, he had returned to wandering aimlessly along the broken roads and tracks of the plains, allowing the camel its head, to plod the now deserted highways of the inland. Harry was lighter, happier for the company of the drooling beast. The camel's farting and gurgling had broken the long slow silences into more digestible intervals—its presence poking a small hole in the elongated loneliness.

Back then he had still felt some exhilaration in that threadbare existence. Wandering and scavenging the country, he had revelled in the hardship—well, sometimes at least. An old fraying man, he played Lawrence, tested against the heat and hell of the vast, shifting desert. He had felt a strange rejuvenation in the utter desperation of scrounging dirty water from the corners of rusting water tanks and from the copper pipes torn from the walls of abandoned homesteads and, occasionally, from the rare soaks that still held moisture deep below the dry billabongs and river-beds. Unlike the past few months, life back then hadn't seemed to hang by such a fragile thread.

Over the past months the precarious balance had tipped. Wandering the fringes of the desert, life had become a long whittled nightmare of unending thirst between the rare finds of water. Jerking across the hills and undulations, rocked by the slow movements of the camel and the dray, in this half-hypnotized state, the admission was slow in coming. But finally he could not ignore it—even his frugal existence out here was now untenable in that collapsing country.

Even with this developing realisation Harry kept moving south, dodging the turn eastwards–avoiding a return across the mountains to the lands of the coast. Another few weeks passed, each day the twisted white and grey trunks of the trees that lined the road seemed to crowd in closer but he could not yet turn his mind to the return to the coast.

* * *

Coughing, Harry winced with the rasp of the thirst in his throat. The bitter cold of the desert night rose up from the soft sand beneath his wadding mattress and burrowed deep into his bones, fuelling the small aches that plagued the joints of his body.

Shivering he pulled the blankets up and under his chin and, with his eyes still closed, his mind saw his breath rising in small volcanic plumes into the dry, frigid air and saw those plumes swallowed by the bulging spray of stars screwing slowly overhead.

There was silence for a moment. Then he heard the familiar shuffle of a large padded hoof off to his right on the low red dune. Among the half-buried trees, the camel shifted its weight from one large, soft foot to the other and huffed softly. The thin, metallic tinkle of the camel-bell sounded once, the tinny note cutting the freezing air before the beast's slow syrupy breath sounded again. The camel's breathing always reassured Harry when he woke in the cold of the desert night.

He fought back an urge to check the condensation trap that he had set out among the spinifex clumps in the swale of the dune. The contraption was next to useless out here, in the bone-dry air–it would take at least until the dawn, still hours away, to collect a few drops of moisture in the tin he had positioned in a shallow hole beneath the small plastic sheet.

Eyes still closed, Harry covered his head with the blankets and, curling into a tight ball, forced himself to breathe slowly through his nose, avoiding the rasp of thirst in his throat, and he slipped gradually back into a shallow, troubled sleep.

* * *

In his dream, Harry's body soared amongst the brooding anvil-shaped cloudbanks which first formed out to sea, then forged in, crossing the long, white, slivered beaches of the coast. Passing high over the vast shining coastal cities, crammed tight against the rubble break-walls that held off the rising sea, for all their size and ominous rumblings, the thunderheads brought little more than sniffs of moisture to the thirsty coast.

Far below Harry saw the once vast coastal rivers, flowing eastward, slowed to intermittent trickles, their broad sand-choked riverbeds meandering fitfully through the patchwork quilt of failing farms and towns, to eventually empty, through mazes of weed-strewn sand bars to the warming sea.

Floating, he followed the cloudbanks inland, away from the overcrowded cities. The land beneath him rose gradually over a hundred kilometres to join the mountains of the Great Dividing Range. Pitched up like one vast arching granite wave, the range followed the coast north to south for a thousand kilometres, a final snare for the tepid fury of the storms.

Having jilted the lowlands, the thunderheads collided with the range's flanks and, corralled by the mountains, squeezed like damp sponges, they coughed up fitful flurries of rain against the forests and fields of the lower ranges.

The foothills of the Divide bore the last hope on that part of the coast. Men and women huddled on the rising lands, working for the Producer Conglomerates, meticulously tending long rows of growing houses made of UV-resistant plastic that produced the crops that fed the heaving, hungry cities.

Above these long rows of greenhouses, flying farther west, Harry's dream took him to the granite talons of the mountains. Rising and cresting, these peaks shredded what was left of the storms, leaving only frayed ribbons of cloud to cross the range to touch the lands of the west.

Forsaking the tattered remnants of the storms, Harry's dream took him beyond the boulder-strewn peaks to the vast western plains. Kilometre after kilometre he crossed the sun-warped chessboard of farms and dying woodlands–the land all broken and defunct–until his journey brought him to touch the ravenous edge of the continent's desert interior.

No rain now fell here. Like a cruel child relentlessly wielding a magnifying glass across the once-productive farming country, the sun's orb had roasted the vegetation, exposing the flesh of shifting red sand. Each successive summer had grown longer and hotter, the respite of cooler winters having slowly vanished. Each year drew more super-heated air in from the west–the scorching winds whipping up the exposed sand and red dirt into gigantic annual dust storms that pushed back eastward, covering the mountains and the coast in a choking red blanket.

Few people now remained in this dying land. Family by family, over long, dry decades, they had finally broken and fallen under the weight of the great drought. Gathering the pitiful remnants of their lives, most had fled, leaving the crumbling weatherboard homesteads and deserted towns to the drought, migrating eastwards to the flimsy salvation of the coast.

Hanging under the cloudless sky, Harry saw a country now nearly deserted. And, with a strange mixture of dread and excitement, Harry looked farther west and saw the sun-blasted hell of the continent's centre. A burning hell had grown in the west and spawned a place of relentless, pulverizing heat. Here the daytime temperature regularly broached sixty degrees, no skerrick of life remained, fallen trees were mummified to fragile shells of tortured wood or left as only powdery outlines on the burning sand. Each year this enormous kiln spread outward toward the mountains and the coast, driving even the hardiest desert creatures before it. Liveable land disappeared year on year, the sun devouring it like a match set to parchment.

Harry's mind shied as he drew closer to the flame and fear filled him. In his sleep he exhaled softly, the breath flowing slowly from his lungs as though it were the last. He lay still in the thin blankets. No shiver or movement escaped him. No groan or cry came. Only the sound of the camel's slow, huffing breath filled the swale of the dune where he camped.

* * *

A bony red kangaroo hopped lethargically away from the road as the dray appeared over a rise. The animal barely managed to reach the fringe of trees before it came to a staggering halt and then slowly stood erect to watch Harry and the camel pass. Harry thought fleetingly about running the exhausted animal down for meat, but he didn't have the strength in him for even a short chase, even when the animal was already so near death. The kangaroo and Harry watched each other for a moment longer then, losing interest, forgot each other as the dray passed on.

The old highway had wound all that day through raw, rolling country of burnt-orange sandstone that broke up through the thin red soil in small fractured outcrops. The country heaved in long undulations that were carved by a chaotic web of eroded creeks and gullies. Dry now, only the wind-blown sand trickled from the gullies where they were cut by the highway, forming deep red fans that made difficult going for the camel.

By the road, occasional clumps of dead, twisted, multi-stemmed mallee trees perched between the rock outcrops, the thin, long-dead trunks of each tree, reaching up from the buried root ball like thin crippled fingers. The broken gullies and depressions were laid with a mosaic of wind-tattered, sharp spinifex grass. Low mounds of tiny brown stones, revealed and polished to a dark lustre by the prevailing westerly winds, frequently lay along the road's path.

To break the monotony, Harry climbed down once to inspect these stones and found in the pile, ancient flake stones and tiny beautiful cutting tools, crafted by the Aboriginal peoples who had lived here over the millennia. He picked up a small, dark, flake stone and marvelled for a long while at the ingenuity of the delicate cutting tool with its still sharp well-formed edge and the ancient hands that had crafted it so perfectly. Tossing the rock down among the others he brushed off his hands and slowly climbed back up to the dray's seat and urged the beast again into plodding motion.

To the east of the dray, as the day meandered on, a low range of deeply folded hills had sprung up from the low undulating country. Harry had watched the humped spine as the road meandered closer, until the range ran parallel only two or three kilometres away and he could discern the dark vertical shadows of gorges carved into the range's flanks.

Through the anesthetising heat of the afternoon, Harry nodded under the shade of his battered, wide-brimmed hat. The camel wandered onward with little urging. The animal too seemed to doze as it placed one large padded foot slowly before the other. Occasionally the tyres of the dray dug into wallows of deep red bull-dust in the road, causing the dray to slew sideways. Woken by the sudden break in the rhythm, Harry would push himself upright in the seat before beginning another slow nodding slump.

The sun was low on the horizon when Harry woke again with a start. The camel had stopped suddenly and stood shuffling from foot to foot in the centre of the road. In the stifling heat, only the camel's soft huffing and the creaking of the leather harness broke the stillness. Befuddled by the heat, Harry looked around, but there was no movement between the chaotic graveyard of grey mallee trunks and larger gums. Rubbing his forehead, he turned to look up the road and his heart skipped a beat.

Half way up the next rise, almost hidden in the shimmering heat haze, stood a white utility parked haphazardly half off the road in the spinifex.

His head throbbed with the shock and potential of the discovery. It was rare and sometimes dangerous to meet a vehicle in this country and he avoided contact with others when he could. He squirmed in his seat, unsure whether to continue or turn back. He removed his hat and scratched his head through his thinning grey hair, feeling lumps of grit against his scalp.

'Fuck it.' Biting his lip nervously, he rose up in the seat. 'I'm no damn good at this shit,' Harry whispered to himself. 'No good at decisions in this fucking heat.'

The camel belched nervously and backed up in the shafts, pushing the dray sideways against the sandy mound of the road edge.

'Easy, eh. Easy,' Harry soothed the camel in a whisper and looked off into the bush towards the low spine of hills. Sitting perfectly still, the reins hanging limp in his hand, he tried to penetrate the veil of heat that clogged the orange and grey of the dead wooded country.

Then, through the shimmering veil he caught a flicker of movement. Three figures danced in and out of focus between the trees as they wandered slantwise from the direction of the range towards the vehicle parked on the road. They were talking in low voices in an unknown language. And then Harry heard a sound that had been missing for many months. One of the figures laughed softly.

Both Harry and the camel remained frozen as the figures closed on the utility. The three men staggered a little and, as they became clearer, Harry saw they each carried a large green jerry can.

Harry caught sight of their dark skin and realised, with some relief, they were Aboriginal. He had encountered these lean, angular people before–seen them sometimes in the distance or passing him on the road in busted-up vehicles. Occasionally they raised a finger at him in silent greeting as they passed, but mostly they failed to acknowledge him, seemingly totally uninterested in why he was wandering out here in the broken land, or where he was going–as though his business was as alien to them as theirs was to him.

As the three men walked clear of the spinifex and approached the utility they stopped abruptly. As one, they turned to stare in Harry's direction and Harry tensed instinctively. The dark figures danced, dissected and reformed in the rising heat, as they stood for perhaps thirty seconds watching the dray. Then, as though bored by his lack of movement, they turned away and, after lifting the heavy jerry cans into the back, they clambered one after the other into the cab.

Harry saw the black cloud explode from the exhaust pipe before he heard the roar as the engine started and the utility slid sideways onto the road through the deep red dust. Another large belch of exhaust erupted as the vehicle did a three-point turn in the dirt and accelerated away from him up a short rise and then disappeared, leaving a rising red cloud in its wake. The noise of the engine slowly died and the country settled again into silence as the searing breeze carried the smell of cooking oil from the vehicle's exhaust to Harry's nostrils.

The camel bellowed, shifting in the shafts but Harry hardly noticed as he eagerly coaxed the camel into motion and the dray lurched toward the spot where the men had been parked.

* * *

Harry's head was ringing again and his legs were jelly with the exertion of the walk from the road. He had led the camel back and forth through the confusion of eroded gullies and spinifex, retracing the tracks of the Aboriginal men. An hour later, reeling with fatigue, he had reached the scree slopes at the foot of the low range, before he stopped, defeated by the increasingly steep slope and the unstable ground. Breathing in short rasping gasps, he slapped the camel's hairy shoulder to reassure the grumbling beast. Ignoring the cloud of dust rising from its hide, he gazed up at the broken cliffs that towered above them.

The country rose in low, broken rock terraces, one after another, to the line of crumbling cliffs. The sinking sun painted a deep red tint across the fractured sandstone rock. Raw and eroded, the cliffs seemed to have been forced violently up and out through the desert crust, leaving scars of scree and rubble at their foot. Giant slabs, some the size of small cars, littered the lower slope among the fringe of dead trees. Just to Harry's left the cliff face was deeply riven by a narrow gorge, eaten out of the sandstone cliffs by the intermittent rains through the millennia. Near where the dray stood, a narrow, dry creek line wandered out in a series of low falls from the mouth of the gorge, to quickly disappear into nothing among the spinifex and twisted eucalypts beyond the scree.

He stood, trying to think—considering his options slowly in the stupefying heat. It was like playing chess in an oven. The heat from the sun, perched only a few inches above the western horizon, still beat relentlessly on his back but it was getting late. The sun would be gone in half an hour or so and it would get cold quickly as darkness fell. It would be dangerous, too, to be climbing back down through the gorge before the moon rose in a few hours.

He chewed his lip thoughtfully and tasted the iron of his own blood from the splits and cracks. His breath caught as it passed his burning throat bringing a harsh cough, and the stabbing pain decided it for him. Harry went to the dray and hurriedly pulled the two empty water drums free and began staggering as rapidly as he could up through the rocky terraces, zigzagging toward the dark maw of the gorge. Several times his feet slipped from under him and he nearly fell, sending small landslides of rock cascading and bouncing around the feet of the camel, bringing a disgruntled rumble from the beast. Each time he fell he spat and cursed softly as he regained his feet to continue the climb.

Covered in dust, his fingers bleeding, Harry scrambled the last few metres on hands and knees, up to the low terrace that formed the bottom lip of the gorge. Kneeling for a moment, he paused to calm his thumping heart and the pounding in his temples. The flat slab of rock where he knelt was stained black in parts with the ancient flows of water. Beyond the long dry waterfall, the narrow crack of the gorge split the cliffs. Up close, the escarpment held clumps of rank, grey grass and an occasional ancient cycad perched in fissures and on the narrow ledges that marked the rock face. The prehistoric plants' dark, fern-like leaves almost looked alive in the shadows as Harry scrambled to his feet.

After the relentless sun burning his lips, the darkness within the gorge seemed inviting. With the two drums in hand, he hurriedly began the climb over the moraine of broken boulders back into the shadows. The air grew cooler as he scrambled deeper but it remained dry against his face. With the lack of humidity his hopes faltered and his heart sank, his mind tumbling eagerly to doubt and defeat. Echoes of his grunts and cursing rang out around him as he quickened his pace against the failing light.

Ten minutes later Harry stood and scratched his head, his route blocked by a two metre high, unbroken step of rock that stretched from one side of the narrow gorge to the other. In the gloom, faced with another hurdle, he allowed a flurry of sharp curses to escape and winced as they echoed around him.

'Shit.'

Stymied for a moment, he turned back to the mouth of the gorge below, and back again to the rock-face blocking his path. He calculated he had at most only another fifteen or twenty minutes of daylight left, but the idea of returning to the dray empty handed to face another thirsty night and the disgruntled gaze of the camel, spurred him on.

Tossing the two water drums over the rock ledge, he leapt up and grabbed the lip above his head and, with a huge effort, dragged himself upward. Scrambling to find holds with the toes of his boots, he managed to squirm his torso above the ledge and, with his strength almost gone, swung his legs over and spread his arms to stop himself falling back to the ledge below.

For a moment he lay panting, face down next to the water drums, before he raised his head. Six feet away in the gloom, a solid wall ran upwards to daylight far above. He had reached the abrupt end of the gorge and, as he stared up at the sheer rock face, his disappointment threatened to overwhelm him.

A thin warbling began in the back of his throat. In desperation his eyes searched deeper into the darkness and there, perched in a crack between two boulders, at the base of the cliff, he saw the twisted silver stem of a tiny, knotted fig tree. Staring at the pale bundle of roots and delicate intertwining branches, his gaze found a smattering of small, and, to his amazement, dark green leaves, and his heart soared. And then he caught the rich smell of the damp and rot that fed the tiny tree and the scent made him instantly salivate. In that rich banquet came an explosion of hope and, with it, a shuddering sigh escaped his lips.

He climbed to his feet and took two halting steps across the flat shelf of rock. And there, at the base of the sheer wall, the fig dipped its roots into a shallow pool, nestled tight in the corner of the shelf. Transfixed for long moment, he stared at the pool and licked his cracked lips. At that moment the tiny pool seemed like an ocean. A vision of fragile beauty, the tiny fig held all the glory of the giant trees of the coast. A simple tranquillity, long missed by Harry, this tiny, fragile oasis brought a lump to his thirsty throat.

He looked back nervously toward the mouth of the gorge, as though he were about to thieve some precious thing. Catching no movement in the dark jumble of rocks below, he turned, hurried over to the shallow pool and knelt at its edge. Pushing his face close to the dark water, he sniffed and smelt the moist rust of iron and dirt. The water was dark and the bottom of the shallow pool was covered with fallen fig leaves, but the water smelled fresh enough. He touched his lips gently to the water and, drinking like an animal, drew it in in long, slow gulps, tasting the earth and rock and the chlorophyll tang of the leaves. The sweet taste flowed through him, the moisture spreading through his stomach and, for a moment, his body hummed with the luxury of it.

After a few mouthfuls he pushed his entire face below the water. He had not felt such wetness for many, many, months. His face immersed, he savoured the water soaking into his parched skin. Like an electrical charge, it tingled in his hollowed, dehydrated pores. It felt as though, like a frog's, his skin itself could draw in the moisture of the pool. Eventually, running out of air, he pulled his face free and snorted, spraying water against the cliff face. Dipping his hands once again, he ran his damp fingers through his knotted hair and over his dirty face.

Slumping back against the cool rock of the tiny amphitheatre, his head under the branches of the fig, he closed his eyes and silently soaked up the glorious humidity resonating from the pool until the growing shadows in the gorge brought him back.

Slowly he filled one of the water drums, scooping the water with a cut-down plastic bottle he had pocketed for that purpose, and then, with great reluctance, he turned his back on the pool, clambered down that high fall and headed back down to the mouth of the gorge and the dray, leaving the other container to be filled on his return the following morning, when he would have more time to savour that small glorious place.

Dragging the heavy container back down through the jumble of rocks and boulders he enjoyed the thought of the camel's excited belching at the scent of the full water drum. Harry laughed softly as he dragged the container out onto the final lip, into the blast of the dying heat of the dusk and saw, far below, the dray silhouetted among the scrub and spinifex.

* * *

The camel stood waiting in the shafts as Harry walked backwards from where they had left the road, masking the tracks of the dray with a dead branch. He didn't know why he hid the evidence pointing to the gorge but, he thought, perhaps the Aboriginal men had left their tracks for him but were expecting him to close the gate after him so to speak—he did not really know, but it seemed like the right thing to do.

He felt bloated by three days of water. His dreams of trickling floods had stopped abruptly. His nights were blank with restful, saturated sleep. He had even, rather guiltily, washed his shirt, which he now noticed was already covered again with a thin layer of red dust after the walk back to the road.

After camping beneath the mouth of the gorge, even the camel was in a slightly less crabby mood. It stood harnessed to the dray, its head held high, gazing off along the road, seemingly eager to be moving again.

That tiny pool, nestled in the hidden corner of the range, had brought some clarity through the muddling heat that had left Harry stupefied over the past few months. As his mind had cleared with the intake of water, he had come to realise his aimless wandering must now come to an end. He must, he thought, at least head east again, moving out of the dying fringes of the spreading desert. There was no hope here now, in the isolation and quiet loneliness, and certainly no freedom in a wandering, thirsty death. The desert, crawling farther from the west each year, driving life before it, would catch him if he stayed, he knew it. His drifting had brought him as close to extinction as he cared to go.

Even the fucking trees have given up the ghost, he thought, even they can't take it.

The cattle and wheat farmers and townsfolk had realised this thirty or forty years ago, the very last of them had gone two decades earlier, as the bores and soaks and dams had finally, permanently failed. He smiled then at his own presumption. He had sought solace among the endless dry when others, who had existed out here for generations, had picked up and fled to the overcrowded, strife-torn coast.

He shook his head as he covered the two full water drums with the tarpaulin. The camel bellowed and burped irritably as Harry procrastinated, fussing around the dray for a few moments longer, kicking the grass-filled rubber tyres and testing ties.

He would, he thought, head back to where life was at least tenable. He would follow the broken roads back to the shrinking ribbon of arable land, clinging to the slopes of the Dividing Range. Heading south and east, he would seek the thin strip between the growing desert of the west and the growing chaos of the cities. He might, he thought, find work on a hydroponics farm or feedlot to tide him over. He had never travelled the southern coast but he had heard it had not been quite as badly affected by climate disruption as the country of the north and east. Perhaps there he might find something–something between the dry death of the desert and the spiralling chaos of the coastal cities but, as he climbed up onto the dray's seat, he was not overly optimistic.

'Right-o then, we're off.' And the camel, without the need of a flick of the reins, started slowly moving off through the pulverised dust of the road.

* * *

Two days travel south and east had brought Harry to the beginnings of the abandoned farming country. Fences, broken and half covered by ever-shifting drifts of sand accompanied the road. Ribbons of dead grass hung from the rusted wire like the lank hair of corpses, and twigs had formed intricate woven piles, trapped against the fence posts above the sand. Huge paddocks, which had once held scattered populations of bony cattle, filled the rolling landscape. Deserted now, the starving herds had been reduced to a horrible collection of bleached bones and mummified skin half buried in the dust. Everything in that country, plant of animal, eventually fell victim to the slowly moving dunes, inching relentlessly forward, to cover the few remaining clumps of saltbush and stunted trees.

But the sight of these drooping fence lines brought a smile to Harry's long pinched face. The evidence of humanity, however broken, brought some life to the silence of the road. Even under the blasting weight of the day's heat he felt a new clarity filling his mind. Each time he rolled over a patch of buckled tar peeking through the sand, he felt his gloom lift a little more.

In the failing heat of dusk he examined the landscape from under the broad brim of his hat for a place to camp in the cleared country. Eventually he came across a clump of dead trees in the corner of a paddock a hundred metres off to the side of the road.

He guided the camel over the low mound at the road's edge and across a broken fence lying twisted in the dirt and around behind the thin copse of trees. The clump would not entirely hide the camp from the road but it still seemed, in a vague way, a little more hospitable than the surrounding lifeless paddocks.

Pouring half a cup of water, he drank slowly in the gathering darkness, before he began to unpack his bedroll, mattress and cooking gear from the dray. The hungry camel violently ripped branches off a sorry-looking saltbush and began disconsolately chewing as he stood waiting in the harness.

Later, as Harry sat beside a small campfire, he listened to the reassuring sound of the camel in his hobbles off among the trees still chewing. Harry had eaten half a can of vegetable soup from his dwindling store on the dray and now sat on his bedroll, poking the fire with a twisted stick. The firelight lit up the grey trunks around him but beyond that there was darkness.

Harry thought of his return to the east and its frenetic, heaving population. He remembered with some trepidation the strife he had fled two years before. The pulse and push and shove of overpopulation along the coast had seemed unbearable then.

He could only imagine the decline the intervening time had brought to those places. The climate refugees would have kept flooding in, the homeless were everywhere even then and crime rates would have continued to spiral as landless people took what they could not afford. Food and water prices had been rising astronomically when he had first left but it would have only grown worse since then. Unemployment and poverty had been breaking all records, cities and towns had already begun the descent into social chaos, colapsing as the shrinking economy faltered, and he could only imagine how bad it was now.

Harry had sensed back then that the thin shell of civility was about to crack irrevocably and he dreaded what he would find, even on the edges of that chaos, now. But he was strangely excited too, by the thought of heading back, tempted by the slightly less precarious existence, and tempted a little, perhaps, by the thought of some more than fleeting contact with other people.

Maybe he could find a few of his old friends still living in the compounds, protected from the crowds of inland refugees. Maybe he would search for his ex-wife, Rebecca, he mused. She had left him years before and he had no idea where she would be now amid the turmoil. He doubted she would have changed, doubted she would be overjoyed at seeing him, even if he did find her. She must have moved on, perhaps she had held onto enough cash and gone to the Enclaves in Antarctica. He thought of others he might find but, he realised that strangely, after all those years in the corporate world, he knew very few people, and that that crowded loneliness suddenly seemed somehow worse than the isolation out here.

He sat lost in thought, his face lit by the dying fire, until with a start he heard the rumble of a car off in the distance. He tensed and stared intently towards the road lost in the darkness a short distance away.

Then he saw the dim beginnings of headlights slowly approaching along the road. He stood nervously, preparing to flee into the darkness but he could not leave the dray and his camp to any passers-by.

Perhaps, Harry hoped, they would just pass. Perhaps the approaching car held the indigenous men who had seemed uninterested in him at the gorge. But it didn't sound like the throaty roar of a diesel motor. He stood indecisively at the fire and prayed the car would leave him be.

The headlights came up over a low crest half a kilometre away and grew as they swerved this way and that as the driver avoided the patches of bull dust. As the car drew level with Harry's camp he thought they would pass him and continue along the road. He realised he should have kicked out the fire but it was too late for that. Then, at the last moment his heart sank as the lights abruptly left the road and slowly crept with a soft whir across the paddock to the edge of the trees surrounding his fire.

'Fuck,' Harry mumbled and his mind began to whirl with anxiety.

The car sat for a few seconds, its headlights lighting up Harry's figure frozen beside the fire. Harry heard the soft chime of the camel-bell in the darkness as the hybrid motor died. There was a disturbing silence for several seconds before the car doors clunked open and figures emerged from either side. Harry heard a soft but gravelly woman's voice call softly from inside the car.

'Be careful, huh?'

In the glare of the headlights Harry could see nothing but figures. One of them grunted in reply and slammed the car door. The two silhouettes moved slowly around to the front of the car and again stopped, facing him, the headlights behind them. Dazzled, Harry raised his palm protectively, and then dropped his gaze to the fire.

'Hey, what're you doing here?' The man spoke in a creaking voice that rang out in the darkness and, when a reply did not come, he raised his voice a little and called again.

'Hey ... '

'Just stopping the night and moving on,' Harry was subdued, not sure how the conversation would turn but buoyed a little by the presence of the woman still sitting in the car.

'Mind if we sit, share the fire for a bit?' The other man spoke. His voice seemed younger than the first but still rasped with the dust of the road.

Harry shrugged his shoulders without speaking and, taking the gesture for consent, the man who had spoken first went back and switched off the headlights before the two tall scrawny figures appeared in the soft light of the fire.

As they squatted across from him, the firelight lit up the two men for the first time. Their white faces were smudged with dirt and their clothes too were filthy with the red road dust. Their faces were drawn and tired, with dark circles beneath their eyes that dug deep into their cheeks. Both men's lips seemed to be drawn away from their teeth in a permanent grimace as though their skin had somehow shrunk in the constant heat. To Harry, this made them look related–a father and son perhaps.

The younger one, the second speaker, had long, matted hair that stood out at erratic angles from his thin face. The older man had a roughly cropped skull, with flecks of grey among the black, uneven stubble. Both men were fidgety and seemed nervous and sullen to Harry but that, in itself, was not unusual out here.

Harry stared across the fire from under his brow and noticed both men wore no shoes. The men's feet were red with the dust and thickly calloused. Their lack of shoes gave them an unnerving air of desperation. Shoeless, to Harry, they seemed more like beasts somehow.

'You from the coast then, eh? You been out here long?' The older man spoke and the two glanced at each other briefly and then looked at the dust between their feet.

'Not long, travelling down from the north,' Harry replied in a sullen mumble. That was all he was giving. He remained standing next to his bedroll, occasionally looking from the depth of the fire out into the darkness.

The conversation died. In the silence that followed, the younger, wild-haired man, retrieved a smouldering stick from the fire and began tracing slow hypnotic circles in the dust before his feet. The slow, repetitive movement of the blackened point, in the building silence, grated on Harry and eventually made him shuffle uncomfortably from foot to foot.

Finally, the man stopped and held the stick still over the fire, spat violently into the dust and glanced quickly at the other and then, in unison, Harry saw the two men steal a darting glance at the dray sitting half hidden in the shadows.

'You got any water?' The older man spoke quietly, staring again at the dirt. 'We could trade something if you've got any. We really need it.' He tilted his head in the direction of the car. The movement confused Harry for a second and he was about to ask what the man meant, when suddenly it dawned on him that the offer was for the woman and, embarrassed, he stammered and went quiet.

'I said, you got any water, buddy? If you do, well ... ' The man looked up at Harry and finally held his gaze through the thin smoke of the fire. Harry shook his head but remained silent. He felt a mounting sense of despair and tried desperately to stop his shoulders from slumping. The two men grew irritated at his lack of response and the younger man's lips drew back over his long yellow teeth in a half sneer. They both stood and pushed their hands into the pockets of their filthy jeans.

Harry and the two men faced each other accross the dying fire. The younger man kicked the dirt with his toe and stared at Harry intently. The older man gazed down at his bare feet in the dust and spoke again without looking up.

'Look, we need water and we haven't got much to trade.' He glanced back at the car again. Sighing deeply, as though exhausted by the stilted talk, he leaned in to the fire, his chin jutting outwards. 'If you got some water we could share it, huh? We don't need much, a few litres for the three of us, eh … if you got some to spare?'

Harry imagined the woman's silhouette unmoving in the back seat. He remained silent for a few seconds longer. Struck dumb, he scratched his head and ran his fingers through his hair and made as though to speak but then closed his mouth again in indecision.

'Listen,' the younger man took a step around the fire and Harry backed off and broke his silence.

'All right, there's a little water in the dray. Give me a container, I can spare a few litres.' He smiled at the two men but his grin felt like a knife gash stitched across his face.

Both men relaxed. Going to the car, the younger man lifted the boot and Harry heard him mumble to the woman briefly before he returned to the fire carrying three plastic soft drink bottles and tossed them across at Harry's feet.

'Ta,' he said in a low, disgruntled voice.

'Yeah, thanks, mate, thanks,' the older man chimed in.

Scooping up the bottles, Harry went to the dray. He would give them some water just to be rid of them, he thought. Pushing back the tarp, he dragged the closest drum to the edge of the tray, making sure he kept the second drum hidden. Holding the plastic bottle in one hand, he tilted the drum and began carefully decanting the water. Looking up, he saw the camel's face watching him at the edge of the light. His hand shook a little, as the bottle grew heavier.

The water level neared the top and Harry lifted the drum to stem the flow. But, as he recapped the bottle, he was suddenly struck from behind. The air was driven from Harry's lungs by the impact of the younger man's shoulder in his back and he fell sideways, striking his head against the dray as he toppled. He saw an explosion of stars, the rubber wheel, the flickering fire and then the dust as he lay, stunned in the dirt.

He felt a wetness creeping slowly around his legs from the spilled water bottle and heard the distant glug-glug as the water flowed into the dust and, far off, a soft curse. He wanted to reach out and set the bottle right but his head swam and he felt vomit climb up in his throat and the throbbing pain in his forehead left him paralysed where he lay. Miles away, he heard the older man speaking softly to the other as they stood above him.

'Why the fuck did you do that?' Harry sensed the older man bending over him. 'He was giving it up.'

'Hold-out bastard. He didn't want to give us anything.' The younger man's voice was hard. 'He's got litres of it under there, I saw. Fuck him anyway, we need it more than he does. If he's stupid enough to camp like this, out here in the fucking open well ... '

'I hope you haven't finished him is all,' the other grunted in reply, poking at Harry with his toe. Groaning, Harry tried to rise on his elbow but a foot held him down.

'Na, look at him. He's coming round.' The younger one leant down and spoke to Harry a few centimetres from his face. 'Stay the fuck down, you piss-weak prick.' And the stars exploded behind his eyes again as another half-hearted kick glanced off Harry's throbbing skull. His mind reeling, he slumped back into the dust. He heard himself whimper and he coughed weakly as he felt the dirt, still warm from the day, against his left cheek. He tried desperately to keep his eyes open, to salvage something from the men, but the ringing and nausea increased and, turning his head, he vomited as he slowly sank into unconsciousness.

A last thought flashed, a banner before his closed eyes—I'm fucked. And in a weird way the thought didn't hold the full horror it should have.

* * *

In his dream the huge glass doors drew apart with a soft hiss and, passing into the vast office, he caught sight of the blue-suited figure of Carlo Mérida far across the vaulted room. Silhouetted against a wall of heavily tinted windows, the diminutive figure stood behind his desk, apparently transfixed by the view of the skyscrapers crowded, row upon row, to the hazy blue horizon.

The sun hung huge in the centre of the windows, boring down relentlessly on the mirrored buildings of the city. Even through the darkened, light-responsive glass the intensity of the light forced Harry to squint as he crossed the enormous office and approached Mérida. He drew close and the immaculately groomed CEO half turned, nodded once without speaking and returned to his silent contemplation of the shimmering panorama.

Standing beside his replacement, Harry looked down on the mirrored canyons of the city and the streets many storeys below, and his thin, jaundiced face wrinkled with unease. The crisp lines, the mirrors and the vast arrays of solar panels, all the pastel colours of the towering cityscape were marred by huge boiling columns of black smoke rising in gouts and surges from between the skyscrapers, billowing up from the chaos of unrest that wracked the city streets. Below their vantage point, unseen mobs ran riot, burning cars and buses, smashing shopfronts and signs, warring with the police and the corporate security squads, in their fury destroying anything representing the Company—a gigantic conglomerate of firms they held responsible for the growing hell of The Failing.

Crowds charged and retreated, rampaging through the streets. Riot squads with water cannon and stun grenades, and drones armed with rocket-propelled tear-gas canisters corralled and manoeuvred, trapping the protestors in alleys and cul-de-sacs to better facilitate mass arrests. Tear-gas trails arched through the glass canyons, bouncing and ricocheting into the crowds of protestors, filling the air with searing gas. In retaliation, the rioters set fire to barricades of overturned vehicles, timber and tyres, creating huge columns of smoke to confound the police helicopters and drones that hovered above.

From above it was almost surreal, but down there, beyond the heavy security cordons, Harry knew the city was rank with discontent. The thick oily smoke, reflected by the buildings and solar collectors, was steadily engulfing the surrounding city. The sight of it forced a soft involuntary sigh from Harry's lips and he closed his eyes for a second against out the chaos.

'Water prices again,' Carlos Mérida, still facing the city, snorted loudly and another short pause followed.

To fill the silence Harry spoke softly to no one. 'At a hundred c-credits a litre, you can't blame them, can you?' Harry's words fought sluggishly through his fatigue. He shrugged weakly and the silence fell again as they stood side by side, dwarfed by the grand panes of glass.

'Brazil and Indonesia are the same. The North American Block... the West Asian Trade Group's even worse,' Mérida shrugged. 'I suppose that's why you resigned ... the terrible injustice of The Failing? Some kind of martyrdom thing?' Carlos Mérida's clipped Anglo-Brazilian accent was infected with the same derision that swam in his eyes.

Mérida turned suddenly. His plump olive-skinned face, turned upwards to glare at the taller man, was reddened by his sense of frustration, his voice fouled with disdain for the weakness in the man he saw standing before him.

"The Failing is not Clearwater's responsibility! You know this, Harry. The market sets the prices, we are as much pawns as they. They ... ' Mérida waved a hand dismissively at the city below, 'The Government should have acted ... Those people are not our responsibility now, they never were. The market ... '

Mérida paused and slowly shook his head before continuing in a lower tone. 'Why throw in the towel? Why throw away all you've built? There is so much more we could do. There are still opportunities going begging out there–Antarctica, Greenland–those places are goddamn gold mines now. Those new markets will keep our profit margins well above ... '

Pausing again Mérida drew breath through his nostrils and his anger faded. 'For Carbon's sake, Harry, you need some help ... counselling perhaps ... a month or two at one of those Heat Retreats. Clearwater could fly you south even.' His tone was measured but his eyes held no sympathy. 'I mean, what the hell will you do?'

Harry had only enough energy to shrug again. He knew the new CEO of Clearwater was not concerned for his health. He only cared about Harry's treasonous betrayal. Mérida and the entire executive would be glad to see the back of him. They thought him soft, even sick, Harry knew that. They dissected his resignation repeatedly, over cocktails at Clearwater's rooftop bar, but his resignation remained utterly beyond their comprehension and, in the end, they simply concluded it was merely some sort of bizarre mental breakdown.

His desertion of Clearwater and the Company infuriated the men and women he himself had hired many years earlier, when Clearwater was still small, before the seemingly endless boom in water prices in the middle years of The Failing. And now, four decades later, they had written him off as some kind of demented Judas. People he had once thought friends stared at him in the corridors as though he were a pariah, fit only to be shunned.

He wanted to yawn hugely and he fought the urge to leave then and there, without another word.

'I'll still retain a large shareholding," he spoke slowly, with little conviction.

Carlos Mérida snorted again, still staring out across the smouldering city. 'If you're out, you're out, Harry. Keeping a few shares means nothing. You'll get dividends paid into your trust account, but that's it. You're a sentimental fool!' His voice rose again, 'You signed the damn papers on some ridiculous whim, you'll have no say in operations any more.' He paused again thoughtfully. 'I don't know, maybe that's a good thing. At this stage of the decline curve, Clearwater can't afford to play these ridiculous games. Protect and consolidate—that's the market paradigm now. Clearwater must build a hedge against ... ' Mérida, unable to speak of the escalating crisis, turned once more from Harry to the skyline of the city.

'People like you Harry are nothing but waste now... nothing but waste. You'll be trodden underfoot like the fools down there—all of them squirming against the inevitable. Why waste the effort?' He stared out the windows, shook his head and suddenly sliced the air with his dark spidery hand. 'We have no time for you, Harry. No time for all your hand-wringing sentimentality.'

Stung by the undisguised contempt, Harry turned away to face the broad granite desk behind them. Fatigue rolled over him. Placing his hands against the cool black surface, he steadied himself and breathed more slowly. The arguments and anger should hold little importance for him now, but still he itched desperately to explain his actions—actions he struggled to rationalise even in his own mind. Yet, at the same time, he felt the overwhelming urge to flee. It dominated him these days, that desperate urge to escape from men like Mérida and their scorn for anything but that all-pervading Company paradigm.

He ran his finger tips along the sharp granite edge of the desk and saw the slack skin on the back of his hands with the smattering of small brown spots. His hands were long and large. Once they had been strong, used to handling wrenches and fitting tools for the rigs. Once he had been secretly proud of those work-hardened hands but that was decades ago. He no longer felt their old strength. His fingers had weakened, like the rest of him, but that, in its own way, was a good thing. Sometimes in weakness there was refuge and escape.

He felt a little stronger, absorbing strength from the solid black stone beneath his fingers. This massive desk had, until recently, been his, and the memory of his first day sitting behind the desk came unbidden to him–the new expansive office in the gigantic new building, all owned by Clearwater outright. Leaning back in his chair, a fresh prince then, tasting the tang of Clearwater's growing dominance of global water reserves, he had revelled in the heady power brought by that dominance.

A little embarrassing now, but back then the warm, youthful grin of success had never left his face. He, and Clearwater, could do no wrong in those early days. The wild places they had seen and the risks they had taken to grow the company's dominance still sent a shiver of excitement through him sometimes. But most of all he missed that life before the boom–the new aquifers they had sought and tapped and drawn in those early days, the smell of fresh water, bubbling up, warmed by the bowels of the earth, spraying and spilling like blood into the dirt around his dusty boots.

The thrill of those lucrative contracts, as governments desperately sought new water, throwing money at any venture with even the slightest hope of finding some made him forget, for a brief moment, the brooding Mérida standing next to him. But the towers of oily smoke rising on the other side of the windows brought him back. Water, or the lack of it, fuelled those fires that raged below. It assaulted him each time he moved in those streets–reminded him of his role in the ceaseless spiral, the profits they had sucked from the mayhem of desperation.

His mind shied away from it now, it was too much to take in, in his present state of mind. He noticed a tall, fluted glass of water that stood on the corner of the desk. The bright light from the windows scattered fragmented rainbows across the black granite. He pointed to the glass and Mérida's cold brown eyes slowly followed his gaze.

'It's all different now,' Harry paused. 'That glass of water ... all the billions we've made from it, it has ... I don't know ... poisoned me somehow. I don't want to be part of that shit any more.' At last a tinge of anger crept into Harry's voice. 'I wish you could ... '

The other man rolled his eyes and snorted like a maddened bull. Mérida's growing anger forced his Brazilian accent to the fore. 'What 'as 'appened to you, 'arry? 'Ave you 'ad some, some fucking breakdown? Talk like this ... ' Harry saw a small white bubble form in the corner of the CEO's mouth as he ranted. 'People think you need committing for carbon's sake.'

Mérida held his eyes again and shook his head gently before he turned back to face the city. He did not turn or acknowledge Harry as the former head of Clearwater turned and, without speaking, walked slowly from the office.

Carlos Mérida stood and felt the unfamiliar anger swamp him as the doors to his office hissed open and then closed. He ground his teeth. Even though the former CEO's resignation had handed him control of Clearwater, Harry's departure still infuriated him. It was as though Harry had betrayed his family, he thought. To waste all this, to throw it all away, it was inexcusable.

Refracted by the endless arrays of solar panels, a deep burnt-orange haze now stained the vista as the morning crept on. Through this disturbing shroud, Carlos Mérida watched as the building's exterior elevator descended slowly from the fortieth floor. Mérida sighed as it finally reached the lobby and watched as, after a moment or two, a small hunched figure slowly crossed the forecourt, skirted the large dry fountain, wove through the security cordon and disappeared into a waiting limousine.

And, finally, the former CEO was gone from the building. Enormous relief flushed away the remains of Mérida's anger and he shook his head to clear the final echoes of their argument. He brushed away a small piece of lint from the arm of his blue silk suit before turning back to the business of the day.

'Voice activate,' he snapped at the intercom. 'Get me the morning trading figures for Horizon.'

Harry cowered a little at the angry faces he saw through the limousine's windows. Normally he was not exposed to this–he usually left by the basement car park–now the crowds broke on the car in a wild surge. The people in the crowd did not recognise him but they knew the car was linked to Clearwater, or at least to one of the many corporations linked to the Company. The details did not matter to them, he and his ilk were all the same cabal of elites. The car had almost broken free, when someone in the crowd spat on the window next to him. Numbly, Harry looked back at the sea of screaming faces, stared at their wild eyes and their bared teeth, their faces red with rage and frustration. He held his face to them, bore their fury unflinchingly, as an older woman let fly another gob of spit.

* * *

He woke coughing and spluttering in a furnace. The taste of sand and grit, and blood too, filled his mouth and nostrils. There was a wall of red beyond his closed eyelids and the sun seared his skin through his shirt like a branding iron. He opened his mouth to groan but the heat spilled in to clog his throat and all he managed was a soft croak. His forehead, where he had struck it hard against the dray, throbbed and each thump lanced down to tie his stomach in knots. And the shit-sour taste of defeat enveloped him as the memory of the two men and the scuffle of the night before, flooded back to him.

'I'm fucked,' he croaked aloud.

For a few moments Harry refused to open his eyes, not wanting to see what the thieves had left of his camp. He lay inert, the stinging tears of frustration hanging at the corners of his dust-caked eyes, cursing his stupidity and laziness in camping so close to the road.

'I'm no good at this shit,' he whined weakly. 'Too fucking stupid.'

One side of his face was caked with dust. The other was crusted with dried blood and ached from the cut in his forehead and the fierce sun he had endured while unconscious. Tentatively feeling the congealed blood with his fingers, he worked his way to a meaty gash above his eye and felt a flap of skin, crusted and dry, hanging open and he groaned fearfully again.

Suddenly, through the roaring in his head, he heard the faint tinkle of the camel's bell and the sound drew him back a little from his hopelessness and he opened his eyes to the searing mid-day sun. Throwing up his arms, he protected himself against the arrows of piercing light that bored into his skull and he croaked weakly again. He climbed slowly to his knees and, swaying unsteadily, reached back to find the hard rubber of a tyre of the dray to steady himself. It, at least, was still there, along with the camel.

Through slitted eyes he slowly surveyed his camp. The tarpaulin hung from the back of the tray and what was left of his belongings—a couple of books, his threadbare clothes, a broken shaving mirror and his spare pots, pans and tin plates—lay scattered around in the dust. Depressingly, but as he had expected, both water drums were gone and his box of food lay overturned and empty in the dirt a few metres away. Three tins of soup stood in a line at the back of the dray, left, he presumed, as a parting gift for him–a stingy recompense for the robbery.

The fire was cold and dead. The pan he had cooked with the previous evening was buried in the ashes but most of his camping gear and the bedroll seemed intact. Harry felt a slight relief that they had left him something. The tins of soup would last for a few days, maybe even a week, but he had no water and his heart sank at the thought of a return to the thirst that had plagued him for months.

Frustration and despair surged and in a weak fury Harry staggered about the camp, kicking at the empty tins and discarded camping gear until, exhausted, he doubled over in the heat, resting his head against the side of the dray. Stumbling back along the tyre tracks of the thieves' car to the road he stood swaying, staring blearily back the way he had come. The three thieves had retraced their path and were now, to Harry's despair, somewhere between him and the gorge.

At least, he thought, the bastards would not find the hidden pool at the gorge. Perhaps he would have told them about it, if they had given him half a chance. But, even as the thought came, he knew it was a lie. He would have greedily guarded that secret place like a gold claim.

Through the pounding in his head, he tried to decide whether to risk encountering the three again and return to the gorge where he knew there was water or to continue on his path south and eastward, toward more inhabited lands and, hopefully, find water there. Lost in indecision, he cursed quietly under his breath.

Harry teetered on rubbery legs as he staggered back through the sand to the dray. He retrieved his hat from the dust and, in a croaking voice, called the camel in as he gathered up what was left of his possessions.

* * *

His head was still reeling as the dray bumped over the broken-down fence and regained the road. Still unable to decide on a direction, he vaguely hoped the camel would sense the closest water and follow its nose. And, as it turned out, without direction from him, the camel turned and pulled the dray in their original south-easterly direction.

Relieved that he would probably not encounter the thieves again, Harry let the camel have its head and fell into a half doze, nursing his pounding skull. By the afternoon his concussion had still not cleared. His brain felt as though it had swollen inside his skull, his vision swam and his stomach heaved rebelliously as he teetered from side to side. Retching occasionally, he choked on the bitter, acid bile churned up from his empty stomach–the foul taste only adding to the burning thirst in his throat.

And now, as the sun was inching down at his back, the camel's shadow stretching out in front, he felt as though he might pass out again. Seemingly oblivious, the camel walked on and, lulled by the dray's rhythm, Harry slumped sideways to lie across the seat in the gathering dusk. But, just as he closed his eyes, he felt the dray stop and, thinking the camel was expecting them to make camp, Harry called to him.

'Hup, hup, get on,' he lifted his head, but the camel remained motionless in the road, 'Come on, fuck you … '

He stared past the camel's bulk, along the road. In his stupor he had not even heard the slow approach of the vehicle now standing twenty metres away up the road. As he struggled to right himself, a fresh dread filled his foggy mind.

Harry studied the vehicle through his swimming vision and, with a flood of relief, he saw it was not the car from the night before but a utility similar to the one the Aboriginal men had been driving. And the distinct smell of cooking oil confirmed his spark of hope. As he watched, the utility began to inch forward, its fat tyres crunching on the sand and broken tar as it edged off the road to pass him. In desperation, he pushed himself upright and thrust out a hand to wave the vehicle down.

The utility came to a stop opposite him and the driver's window slowly wound down. An old, dusty, black face stared back at him and Harry tried to smile. There was no response in the man's grey bearded face. His large black eyes simply stared at him from under dense, bushy eyebrows, any expression hidden in the deep network of creases cut around the man's eyes and mouth was unfathomable.

The two passengers crammed into the front seat, both black men, one grey bearded and the other younger and clean shaven, craned their necks to look at Harry from under their broad, sweat-stained hats. After a second or two silently examining his bloodied face, they sat back and gazed out the windscreen.

'I need some help.' Harry croaked through the pounding of his head.

The driver stared at him for a moment, his eyes still blank, and then he spoke quickly, in language, to the passengers. The younger man in the middle nodded and reached down between his knees. He passed a dented plastic bottle to the driver who reached out and passed it from the window to Harry's outstretched hand. Harry, took the full bottle, rasped his thanks and attempted a crooked smile again.

'We have nothing for that cut, mister,' the driver spoke flatly. 'You'd better … '

'Is there a chance of water ahead?' Harry asked desperately. The Aboriginal man turned to the passengers to consult rapidly in their own language before he replied.

'Keep going half a day, maybe a bit more, along this road. There is a place … a white painted gate and a sign that says "No Water". You'll see the house from the road. Ask there. They're good people, they might help you.' He looked Harry up and down and then turned as though to drive off but Harry raised his hand to hold him.

'How far is it again?' He squinted and swayed, steadying himself on the seat.

The man shrugged his shoulders but his brow wrinkled in worry. 'Half day for you is all I can say,' he looked down at the dashboard of the utility. 'Speedo's busted.' He stared into Harry's dirty face and frowned, 'Get some of that water into you quick smart or you'll be in the shit.'

Harry let his hand drop and weakly thanked the men. Inside he sobbed, not wanting the men to leave him, but he said nothing. The window was wound up and the utility's engine roared, gears crunched and the vehicle slowly moved off, leaving behind a cloud of black smoke. Harry watched it disappear in the rising dust, cradling the bottle of lukewarm water in his lap like it was a newborn baby.

* * *

His head had improved slightly as the camel had plodded through the night and on again into the rising heat of early morning. His spirits had lifted a little too, when he occasionally opened his eyes and saw the country slowly growing less forlorn. Fences more often crossed his path and the dray rumbled across an occasional cattle grid, full to overflowing with sand. The road wandered through country studded with skeletal cypress pines and a scattering of tortured red ironbark trees. Most were long dead, but an odd tree here and there held some semblance of life—an occasional branch with a few leaves that still held a tinge of green.

But at midday his mood darkened again when he crossed an area of cypress woodland that held the blackened scars of bushfires. In places the entire landscape was pin cushioned with thousands of blackened toothpicks. From the road, looking across the rolling hills, ash and cinder covered everything. Long black shadows lay in lines along the sand where entire trees had burnt to charcoal in the intense heat of the blaze and even the sand of the road had turned a burnt orange, stained with the ash spread by the wind. He passed two burnt-out homesteads, their wooden frames collapsed like pick-up sticks, their rusting corrugated iron roofs so deformed by the bushfire's intensity that the sheets had sagged like carelessly draped bed sheets, over the remains of the blackened timbers.

He remembered hearing of these great fires years ago. They had raged uncontrolled for months in the dying, tinder-dry forests of the west. No water could be wasted to fight them. The land had been so dilapidated and the heat so fierce, it had made any attempts at fire fighting utterly hopeless. People, some of the last out here, could only watch the infernos rage, exploding and surging, leaping from ridge to ridge, consuming all in their path.

He had seen news footage of families fleeing across the hills to the coast, the western sky cloaked in a bright orange, atomic glow, as pillars of smoke rose to blanket the sun for weeks on end. Many people fled and most never returned to the blackened apocalyptic landscape. That had been the beginning of the last exodus to the coast, the fires were the final nails in the coffin of the western lands. And, with a grimace, he noted that, decades later, there were still no green shoots or regrowth here.

Late in the day the road finally left the blackened land behind. The dray meandered onward through the failing afternoon, through small rocky paddocks that held the odd clump of dry, grey tussock grass perched among the shifting sand. The sand drifts still consumed the road in many places but there were longer expanses of cracked bitumen making it easier going for the camel. The sun still seemed to burrow into the wound on Harry's head as they neared a range of hills that dissected the road a few kilometres ahead.

Still bleary, Harry took an occasional sip of water from the bottle, watching the spur of hills slowly approach. From a distance the coming hills seemed to be formed of a darker rock than the surrounding country. The spur, perhaps formed of a granite or basalt, had been forced up through the surrounding strata. Nothing appeared to grow on the nobbled slopes, the iron barks and cypress pines that had grown on the sand ridges disappeared from around its feet as the country rose up to meet the spur.

As the dray drew closer Harry saw a dilapidated white homestead, with a red, rusted iron roof, sitting off from the road but free of the fringe of twisted iron-barks and cypress pines. Before the house, lay a small fenced yard and a rutted track from the yard led down to the road proper.

The house seemed tiny, half hidden at the foot of the dark jutting talon of hills. Atop a low rise, Harry reined in the camel to watch for a minute or two. The camel belched loudly and shifted impatiently from foot to foot as Harry strained his bleary eyes, waiting for some sign of habitation, but he caught no movement in the rippling haze. And, the heat getting the better of him, he called the camel back to its plodding progress toward the house.

Small willy-willies stirred the paddock as the dray slowly approached the homestead. Through the dust, a sudden movement caught Harry's eye. A figure had emerged from the shadows of the homestead's veranda and strode purposefully along the rutted track towards the road. Reaching the farm's gate the figure silently waited with his foot resting on its lower rung for the dray to draw level.

Harry had no option but to continue. His blurry gaze fell on the 'No Water' sign, roughly painted in white on a broken plank that hung on the gate. Despite the message, his hopes rose as he remembered the Aboriginal man's directions. He pulled the camel up abruptly as he reached the gate, drawing a scowl from the waiting man. Harry's mouth flapped open to speak but the man held up a hand to cut him off.

'There's nothing here for you, no water, nothing.' The middle-aged man stared coldly at the dray stopped the road. His round sunburnt face was hard under the brim of a faded green baseball cap, his small hostile eyes stared right through Harry as he slumped on the seat. The man wore long faded blue overalls with a small insignia on the breast. He scratched his bristled cheek with one finger of his broad, meaty hand and studied Harry from behind black, thick-rimmed glasses.

'Listen ... ' with a huge effort Harry slid to the side of the seat and made to climb down.

'Don't bother getting down. It's like I said, there's nothing here for you. Keep heading south, or east, you'll find people there.' The man's hand fell to the gate latch and rested there. Stammering in protest, Harry teetered on the edge of the seat, his boot slipped and he fell in a tangled heap beside the dray's front tyre and lay there, breathing heavily in the rising dust. The camel turned his huge shaggy head, looking back at Harry's fallen form and then, as though embarrassed, looked ahead again.

The man behind the gate did not flinch as he watched Harry fall. He remained mute as Harry tried several times to regain his feet. Only managing to make it to his knees, Harry looked up at the man in faltering desperation.

'Look, all I need ... ' his voice rasped like sandpaper as he spoke to the cold face that hovered above him. 'All I need is ... '

The man held up his hand again to silence Harry's pleading. He started to speak, his face grown fierce, but he was cut off suddenly by a shout from behind him.

'What's happened, Samuel?'

Another face appeared over the man's shoulder and stared down at Harry. The face was long and narrow and half the age of the other. Under an unruly mop of blond hair, a pair of bright, green eyes sparkled. The face seemed to shine a little in Harry's faltering vision and a wash of relief flooded him, as he sensed that the younger man's arrival might herald some salvation.

Samuel scowled again and half turned to speak to the younger man. 'Don't get involved, Finn! Just leave it, eh?' But the older man's voice had become more subdued as he finished the sentence.

Harry fixed his attention on the new face and pleaded with the last of his waning strength. 'Look, all I need is a little water, just to get me on towards the coast.' He raised his hand to his forehead and touched the flap of skin hanging from the wound and pain shot through his skull like nails and he groaned aloud. His head swam with the effort of speaking but his persistence was rewarded as the young man's face creased with concern.

'Look at him!' Finn pushed past Samuel, opened the gate and rushed to Harry's side and helped him to stand, keeping a firm grip on Harry's forearms as he wobbled unsteadily on his feet.

'Listen ... all I need ... is some water if you have any to spare. I ... I was robbed and beaten two nights ago. I could use a couple of litres maybe ... to get me by. I ... ' out of a growing sense of desperation he changed tack. 'The Aboriginal men ... they said you were good people, that you might help.' He spoke rapidly, giving neither man the opportunity to break in.

Samuel, his large hands still gripping the gate, finally growled through clenched teeth, 'I told you already, there's nothing here for you. Keep on east and you might get help. You'll be ... '

'Samuel! You can't send him on, not like this. Look at him! Come on, Dad, what's the risk? We can help him, can't we?'

'I said forget it, Finn. Look at him. If we let every useless bastard in, where would we be? You know it's best ...'

He petered out seeing the look of dismay cloud his son's narrow face. Father and son stared at each other for a long moment, Harry teetering next to Finn, then the father's gaze faltered and fell and he sighed. Rubbing his face with his hand he stepped back away from the half-open gate. 'He can go up to the house, that's all. You bloody hear me, Finn? He goes no farther and that's my final word on it.'

Samuel shook his head and, turning his back on them, stalked off up to the homestead. Finn silently helped Harry scramble up to the seat of the dray again and opened the gate. The camel seemed to sense the opportunity and turned without coaxing into the rutted driveway and wandered along the track, the reins dragging along the ground, following the young, mop-haired man toward the homestead.

* * *

Harry slept fitfully on a fold-out cot in the corner of the kitchen until the sun had risen high over the ridge behind the house.

Finn had taken a rag and, as best he could, cleaned the blood from the comatose man's face and hair. Finn winced as the deep cut was finally freed from the congealed blood and a crescent of white bone showed through the angry lips of the gash. Then, with great care, his tongue poking out in concentration, he stitched the puckered wound with a needle that he had sterilised in the heat of the kitchen's wood fire and some red cotton thread from a small tobacco tin that served as their first-aid kit. Harry had slept through it all, lying in exhausted oblivion as Finn dressed his wound.

Finished with his first-aid, Finn had sat at the table and watched Harry, sprawled out on the camp cot as dawn crept through the house. Harry's long sinewy arm hung over the edge, his hand resting on the dusty timber floorboards. In the quiet, Finn heard a small rattle come at the end of each of the old man's slow breaths.

Harry's deeply lined face was tilted to the light of the kitchen lamp and his thin chest and shoulders were exposed above the dirty grey sheet. His arms, chest and neck were wrinkled and red with sunburn where they had been exposed beyond the protection of his shirt. But where his shirt had hidden his skin, he was pale and pasty looking. Finn frowned at the sight of his arched ribs and deeply concave stomach. The skin seemed to be stretched tight, almost to the point of tearing, over the curved bones of his chest. His body told of a long count of days on the western plains—of long intervals with little food or water.

The man's long, wispy hair spread like a broken hallo across the yellowed pillow. His face was weather-beaten, narrow and haggard. Square cheekbones jutted out above hollow, sunburnt cheeks and his long, narrow nose split his face like a carving knife. His high forehead was deeply lined and showed several, small, red, skin-cancer blotches near his receding hairline. Under the thin grey eyebrows, his widely separated eyes moved ceaselessly behind thick leathery lids.

To Finn, only the sleeping man's mouth held any hint of a life outside the bone-cracking torture of the desert. His lips seemed thick and soft beneath the cracks and blisters. The carved craggy lines at their corners somehow lent a hint of softness to the ruins. To Finn, the character in those lines spoke of somewhere else, of things and places beyond Finn's isolated existence.

Occasionally the man's full lips drew back in a grimace, revealing long, square, yellowed teeth. Finn's forehead wrinkled in worry as the man rolled restlessly in the cot. An outstretched arm was flung back, thumping against the thin plaster wall behind the cot but the man did not wake. Only his eyes moved at increasing speed behind his lids, as though his mind raced with frenetic, fevered dreams.

With the morning Samuel returned. He scowled, seeing the fresh, clean, puckered skin of the stitched wound. He looked from the wound to Finn and shook his head as he and Finn began preparing a meagre breakfast of canned tomatoes and beans on the wood stove in old blackened pans. They worked quietly around each other, moving slowly back and forth in the already heavy heat of the kitchen. Finn finally spoke as he carried three plates to the small table.

'Couldn't we bring some of the better stuff up for him. Some decent food would do him some good,' Finn glanced sideways at his father across the table.

In the combined heat of the morning and the cooking stove, clad in singlets and old faded shorts, both men formed their words with halting deliberation. Turning from the table, Samuel paused and stared at Harry's sleeping form, sluggishly trying to construct a rational argument.

'Enough, Finn. Don't waste time on him. He'll be gone in a day or so. We're not a bloody charity.' A worried frown crossed Samuel's face, 'He's been sleeping for hours.'

'Must have concussion or something,' Finn replied quietly.

'He goes as soon as he can walk, Finn. That's my final word on it,' he didn't look at his son as he laid out the cutlery on the formica table-top. 'And she'll tell you the same, you know it's the only way.'

Samuel's movements were rigid with disapproval and Finn knew that he was skating on thin ice with his father. His eyes flitted to the cot as the man's arm suddenly flopped out from under the thin sheet. But Finn's eyes registered his disappointment as the man continued to sleep.

'There's no harm in him, I don't think so anyway. We have to help him, he wouldn't have lasted another day like that,' he mumbled sullenly, but Samuel refused to be drawn as he clattered grumpily about the kitchen.

* * *

Harry woke to the scrape of knives and forks and the soft sounds of people eating. His memory slowly came back to him as he lay listening. He remembered staggering into the kitchen, pulling off his bloodstained shirt and stumbling from a chair to the cot the younger man had made up for him and then nothing more. His body ached from the torpor of unconsciousness and his head throbbed softly but, with some relief, he realised much of the miasma of the past few days had finally cleared.

He did not open his eyes at first but listened cautiously to the sounds around him and tried to search the room from memory. He remembered a table in the centre of the kitchen and some mismatched dining chairs scattered around it. There was an old blackened wood-stove next to the sink and there was, he thought, a faded butter-coloured kitchen cabinet, maybe with plates and bowls stacked haphazardly on its shelves, opposite his cot.

The soft noise of people chewing and the scrape of cutlery seemed to drag on endlessly but Harry was happy just lying in the security of feigned sleep. He was content to lie in the stuffy cocoon of the sheet and listen to the quiet familiarity of the doings in the kitchen—simple sounds he had not heard for years. The smell of the food made him salivate and he swallowed the moisture greedily to ease the dryness in his throat.

He floated, waiting patiently to hear the people in the room speak and perhaps discern some idea of who they were and what was in store for him. And, at long last, his patience was rewarded by the surprising sound of a woman's voice.

'I'm no goddamn mechanic, Samuel, you know that. I've pulled the motor down twice and can't find the problem.' The woman whispered but her voice was gravelly and clipped. Her comment was met with two consecutive grunts.

'We're in a bit trouble if we can't fix it, Nettie. We'll have to give it another go. I'll come up and look after we finish here.' Harry caught an edge of worry in Samuel's voice, his words ending in a long, tired sigh.

'I could have a look,' Finn's uncertain voice cut in. 'If you think it might help, I mean.'

There was a soft snort from his father. 'What'd be the good in that? You know less about the damn thing than we do. Just stay here, Finn, and keep an eye on him. You brought him up here, so he's your problem now.'

'If you think … I don't mind.' There was an injured air to the younger man's voice and the conversation petered out for a few moments before, in a more conciliatory tone, the woman's broke the deadlock.

'Dad's right, Finn. If he wakes keep him here until we get back, eh?' She paused and sighed and Harry heard a hand fall heavily on the table as Finn grunted disconsolately before she went on.

'Look I know it would have been wrong to let him carry on in that condition,' Samuel harrumphed loudly but, ignoring him, she continued. 'But you understand don't you, we've helped him enough just letting him come up here?'

'Listen to Nettie, Finn. Keep your eye on him,' Samuel interjected and Harry heard two chairs scrape the floor as father and daughter left the room. He heard a screen door creak and slam and then silence fell on the house.

Harry felt some relief at Nettie's words. At least they meant him no harm. They would see him on his way as soon as he was able and that was more than good enough for Harry.

Reassured, Harry began to drift, listening to the clatter of plates as Finn cleared the table. He heard the deep heavy clunk of what he instantly knew was a full water drum and then, as he fell again into sleep, he heard the chugging of water as the young man filled the sink.

* * *

Standing shakily next to the cot, Harry ran his cracked fingertips over the puckered edges of the stitched wound in his forehead as Finn re-entered the kitchen. The young man stopped abruptly in the doorway, startled to find him awake. The young man's face slowly brightened after his initial surprise and he smiled shyly at Harry.

Silently, Finn crossed to the kitchen bench and half filled a tin cup with water from the drum and, without asking, passed it to Harry. Harry downed the warm water in three long gulps and passed it back. The two stood facing each other in the blanketing heat of the room. Harry noted a strange metallic but not unpleasant taste to the water as he ran his tongue around his mouth.

Finn filled a plate with food from the stove and placed it on the table. He nodded to Harry and the old man sat himself eagerly before the food, hesitating momentarily before he began to devour the leftovers. The meal quickly filled his shrunken stomach but he continued to shovel in the remaining mouthfuls from the plate without looking up. The gaunt, grey-haired man's ravenous hunger seemed to please Finn and he smiled again as he sat opposite and watched Harry finish.

'Are you from out east?' He broke the silence with a voice overflowing with a desperate hunger for news.

Finn's sudden question took Harry by surprise. He looked up from the empty plate and, wiping his face with his hand, he grunted and nodded in reply. The younger man's enthusiasm seemed to draw Harry's new found energy from him and the sudden sating of his appetite made his mind sluggish as he struggled for something to say.

'Finn Bishop,' Finn leaned farther across the dining table and held out his hand. Inspecting it before he took it, Harry noticed the young man's fingers were unusually white and a little plump for someone who lived out here in the dust and dirt. Finally he took the outstretched hand and shook it half-heartedly.

'Harry.'

They sat for another minute—the heat feeding the silence between them. Finn frowned and scratched at his cheek and, leaning back, he tried to smooth his wild mop of blond hair but, despite his efforts, the long matted strands sprang instantly back to disorder. He dug up some courage and spoke rapidly almost stumbling over his words.

'What's it like back there? You know back on the coast,' Finn leaned in again, unabashed in his eagerness for news.

'Like? What d'you mean, like?' Harry stumbled at the unexpected start of the conversation.

'You know … the cities. All those people back there. I've never … It must be kind of wild … or something … lots of stuff happening … I don't know.' He shrugged his thin, bony shoulders and then, almost as an afterthought, he blurted out, 'Everyone's gone over the Divide, you know, to the coast. Dumped everything and gone.'

Harry saw the unmistakable glint of curiosity in the young man's eyes. But he only grunted in reply, watching Finn fidget in his seat. Harry felt a peculiar spark of anger at Finn's unfettered enthusiasm.

'I haven't been there for two years, more maybe.' Harry stared down at the table, 'If it's anything like when I left, it's a shit hole.'

Finn's face fell. 'Well, I suppose it must be crowded but still ... ' His index finger traced a crack in the table-top. 'Why have ... why would you come out here. I mean ... there's nothing out here, not now. No people, no farming, no towns, just hopeless stragglers and drifters ... '

The young man looked up nervously and Harry saw his gaze dance around the room in desperation. Finn rose abruptly and went to the sink carrying Harry's plate. 'I didn't mean you. I just ... '

But Harry felt no insult. He felt nothing. The food had made him drowsy—his eyes had become bleary and burned in the thick dry air. Like a wave, the fatigue rose up again and dragged him downwards.

'There's nothing for you there ... on the coast. The water's failing there, too. Nothing's working. Things ... I don't know ... it'd just be chaos now ... too many people fighting over the smallest things. The Failing, it's torn it all apart ... ' Harry sighed and fell silent, finding it far too hard to explain it in the heat.

The younger man turned quickly to face him and there were glowing coals in his bright blue eyes. 'There's nothing here either, Harry,' his voice whined with frustration. 'There's nothing here either.'

Harry opened his mouth to speak but shut it again. Wanting to placate the younger man, to tell him something to ease that whine, but he couldn't find a spark in himself to give.

Absently he scratched at the stitches in his forehead. 'You stitched me up?'

Standing at the kitchen bench Finn nodded sullenly.

'Thanks for that.'

Harry climbed slowly to his feet and walked to the cot. He sat at its edge for a second before he lay back and pulled the sheet over himself and closed his eyes. He listened to Finn shuffling about the room and knew the young man was disappointed by his negativity, but Harry could conjure nothing to brighten the younger man. Finn, blinded perhaps by his desperation, would refuse to see it, no matter what he said. The young man saw only something different, something bright and new and exciting. Harry saw the treacherous mirage. He wanted to shake Finn—rid him of that desperate hope—but he did not have the energy to bully the younger man out of his futile dreams.

* * *

Harry woke, his body soaked **in** sweat. His head felt completely clear for the first time in days. He climbed gingerly to his feet and crossed unsteadily to the kitchen sink, where the drum of water stood. In the dim light he filled the cup, the luxurious glug of the water made him smile a little and then, raising the cup to his lips, he drained it slowly. He felt the water seeping through him, seemingly infusing each desiccated cell of his body, one by one. Replacing the cup gently on the shelf, he stood for a moment in the kitchen listening to the soft humming of the heat inside his skull.

He began wandering through the house. Through rooms all thick with a stale mustiness, his bare feet felt the dust and grit lying thick on the raw wooden floorboards. In the dim light he poked his head into each of the three bedrooms along the hallway that led from the kitchen. Each room, despite being full of old furniture—beds, wardrobes, chests-of-drawers and the like, held few personal items. None of the rooms seemed as though they had been inhabited for many years. Every surface was covered with a deep layer of red dust. Only the floors between the furniture showed the wandering trails of footprints tracing paths in the thick layer of dirt. He felt a weakness come over him again as he wandered, trailing his hand along the wall, towards the front door that stood at the end of the main hallway.

Hearing the sound of voices outside, Harry stopped and, leaning heavily against the wall, he listened in on the quiet conversation through the closed door. The words were muffled at first, but after a few seconds, as he listened more closely, the woman's voice, Nettie's voice, became clearer.

'I can't work it out. I'm no bloody expert–I can fix the small things but this is beyond me. I'm surprised it's run this long with so few problems,' Nettie grumbled and Harry heard a chair creak.

'But what's going to happen then, what are we going to do? Without the pump to pump water we're–'

'Finn!' Samuel's hiss cut the younger man off. 'We're trying to work it out. Calm down and stop fussing.'

There was quiet for a few moments before Nettie continued, 'Well, there's no more I can do with it. We might have to rig up some sort of manual system or something.'

'That's ridiculous, Nettie,' Samuel whispered. 'There must be a way to repair it.'

Afterwards Harry wondered what had come over him when he pulled open the heavy door with the stained glass window and blundered through the fly-screen, out onto the veranda.

The searing light of day blinded him momentarily and he raised his hand in front of his eyes. Three startled faces stared up at him from where the family sat around a small rickety wooden table. Samuel's chair fell backwards with a crash as he stood, his face crossed by a deep frown, 'What the … '

'Oh … you're up,' Finn stood up more slowly and reached out as though to place a hand on Harry's arm.

Stony-faced, Nettie remained sitting. Her eyes were almost hidden by her dark frown. Harry saw the similarity of her long, narrow face to Finn's at a glance. She was older than Finn, perhaps in her early thirties. Her face was more deeply tanned by exposure to the blistering sun and, unlike Finn's youthful complexion, there were the beginnings of lines creeping around her eyes and thin mouth, but her long nose and her high cheekbones held the same defined bone structure. Her hair, long, dark and wiry thick, had been carelessly tied back but remained somehow as unruly as her brother's sandy mop. Her eyebrows too, like Finn's, were thick above her half-hidden eyes.

Harry was immediately struck by her proud hawkish grace. Even before The Failing, life on the plains was hard on faces. People out here wore their years heavily and often betrayed little through the thick reserve born of their hardship. But Harry could see she was a proud woman beneath that scowling veneer. Sitting rigid in her chair, she refused to turn toward him but gazed instead, out beyond the shade of the veranda, towards the red dirt of the paddocks and the dark slash of the spur running out from the hills.

Turning away, uncomfortable under Samuel's scrutiny, Harry screwed his eyes up against the fierce light to discern something more of the landscape he had only seen as a blur on his arrival. Beyond the shade, the sun blasted down on the small fenced garden and the dirt paddocks farther out.

As his eyes grew accustomed to the light he made out a jumble of garden beds, lying between half buried, broken concrete paths. The old beds were edged with peeling white-painted stones that now stood haphazardly like tiny memorials to the garden's better days. Once, long ago, the derelict gardens must have contained well-tended beds of roses and shrubs and even herbs maybe, but after years without being watered, there now remained only bankrupt dirt, pulverised by the hammer of the sun to a fine, moribund powder.

The faded timber picket fence surrounding the house and garden was broken in many places. Palings lay one on top the other on the ground where they had fallen. Drifts of red sand had invaded the garden through the gaps. The huge grey timber corner posts, protruding from the encroaching sand at obtuse angles, were split and cracked with the slow desiccation of the long dry. Bathed in the grilling sunlight, the garden jarred Harry, bringing home afresh the demise of the once grand farming country.

Then, to his relief, he saw the camel and the dray standing tied to a post. The animal chewed disconsolately and glowered back at the house from under its long lashes. Harry's gaze returned to the three sitting around the table and he spoke at last.

'I know a bit about pumps. If you like I could have a look ... ' Harry's words trailed off. He shrugged, stuffed his hands deep in the pockets and leaned back against the doorframe. His legs had suddenly begun to feel like rubber under Samuel's unrelenting stare.

'It's none of your damn business.' Samuel glanced down at his daughter sitting across the table from him as he spoke.

Still staring out into the distance, Nettie spoke slowly, 'If he's walking around, he's well enough to leave.'

'But he knows about ... ' Finn blurted but his voice died as the two turned to glower at him.

'If he's well enough, he can be on his way,' Samuel turned to Harry. 'Look, we've done you a good turn, right? You were in a bad way yesterday, a very bad way. Probably would've been dead by now but for us. Now you're on your feet, it's time to get going. No hard feelings but we don't need you here.'

As Samuel spoke Nettie stood and faced Harry for the first time and Harry shuffled his feet, uncomfortable under her piercing gaze. Her eyes were almost completely black and a little too large in her face. Her stare was cold and unnerving, as though she looked right into him, causing what little confidence he had to slip away.

'Look, I'm grateful for your help, really I am. I just thought … it sounded like you needed mechanical help and I know something of water pumps and things. But it's no skin off my nose, no problem at all.' He began to back up through the front door. 'If I can get a couple of litres of water maybe … if you can spare it … I'll get out of your hair.'

After living alone for so long, being around these people made his head ache terribly, but Harry felt a little disappointed too. Even though they made him uneasy, it had been a long time since he had stayed in a house–in a real bed–and the thought of some company tempted him a little.

He felt the heat rise in his cheeks like an embarrassed child. Anger flared in him at their outright rejection of his offer, and at his own utter stupidity in making it.

The three stood staring at him as he turned to walk back to the kitchen to retrieve his remaining clothes. Only Finn looked a little disappointed. Harry saw his face fall as the young man lowered his gaze to the bleached boards of the veranda.

Walking quickly to the kitchen, he picked up his clean shirt, socks and boots from where they lay neatly folded on the floor next to the cot. As he dressed and sat to put on his boots he could hear them talking in raised voices outside. Their words were indiscernible but, from their tone, Samuel and Nettie had taken sides in an argument against Finn.

Boots finally on, he stood quietly waiting for the discussion outside to end. Glancing around the kitchen, his eye was snared by a photo of Samuel, Nettie and Finn standing with another woman outside in the garden. He presumed the woman was Samuel's wife and the mother of the two siblings.

The photo was yellowed at its edges. Nettie and Finn were young in the picture–the girl, seventeen or eighteen, the boy maybe ten or twelve. But more revealing of the picture's age, the garden in the background behind the figures still bore a few pitiful splashes of green. There were pale, drooping plants, not in flower, but still alive at least, and the well-tended beds were turned and mulched with a miserly layer of straw.

The mother's face was long and thin, with the same narrow nose as Finn and Nettie. She stood, dour and stiff, behind the other three, as though she carried a weight on her shoulders. Her eyes, large like Nettie's, were blank and emotionless and her face sagged slightly with age and fatigue. The woman's skin was unusually pale for someone who had spent any length of time west of the Divide.

Harry stood and stared, chewing his lip thoughtfully over the family portrait and the fading smattering of greenery that had now completely disappeared from the land outside. After a while he began to search the kitchen cupboards for a container of some kind to fill with water but then thought better of it. Perhaps he shouldn't help himself given the sullen mood outside.

Returning to stand in front of the picture, he heard the conversation outside die. The front door banged and footsteps approached along the dusty floorboards of the hall. Sighing, he straightened his shoulders and turned away from the picture to face the door.

Nettie appeared quietly in the doorway and put a thin, wiry arm up and leaned against the doorframe, her face remaining hidden in the shadows of the hallway. Tall against the frame, her body seemed bony and angular beneath the same baggy blue overalls the other two wore. She stood silently propped like this for a moment before she spoke.

'We'll give you twenty litres of water if you fix the machinery, that's it. If you're full of bullshit–if you don't fix it–you get nothing. You can sleep in here until you're done and we'll give you a meal a day.' She paused and stared at him with her cold, black eyes, 'Once the job's done you're gone. Take it or leave it.'

'Look I ... ' Harry started to protest but she turned on her heel without another word and disappeared down the hallway.

Left standing there, Harry slowly shook his head and moved to sit heavily on the cot. He stared at the red dust gathered in the cracks between the floorboards, bemused by the meat-cleaver hospitality of the father and daughter. His face itched with the heat and he began rubbing at it with both dry cracked palms and he groaned aloud into the stifling kitchen air, once again besieged by the same excruciating human inscrutability that had originally driven him from the throng of the coast.

* * *

Dragging a tangle of brittle sticks and branches from a garden bed behind the house, he threw them down in the dust in front of the camel. The animal looked blankly at the meagre thorny pile, then raised its head and stared coolly at Harry, before gingerly groping the twiggy tangle with its thick leathery lips.

'It's all I could fucking find, you damn ingrate!' Harry watched the animal begrudgingly chew the dried vegetation between its big yellow teeth–the beast not amused by the thorny, desiccated meal.

The day before, after Nettie had left the house, Harry had seen no one else. He had slept through the night and dozed intermittently through the morning, watching the shafts of dust-laden light creep across the floor as the day drew on through midday toward dusk.

Despite the oven of the house, he had remained inside until he felt the temperature drop a degree or two then, rousing himself from the tangled sheets, he had sat on the veranda steps and gazed out across the paddock to the black spur. Nothing stirred across the expanse of parched ground except the sporadic stuttering willy-willies kicking up the loose dust and one lone speck of a bird, briefly rising above the broken rock of the spur only to quickly disappear again in the shadows beyond the range.

Harry enjoyed the forgotten luxury of just sitting on the steps as the sun at last disappeared. Watching the final light melt into the gloom of a burnt orange dusk, he had heard a sudden resounding crack off across the paddock. The change in temperature had caused a brittle, long-dead gum tree to finally splinter and he had numbly watched it slowly topple, raising a distant cloud of dust as it hit the ground. The mummified tree's fall had ruined the brief tranquillity he had felt and he hurriedly returned to the musty kitchen to lie, drained, on the cot.

Now, in the blossoming heat of the morning, he turned from the slowly chewing camel and looked toward the hills. After examining the gnarled spine of the black basalt spur for several minutes a movement caught his eye among the scatter of large boulders and a vehicle appeared, bouncing along a rutted track that wound down through the outcrops to the paddocks. He held his hand up to shade his eyes as the vehicle reached the paddock and, dislodging an enormous billowing dust cloud, zigzagged back and forth across the flat of the valley.

As it drew closer, Harry saw that the vehicle was a small white golf cart with a rather jocular, fringed sun-canopy shading the two front seats. The cart seemed incongruous as it bounced on fat balloon tyres across the last few hundred metres of dirt and into the house's rocky driveway.

The dust cloud engulfed Harry and the camel as the vehicle stopped before it was swept away in the heated breeze. The white fibreglass sides and canopy of the electric golf cart were covered in a thick layer of red dust. Behind the two seats a wooden platform that served as a storage tray had been attached. A tangle of shovels, wrenches and fencing wire was piled on the tray. Through the dust-smeared windscreen, Harry saw Finn's smiling face peering back at him through a ridiculous pair of old-fashioned flying goggles.

Like a clumsy spider, the young man slowly extricated his long frame from the cramped cart before he removed his goggles and looked to where Harry stood near the broken fence. Wiping his hands on his overalls, Finn smiled shyly at the silent man but Harry failed to return the gesture.

Finn shuffled his boots and eyed the camel, still crunching through its meagre meal. 'You sleep OK?'

'All right.'

After an awkward silence, Finn frowned uneasily and began speaking rapidly. 'I've come down to pick you up.' He waved his arm toward the range behind him, 'It's not far really, ten, fifteen minutes maybe.'

Harry shrugged.

Finn wiped his hands down his dirty overalls again and shuffled about. 'Well … um … I guess we should get to it then.' He waved a thumb at the cart and turned to climb back into the cramped seat.

'What about the camel? Have you got something it can eat?' They both glanced at the animal and the skeletal branch hanging from its mouth. Finn ran his hand through his unruly mop of hair and glanced at Harry quickly.

'We can probably find something. Will it be all right here today, tied up like that?'

'He'll be right today but he'll need food tomorrow or the next day.'

'While you're fixing the ... err ... machine, we'll find something for it.' Finn climbed behind the steering wheel and Harry squeezed in next to him. The camel stopped chewing long enough to watch them bounce away through the yard and out across the paddock before he lowered his head again and resumed eating.

* * *

Despite the loose, pulverised bull dust, Finn drove the cart at full speed across the paddock, his face screwed with concentration behind his comical goggles, the cart slewing to one side then the other as he fought desperately to keep it under control. Harry frowned but said nothing, tightening his grip on the side of the wildly bucking vehicle.

The rising ground became firmer and the billowing dust dissipated a little as they approached the spur. Outcrops of dense black rock appeared through the red dirt and the cart slowed to a crawl as Finn navigated between the outcrops scattered on the rising slope.

Studying the dark rock as the cart passed close to one outcrop then another, Harry saw the rock was indeed of a different kind to the surrounding yellowed sandstone country. Up close, the dark bedrock looked like basalt that had been forced up through the shallower sandstone crust. The dark stone mounds, protruding through the thin, rocky soil, lacked the deep cracking and flaking of the sandstone, instead swirls and smooth bubbled ridges covered the exposed surfaces, perhaps indicating a volcanic origin. To Harry, the dark volcanic rock seemed to brood in bubbles and frozen eruptions—as though the blood of the earth had spilled and then congealed in large globules on the surface.

Small pores, like tiny gaping mouths, pockmarked many of the outcrops and the tortured shapes made Harry grow uneasy again.

They slowed to cross a rock-strewn section of the trail near the crest of the spur and Finn suddenly stopped the golf cart and turned to Harry.

'Um, sorry, Harry … but from here on you'll have to wear a blindfold.' He reached into his pocket and produced a dark, crumpled piece of fabric.

'Blindfold! What do you mean blindfold?' Harry grew angry at the ridiculous request.

Finn shrugged nervously, 'It's just the rules. I … '

'Why?'

'Samuel said you have to, coming up here,' Finn ran his hand through his tangled hair. 'You'll be quite safe really, we don't mean any insult or anything, it's just … well, it's just the way it is.' And Finn smiled crookedly, in an attempt to reassure the older man.

Harry stared back, mulling it over. Even the presence of the good-natured young man didn't make the thought of it more palatable and he briefly thought to refuse, but the promise of two full water drums pushed him reluctantly to agree. Shrugging in defeat, he scowled as Finn reached over to tie the blindfold over his eyes.

The world went dark and Harry instantly became claustrophobic. He settled uneasily back into the seat, grabbing the cart's side for security, as it began to move forward across the rough ground.

'What is there to hide out here?' The bouncing of the golf buggy made his voice vibrate comically as he probed for information. 'You have nothing to fear from me, you know. I couldn't give a damn what you're doing out here.'

'I know that, but … Samuel and Nettie, they want it this way so … '

Harry heard the discomfort in Finn's voice and changed the direction of the conversation.

'So Nettie and Samuel–they're your family, eh?'

'That's right,' Finn sighed softly. 'They're OK, you know. They seem a bit grumpy, but they look after us–it's tough out here so they have be tough too.'

'How many people are there here?' Harry prodded, but he felt Finn stiffen at the question and there was a silence.

Harry grunted. 'Why haven't you gone back east? What's holding you all out here?'

'If it was up to me I'd be gone tomorrow! ... but ... ' he flared. Harry could feel Finn baulking at being drawn to say too much, so he changed tack again.

'The country's dead, eh? Must be thirty years or more since the last decent rain out here. It's a hell on earth, huh ... hell on earth,' Harry talked to keep his claustrophobia at bay. He could see nothing of their journey but soon he felt the terrain become steeper again under the cart as they wove down the far side of the rocky spur.

'You're right, this country is dead,' Finn's exuberance had been quenched. 'That's why I asked about the east. I want to go there, see? The cities and all that ... I've never known anything but here, And mum left years ago ... I could...' he muttered disconsolately. 'There must be something on the coast–something more than this ... mustn't there?'

'I don't know,' Harry flinched from talking of the east and of Finn's absent mother. 'There's more time back there, I guess. There's still a little water ... well, sometimes. The de-sal plants produce just enough to keep things turning over. But there are too many people crammed onto the coast, Finn.' His brow wrinkled. 'There's more time than here, that's for sure.' He shrugged in the darkness of the blindfold. 'But the water's failing there, too.' He turned instinctively toward the young man to reassure him.

"No, no ... I don't mean the water!' Finn's voice rose in frustration. 'There must be music, movies, people like me ... young people ... back there. People doing things ... I don't know, art, theatre, protesting even.' He paused as he steered the cart around another outcrop. 'Just to sit and talk ... that'd be enough ... just to meet people.' He sighed, a little embarrassed at exposing his eagerness.

When he spoke again, his voice had collapsed into despondency. 'There's nothing here for me, Harry. I knew people on the coast when I was a kid ... when the internet was still working ... we used to talk back then ... but even the net rarely works these days ... weak signals and satellite blackouts ... I haven't heard anything for years. They could be dead for all I know,' Harry let Finn rattle on. 'Nettie and Samuel, they don't get it. They're satisfied with hiding out here, but for what? There's more to life than waiting ... I know there is. There's more to it than just hoarding all tha... '

Abruptly, Finn bit off his words and swore under his breath and then sulkily said nothing more. Feeling for him, Harry abandoned his efforts at conversation and slumped back into the seat. Behind the shifting shadows of the blindfold, he worried at what these people were doing out here. Something big was going on, he thought, to stay on in this hell they must be sitting on something that gave them some kind of hope.

The buggy's route levelled out and they bounced across what Harry sensed must be flat paddocks again. Then the cart slowed suddenly and the light dimmed as they came to a halt under some kind of shelter. He heard Finn's footfalls crunch as he crossed in front of the cart and then Finn's voice was close to his ear.

'Here we are.' The flatness of despondency had lifted, replaced by Finn's usual rapid, lilting speech. 'I'll hold your arm and guide you. It's not far and you'll be fine if you follow my directions.' He laughed nervously as Harry climbed clumsily from the seat.

The light flared again as they passed into the sunshine. Harry had left his hat behind and the heat thumped down on his shoulders and head as they walked. He stumbled once and, putting his arms out to the sides to steady himself, his fingers met what he thought were glass walls on either side.

'What … ' he almost asked but thought better of it.

Finn gently pushed him forward again. 'It's not far now … just keep moving.'

They walked for a few more paces until Finn pulled gently on his shirt. 'Stand there for a minute. Don't move and I'll be right back.'

Harry heard the jingle of a large bunch of keys. He felt unsteady, blindfolded in the searing heat, and he wobbled a little as he heard a heavy lock snap and a metal handle shriek as it turned. He heard large metal hinges squeal and, finally, a resounding thump as a door opened to its limit.

Finn pulled at his shirt again and they went forward again into darkness. Harry stumbled over the threshold and walked a little farther before he stopped abruptly and Finn bumped into his back.

The air felt cool and strange in the darkness. At first Harry could not say why. They took a few steps more and his feet met a metal walkway of some kind, he sensed a large space had opened up around him and he felt vertigo rise up until Finn's hand guided his to a metal handrail. From behind the blindfold, he stretched his senses outward trying to gain some idea of the place. And suddenly his mind grasped the shocking enormity of the place where he stood. There was an incredible, all-enveloping, humidity saturating the air around him.

The moisture-laden air touched Harry's face and arms and filled his clothing. Holding his breath in shock, a soft sound suddenly shredded the silence around them. The sound–the deep resonant plop of a single drop of water falling into a massive pool somewhere below where they stood–shook Harry to his core. The echoes rang in his ears, reverberating again and again, back and forth across what, Harry guessed, was a huge vaulted room or a massive cave of some kind. Harry stood frozen to the spot and played with the sound in his mind. He had not heard a sound like that for many, many years.

The cool density of the air–the thickness of it in his nostrils and throat–was almost suffocating. The silken touch of the humid air caressed his bare skin and goose bumps sprang up over his body as he heard another drop hit the water's surface maybe ten metres away. The echoes again repeated, making his heart race and his mind whirl with the utter decadence of the immense quantity of water that must lie below him.

'Come on, Harry. We can't stay here.' A cacophony of echoes reverberated around them as Finn pushed him forward and they both clanged slowly across the steel gangway high above what, Harry thought, must have been the largest volume of water left west of the mountians.

How it had slipped below the prospectors' radars, Harry could not fathom, but his mind boggled at the potential value in that vast pool of liquid gold.

* * *

After Finn had closed a door behind them and removed the blindfold, Harry could not focus on the dismantled pump that lay before him. The sound of that fat drop hitting the pool drove him mad. He circled it and poked at it as though it were some trick or snare for his unwary mind. The potential possibilities of such a find and, inevitably, the whirling calculations of profits came unbidden to his mind.

To distract himself, he picked up a steel bearing from the pile of parts scattered before him and examined it, turning it in his hand in the weak light of the single hanging bulb. Snorting, he put it down again and flicked through the dog-eared pages of the water pump's maintenance manual. Staring blankly at the complex diagrams, he sucked his teeth as Finn, leaning against the wall of the pump room, looked over his shoulder.

The heavy-duty electrical pump and the pipes running from it took up much of the metal floor in the tiny box of a room. Released from the blindfold, Harry's eyes had been confronted by the pump's heavy, red, steel casing that sat amid a chaotic circle of dismantled parts. In one corner lay a half-open, battered toolbox with a clutter of rusty mechanic's tools spilling from its drawers.

Dismayed by the chaos, Harry had run his eyes over the rest of the tiny room. The sheet metal walls around him were stained with long rainbow ribbons of rust. Even the low, sagging, metal ceiling had short stumpy stalactites of rust hanging from it. There were no windows or furniture in the pump room, only the dismantled pump and the thick, grey, bandaged intake and a thinner outlet pipe to the surface and a thick, plaited electrical cable that brought power to the pump from an unknown source. The air was thick with moisture and the metallic tang of rust sat on Harry's tongue as he studied the dismantled pump.

Harry's eyes, usually dry and painful from the desiccation of the desert, felt as though they were brimming with tears. After the relentless heat and brittle dry of the outside world, the dampness and cool of the room made him shiver as he sat mulling over the tools and the chaos of engine parts. As he picked parts out of the pile in front of him he itched to ask about the water. Finally, unable to shake the thought of it, he threw down a tangled nest of wires and turned to glare at Finn.

'Why the fucking pantomime? Why the blindfold? You seriously thought I wouldn't guess?'

Finn pushed himself upright from where he leaned against the wall but said nothing. Shuffling nervously, he ran his hand through his hair.

'I mean … ' Harry held up his oily palms. 'I don't give a damn really. It's your business but … '

'All you're doing is making it more difficult for me!' The young man scowled. 'Just fix the pump. Don't ask about the rest. I … Please, Harry, just fix the pump. It's how they need it to be and that's all you need to know.'

Harry stared at him for a second before turning his back. He managed to focus on the diagrams in the manual for half an hour before Finn, growing impatient, interrupted him.

'Can you fix it?'

Harry snorted in disgust, 'It's impossible to tell with it in a mess like this. I mean, look at it,' he huffed. 'I know this model reasonably well. It's old, so I know it. With the manual–if you've got a half decent workshop, and electricity … I think I can probably fix it. It might take a while though.' He looked up at Finn and saw his face brighten, 'Maybe a week, maybe two,' he shrugged noncommittally.

'We have a workshop, small, but a pretty good one,' Finn rubbed his hands on his blue overalls and smiled in the weak light. 'Two weeks, huh? When it's fixed you'll head off east again, I suppose?'

Harry only grunted in reply.

Finn hesitated, 'So where will you go? Back to the cities, the way you were going?' The unbridled desperation in the young man's voice irritated Harry again.

'Shit, do you ever let up?'

'Well … I just … '

'Maybe, maybe not. Might go south-west, down through the salt lakes.' Harry said it more to annoy Finn than anything else.

Finn's face fell. 'Why? Why not go east? I mean … there's nothing towards the salt lakes … only more desert– its bad down there, they say. The land's all contaminated or something,' he hesitated again for longer this time. 'You know. I could tag along, if you went east … if you want company that is.'

The question hung in the air as Harry examined wires leading from the motor's control panel. He left it a while before he replied almost enjoying the younger man's squirming.

'No, thanks … fine on my own. Why would you go east anyway? You've got the … well, all this here. People back east would kill for what you and your family are sitting on here.'

Finn slouched back against the wall, saying nothing and occupied himself by staring down at the scattered parts of the pump. He seemed about to speak several times, his mouth flapping open like a carp's, but changed his mind each time. Ignoring him, Harry went back to the pump and began slowly sorting the parts into some sort of order.

A short time later Finn broke the silence, in a sulky monotone telling Harry it was time to go and producing the blindfold again. Harry wiped his hands on a filthy rag he found on the floor and stood.

'Is that really necessary now? I know your bloody secret. I don't care really and I won't tell anyone, if that's what you're worried about.'

Finn shook his head vigorously. 'If Samuel found you without a blindfold down here he'd crack it. Sorry, Harry, I have to. I know it's stupid but … ' He raised the material and motioned Harry to turn his back as he retied it over his eyes.

The claustrophobia returned when he heard the door squeal. He grew nervous for a moment before he felt Finn touch his arm.

'Come on,' Finn guided him back onto the clanging metal walkway.

After a few paces Harry pulled against the younger man's grip and stopped.

'Please, let me see it. Let me see the pool.' Desperation flooded Harry's voice.

The younger man hissed but said nothing. He grabbed again at Harry's sleeve but Harry batted his hand away.

'Please, it can't do any harm … I already know what you're hiding here.'

'But Samuel said … '

'Listen, Finn, I won't say a word, really, not a word. Please … I have to see the water. It's … it's what I do … ' He paused and then spoke in a softer, wheedling tone, 'Look if you come east, and I'm not saying you can but … well … we'd have to trust each other, eh?'

Another drip hit and echoed from the pool below. And, as the echoes died, far off, the sound of small ripples lapping against rock came back to them. At the sound Harry grew wild and reached up and tore the blindfold from his eyes. Finn reached out half-heartedly to stop him but, seeing Harry, open mouthed, blinking as he took in the cavern's vaulted interior, the young man dropped his hand to his side.

'My God … ' Harry gasped as he gazed at the huge cavern.

The pair stood between the two handrails on a narrow metal gantry that hung between the door in the cavern's wall from where they had entered and the door of the pump room. Harry leant against the rusted handrail and gazed out across the dimly-lit pool. His gaze followed the row of lights out across the rough rock ceiling to where it met the opposite rock wall, maybe thirty metres away. The raw, angled roof and walls were cleaved and chiselled in great gouges as though huge machines had hewn the vast cave from solid rock. On each small angle and protrusion of the ceiling, tiny bright sparkles danced in the light. Each low point of the roof seemed to hold the waiting birth of a water droplet. Each drop hung for an agonising pause, until one, far off across the vault, fell and with a deep, explosive plunk, hit the black surface of the underground pool.

Harry gasped again. Here, encased in the raw basalt of the spur, was a giant obsidian jewel. Thousands–no, much more–litres of liquid gold lay hidden here. Harry had heard nothing of this place in all his years at Clearwater, nothing. If they had only known of this oasis, they could have ... His mind began to race with the value of the water but he cut the thought off.

Finn watched the man gape and saw the conflicting emotions flit across his face. He felt a smile build but stifled it. He watched the old man's hand slowly rise and involuntarily scratch his hollow, shaven cheek.

'See ... this is why ... this is why we keep it a secret.'

Harry looked over at Finn–his eyes glazed and he shook his head, 'Do you realise what you have here? Do have any idea of its worth to the companies. Do you?'

Finn looked to the door nervously. 'Of course we do, that's why Samuel makes us keep it a secret. If others knew ... they would come and ... ' His face fell with the thought of it. 'Samuel's right. People might come ... and take all this.' He waved his hand out across the space. Another drip fell. 'It's our lives... '

'But others need it ... ' Harry paused for a second and stared into the young man's face and saw his forehead crease with worry.

A younger Harry would not have cared about these people, but the old, tired Harry just shrugged his shoulders and turned again to the pool. He breathed deeply, sucking in the moisture, sucking it down deep into his lungs, savouring it.

Finn stared down at the pool for another second before whispering, 'Come on. I have to put the blindfold back on before somebody comes.'

Finn grabbed the blindfold from Harry's hand and raised it. He could see Harry's long bony hands grip the handrail but, after a brief hesitation, he turned away allowing Finn to tie the material over his eyes. He guided Harry to the door and pulled it open with a screech and a hot blast of dry air punched them as they emerged. Harry flinched from the furnace, his skin and mouth protesting the loss of that blessed humidity.

'Remember, Harry, don't tell Samuel you've seen the Cistern. Tell him or Nettie, and I'm in for it,' with that he pushed Harry out into the sun.

The vile heat drew the air from Harry's lungs and his mouth opened and closed soundlessly. The image of the pool seemed to shrivel and curl under the barrage of heat and light but his mind fought back. Still whirling with the possibilities, Harry clung to the memory of that vast pool and, most of all, the wonder of how it had remained unexploited during these desperate times.

* * *

Samuel's face was screwed into an angry scowl as he stood before Harry and Finn on the veranda. He had not been told of Harry's knowledge of the Cistern—he had not needed to be. He knew it simply by seeing the look of wonder on Harry's face—it was impossible for the old man to suppress it.

In disgust, Samuel turned away to stare out at the darkening landscape. His hand gripped the veranda rail and like snow, powdery paint fragments fell to the grey, buckled veranda boards. Harry saw his head shake imperceptibly before he whirled back to confront them.

'You're a bloody fool, Finn! Why would you risk our life here? He's nothing! You risk the entire Centre because you think he'll take you east. You think ... no, you don't think ... and that's your bloody problem. You are a fool!' Samuel's round, bristly face reddened and his cheeks shook with barely supressed rage. His mouth moved as though he savagely chewed his words before he spat them out. It shocked Harry to see the father's anger so strong and he spoke up, thinking to take the heat off Finn.

'Look ... look, it wasn't his fault. I'm not sure what you think, but I heard the drops falling. I felt the presence of the water. I mean, it's not hard. I removed the blindfold myself. I had to see ... '

Scowling and red faced, Samuel turned on Harry and snapped. 'Damage is done. You know about the Cistern now. Nothing can change that.' He paused and took a shuddering breath. He turned his scowl to Finn but still spoke to Harry, 'Can you fix the damn pump?'

Harry nodded, happy for Samuel to call a halt to the argument. The three of them stood there in silence. Finn shuffled nervously and the camel belched by the fence as he chewed a brittle branch. In the silence Harry hesitated, unsure, and then turned and wandered back to the oven of the kitchen and slumped back on the cot.

As he slowly relaxed, his head propped on the musty pillow, a trickle of sweat dislodged from his hair and ran in fits and starts, down through the dust to his dirty collar. Harry's mind sluggishly followed its trail. He lay listening as Samuel and Finn fell to arguing once again. In the heat, the raised voices made his head buzz. There was a cutting venom to Samuel's rancour and his son's voice fell under his father's, softly pleading.

'I couldn't help it, Samuel. He tore the blindfold off before I could stop him, I ... I mean, what was I supposed to do ... tie him up or something?' There was a short silence, as Samuel seemed to consider the suggestion.

'Yes ... Maybe ... I should have sent Nettie or gone myself ... It was a mistake, I knew you weren't ... '

"But, Samuel ... Nettie couldn't have ... She ... ' Finn's voice faltered.

'I've told you before, you're too bloody soft ... you let him, an outsider, walk all over you. You're soft with all that silly crap about the cities ... ... just like your damn mother was,' Harry heard Samuel sigh loudly. 'Like a goddamn puppy, whimpering at that fool's feet, you put all we have here at risk! You can see it in his eyes–all he sees are the c-credits. You see it, don't you, Finn? Men like him are like dogs circling around a bone. He could bring others here. He doesn't give a fig about you or Nettie or any of us. You've got to get it into your head ... men like him, they're leeches, Finn!'

Harry felt his face burn as he heard the father snort violently in disgust.

'But what could I do? You said to take him ... ' the younger man's voice was a dismal whine now.

'Forget it, Finn,' Samuel groaned. 'Just forget it. The damage is done. Just keep an eye on him, do you hear me?'

There was no audible reply. Samuel's boots scuffed the boards of the veranda steps then dug into the dust of the yard and finally Harry heard the rattle of the golf buggy bouncing across the yard.

Harry felt bad for putting Finn in the shit, but the vision of the cavern diluted his guilt. He stretched slowly on the narrow cot and felt the sharp pang in his side again. He rolled over and stared at the door to the hallway, waiting for the thin figure to appear. Glancing across at the picture on the mantle, he pondered the image of Finn's mother–it had probably not been an easy parting judging by the sour bile in Samuel's voice.

Harry grew thirsty and contemplated pouring a cup of water from the drum when he heard the door to the veranda creak and slam. He heard the scuff of Finn's work boots in the doorway but he didn't look up. The young man crossed silently to the cupboards above the sink and clattered around searching through the food tins and threw two down on the bench. Harry felt Finn's eyes on him. There was a long silence and no movement in the dusty heat and Harry finally dragged his head from the crusty pillow and looked at the man standing across the kitchen.

'You want me to help?' Harry's voice croaked in his own ears.

Sulkily pulling a pan from beneath the sink Finn said nothing. His face was ashen as he slowly opened the cans with a rusty can-opener and vigorously slopped the contents into the pan on the stove. The fire was down to only a few glowing coals, but it was enough to warm the food. Leaving the spoon standing in the battered pot, Finn turned to Harry.

'Don't worry about Samuel, he's just careful about anyone coming here,' the crack in the young man's voice belied his words.

Harry swung his feet over the side of the cot and sat up with his elbows resting on his knees but said nothing.

The two ate silently sitting across the table from one another and then, when they were finished, stared into their empty bowls. Harry reached for a glass of water and spun it slowly in his fingers.

'Why is it here, Finn? The Cistern I mean. How has it remained hidden through the last rush? I know the prospectors came through this country. How did they not find it?' He sought the young man's eyes but Finn's gaze remained locked on his plate. He merely shrugged. Then slowly he looked up to Harry's questioning frown and began to speak.

'Samuel could explain it better than me. He took over the manager's job at the Centre before we were born. Back then he was a sort of a foreman, I guess.' Finn's face brightened a little as he began to tell the story. 'We lived here, in the house with Mum. Me and Nettie grew up here, roamed out in the hills, even swam in waterholes back then.' He leaned in toward Harry and whispered, 'Back then you even heard frogs croaking in the reeds–not all the time, but sometimes. It was good then, before the last waterholes dried up. The kangaroos and wallabies were still here. And even cattle came down to drink. We used to watch them from the water.' He stopped for a moment his eyes glazed with memory, his long thin fingers splayed wide on the table.

'This place was some sort of experiment–begun before we came–even before the first water crisis I think.' He drew a breath and wiped the dust from his cheek. 'The Cistern was part of an experimental water extraction program–a new process. They set up the Centre to test a new plastic or something–a hydrophilic polymer, but I don't really understand all that stuff.'

Harry frowned, not recognising the term and Finn paused before elaborating. 'The way I understand it, it was a kind of plastic, a polymer that draws water from the air to its surface in some sort of chemical reaction. Samuel says when the polymer is exposed to even the smallest amount of moisture in the air it draws any water from it. The water pools in droplets on the polymer's surface, but it isn't absorbed.'

Finn watched Harry's face grow bright with the dawning realisation of the potential of such a thing and the younger man smiled with pleasure. 'Amazing huh? They developed this polymer coating and came out here to undertake trials in the hills behind us, above the Cistern– the darker rock here helped the process I think.' He shook his head in wonder. 'They dug the cavern from an old mine shaft and coated the rock on the hills above it with the polymer. They bored holes through the rock to channel the captured water downward, to be stored in the Cistern … or it did in the beginning at least. It slowed to almost nothing five or maybe six years ago—the air is just too dry now, Samuel thinks.'

Finn sat for a moment chewing his lip before he continued. 'There's still more than enough in the Cistern though. It will last decades, more maybe, enough to pump up and into the gardens and for the old research station, where we live now. We even have enough for showers once a week. This house is really just for show … you know, to put people off.' He smiled again at Harry's incredulous face.

'But why … why isn't it … why haven't I heard of this before?'

Finn shrugged and frowned. 'Samuel can explain it better than me. They kept it secret—only the people here, the government and the private sponsors knew. It was all hushed up in case it failed. But it worked … in the short term. The tests were a complete success for a few years but over time the polymer's collecting efficiency declines and, well, like I said, its too dry now even for this, you can't get water from a stone as they say.' He glanced up quickly but Harry did not smile at the young man's joke. 'The polymer still drew water out of the air, still does now, but much slower … not enough to be commercially viable. The government money dried up decades ago, the private sponsors refused to keep it going.'

Finn stuffed his hands into the pockets of his ill-fitting overalls and leaned back in his chair. 'Like I said, Samuel could explain it better. He understands the way things worked back then. He says that after the polymer's efficiency declined none of companies wanted to touch it— no profit in it.' Finn's brow wrinkled. 'Samuel says they shifted their efforts back to prospecting and tapping the last remaining groundwater reserves.'

Harry knew all this, could see the truth in the young man's words. The focus of those times, in the midst of the frenzied desperation of The Failing for corporations like Clearwater, was on where the money was—the lucrative government exploration contracts to find other untapped aquifers, not on technical stuff like this.

'Anyway,' Finn continued, caught up in the telling of it. 'The companies ditched the project, the Government cut funding and, well ... we were kind of forgotten, I guess, in all the chaos of The Failing. Samuel and a few of the other scientists and maintenance staff stayed on when most of the others who worked here moved back to the coast. Nettie and me ... we were still very young back then. We grew up here. There are ... ' he hesitated. 'There are only a few of us left now.' And then a scowl flitted across his young face, 'And we've been rotting out here ever since, except Mum, she ... ' He stopped talking abruptly, glancing nervously up at the door.

Harry slumped back in his chair, incredulous, but he knew exactly how it could be that the project had been forgotten. It was a chaotic scramble then, new ideas picked up and then discarded in a frenetic search for solutions to profit from. The rivers of government money had seemed almost inexhaustible twenty or thirty years ago. It would have been so easy to write off something like this. He shook his head, the loss of such a thing, the stupidity of it resounded in his mind.

Then he chuckled to himself and Finn stared at him in confusion. It was, as always, the way with them—the corporations always cutting off their damn noses to spite their faces. This system could still have worked, back on the coast, Harry thought. Back then anyway. If only they had persevered, he thought, they could've taken it further, refined it or improved it, maybe. But the greedy bastards were never interested in things like this, not without guaranteed profits at any rate. And as Finn watched him, Harry chuckled softy to himself again and shook his head slowly in resignation.

'When will it be fixed?' Her shout made Harry jump as he bent over the screeching lathe, fashioning a thin metal sleeve to replace a worn water line fitting. He turned and saw Nettie standing in the doorway. He smiled involuntarily but she did not return the gesture and then he reached down and pressed the lathe's cut-off button.

'Two or three days, I'd say … a week at most, maybe … by the time I put it all back together.' He leaned against the machine and wiped the sweat from his face with his sleeve.

'Finn said it's the impeller rotor bearing or something.'

'Yes, that and a few rusted or broken wires in the motor itself and some worn seals and corrosion. I made some new parts for the pump impeller and some new gaskets for the leaking seals. The pump's pretty far gone but it'll hold for a while now, I think.' He paused. This was the only conversation he had had with Nettie in the week he'd been there.

He presumed she wanted as little communication with him as possible, so he was surprised when she stepped over the threshold and approached across the oil-stained concrete floor. Stopping a few metres away, she inspected the jumble of parts resting on the bench for a moment before she looked up and pinned him with her dark, over-large eyes.

'He wants to go with you, wants you to take him.' Her voice was flat but Harry saw a frown wrinkle her forehead below the wild tangle of wiry, brown hair.

'I won't take him, I don't want the company.'

'He's bloody desperate,' she continued, ignoring him. 'You should stop playing with him and tell him the truth, damn it! You know what's happening on the coast. Coming from you … he might forget about all that bullshit!'

'Don't you think I have?' Harry looked at her thin angular face as she stared at him. In her anger, the smouldering coals in her eyes grew bright and her thin cheeks wormed with the grinding of her teeth.

'How'd you know about pumps?'

Harry shrugged, immediately wary of the sudden swerve in the direction of the conversation. He swung back to the lathe to avoid her gaze. 'Here and there, you know just picked it up over the years.'

'Bullshit.' But she didn't query him any more.

'You can't blame him for dreaming. What's here for him, from his perspective anyway?' Harry spoke softly.

She stared for a moment, her face stony, a finger tracing a circle in the grease on the bench top. But when she finally spoke her voice had mellowed a little.

'He'll fucking beg you, you know. He's a sucker for all the glamorous crap about the city. He's not old enough to know better. He's heard stories and seen pictures, you know, on the net. But seeing that chaos, in pictures and streams, doesn't change things for him—he thinks it's just a big adventure. He's fucking mad for it.'

'I can see that, Nettie. I told you, I wouldn't take him. I'm probably heading south anyway, not east. I can't go back to the coast, not yet.'

Her stiff shoulders slumped a little. 'The city will eat him alive,' she stopped and breathed deeply. 'I don't know what to do with him. He's so damn hopeless.'

He stepped forward, but only a step. 'Go with him, maybe. What's here for you anyway? The Cistern won't stay hidden forever, you must know that. It might take them years but eventually the prospectors will find you. And they will take it—it's worth too much to them to be left alone.'

'Fuck you! If we're careful, they won't find it.' Her anger was only half-hearted—he could see she knew there was some truth to what he said. 'There's nothing out there anyway. This is it for us. The Centre is an oasis ... surrounded by that hell out there. And it's ours ... we'll hold on to it.'

She stared at him, her brow furrowed, her long-fingered hands curled into bony fists before her. 'You know there's nothing to be gained in leaving. Out there's a goddamn blast furnace. If there was hope on the coast ... you wouldn't be here.'

'No, you don't underst ... '

She held up a hand, halting him. 'Where would we go? Come on, tell me, where could we go that would prolong the inevitable, any more than here? Where is there left? The Centre is a last refuge against all that hell out there.' She drew breath before she continued a little more softly, 'Samuel will not leave here and neither will I. The western lands are broken, but the east is only a few years behind. Everyone with any real money has gone to the refuges at the Poles.'

'That's right, the Poles ... you could ... ' Harry broke in weakly.

'How? We have no money to go, all we have is held in that Cistern and we don't even legally own that. You tell me, Harry, tell me where is there left to go?'

And his mouth flapped open and then closed again.

'You wander around out here. Why?' She waved away the prospect of an answer. 'That's fucking fine for you. Do what you want, but don't lead Finn on. Tell him the honest truth about what's happening in the cities. Don't send him into that shit.'

She stared at him, her eyes full of anger and pleading and Harry's gaze fell from hers and he mumbled, 'Like I said, I won't take him with me, Nettie. I like it too much, being on my own.'

He was not allowed in the cool-houses where they grew the food to feed themselves but often, as he passed on his way to or from the pump room, he would pause and find a gap in the condensation of the misted windows to look in at the rows and growing-racks that made the Centre's protected gardens.

When he had first looked inside the growing houses his body had shivered with the sheer luxury of it all. He had not seen plants like this in years—long rows of tomatoes and beans, low clumps of potatoes and even zucchinis grew under the shade cloth in the cool glasshouses. Once he had looked in and found the looping lines of water hose were on, spaying fine mist over the beds. The sight of the thin mist, like a light rain on a spring day, brought memories of long ago, and a spasm of sorrow shook him.

One morning he peeked in and saw a figure bent over a tray of seedlings. Nettie's thin frame was turned away from him, yet he recoiled and pulled his face away. But her figure soon drew him back. He watched her working quietly in the cooler air fed channeled from the Cistern, her hands among the small green plants, delicately re-potting them into the larger trays. He had never been a gardener, never enjoyed growing things. He had never had enough time or enough patience. But now, watching her gently handle each seedling, her movements slow and composed in concentration, he could see the subtle joy of it reflected in her small economical movements. Wiping the rich, black dirt on her overalls, she sat back on her haunches in satisfaction. She squatted for a long time, her hands relaxed on her knees and, enthralled, he was unable to turn away.

Nettie's sharp, angular beauty was softened by the lushness inside the cool house. He wanted to speak to her but squashed a sudden urge to call out to her, to say hello. The thought of the tranquil moment being ruined by her scowl and her anger at his prying drove the fleeting desire away.

Watching Nettie, he lingered too long, and heard the crunch of boots on the gravel and turned to see Samuel watching him, a dark scowl on his face. They said nothing to each other. Harry held his eye only briefly before guiltily glancing away and hurrying off. Samuel stood and watched him go and then strode off toward the small huts of the living quarters.

* * *

Running his hand over a jutting protrusion of black basalt rock, Harry felt no rough surfaces on the angular outcropping. The surface felt strangely plastic, almost silken–not shiny as he had imagined, but slippery like powdered graphite under his slow-moving fingertips. Entire exposed areas of the rock ridge were coated with the polymer. In the larger cracks and depressions of the outcrop, he noticed there were holes–the perforations drilled to draw the water from the polymer-coated rock surface as it ran to the low points. The entire expanse of undulating rock, perched directly above the Cistern, glistened lightly, as the sun slowly set out on the plain.

Late in the afternoon Harry had wandered up to see the polymer for himself, and seeing it, caressing the silken polymer-coated stone, brought back his wonder at the audaciousness of the project. From his vantage point he looked down at the Centre nestled in the small cul-de-sac valley below. The cluster of tiny buildings, their roofs covered in solar panels, was crammed at the back of the narrowing valley. The tool-shed and workshop were ringed by the two long, low, glass cool-houses. A small group of huts, home to the seven or so people who lived there, was squashed into the innermost part of the narrow defile. Outwardly the barren looking valley sold no hint of the vast volume of water the residents of the Centre perched above. With all that water, he mused, the group could have tripled their growing houses, even quadrupled them—fed dozens more people using the water hidden in the heart of the rocky spur.

He and Finn had talked of the workings of their small community over the last few days as they sat in the little rusted room, rebuilding the pump. The entire thinking of the little society seemed to be focused on concealing the existence of the Centre and the Cistern. The Centre had remained hidden for decades, concealing the water from passers-by, lest someone came who would try and take it from them. They trusted no one it seemed but each other. Any benevolence would, almost certainly, be punished—that was their thinking—and Harry thought they were right in that. There was little room out here for altruism or generosity.

Lost in thought, he gazed down at the Centre as the light fell and wondered at the luck of those people sitting down to their dinner below—hiding such a secret in these blasted lands, for so long. Shaking his head, the last of the sun gone, he stood slowly and worked his way along the spine of the ridge through the jumbled rock shelves to the track that led back to the house and to his ration of water and a now-cold plate of food.

The pump was fixed. He would leave the next day, having earned his two drums of water. The cut on his forehead had healed without infection and he had, he thought, put on a bit of weight with the extra food. He felt a little lighter for the break in his travels. Even the camel had plumped up a little and seemed better for the bundles of leaves and garden scraps Finn had brought from the gardens each evening. He sensed Finn wanted him to stay on, but Samuel, Nettie and the others wanted him gone.

Harry felt a little torn by the place. He itched to get on the road again, move off on his rambling journey along the roads to the southeast, but the Cistern drew him like a wasp to a packet of sweets. He could still feel that moisture against his skin as he lay each night on his cot in the stifling heat of the kitchen. He could feel it eating at him now, but he fought off the urge to ask to stay. Deep down, he knew what their reply would be, and he felt, too, that the community was just a tempting mirage for him. His journey still lay before him.

* * *

The throbbing pain beat deeply in Harry's side as he lay after waking. It was cooler in the early morning but still he found it difficult to breathe in the hot, stale air of the deserted house. To escape the heat and the pulse in his side, he climbed stiffly to his feet and wandered through the house to gain the shade and the cooler air of the veranda. He pushed open the screen door with a long screech but he stopped mid-stride on the threshold, his heart sinking in his chest.

Out across the paddock, a hundred metres beyond the rails of the broken fence, stood three large vehicles. Framed by the dark line of the spur, the dirty white vehicles seemed to have risen up from some long hibernation, out of the earth itself and, the dust trickling from their flanks, they waited.

These vehicles were familiar to him—he recognised them like you would recognise your own childhood house. The three trucks, perched up on huge treaded tyres and high-lift all-terrain springs, were water prospecting vehicles. He had spent many hours and thousands of kilometres in similar trucks in the old days, searching for water. And he was not in the least surprised by their presence here now. Their appearance, however ominous, merely seemed a depressing inevitably to Harry.

Monolithic and silent, the vehicles rested like great humpbacked beetles crouching in the dust. One truck sported a long tail—a stretch of broken fence and a fence post trailing from its rear bumper, probably collected as the vehicle had lumbered off the road and through the dilapidated fence. Their deep tyre tracks cut unwaveringly across the barren paddock.

Harry exhaled slowly. Under the thick coating of desert dust he could just discern the large CLEARWATER HOLDINGS stencilled on their doors. The windows of the three trucks were darkened with dense protective tinting but, without even seeing them Harry knew the men inside—not personally, he was pretty sure of that, but he knew their ilk from long experience. And knowing these men, knowing how they worked, made him squirm uneasily with the awful certainty of what was to come.

It rushed at Harry now. From his memory, he could hear the clang and clatter of metal and, behind it, the quick, efficient silence of the men unloading their long drill rigs and pumps. He heard too, the echoes of the altercations that inevitably followed the appearance of these men. Harry felt a wave of tiredness and the pain in his side began to beat more sharply.

He staggered back to lean heavily against the doorframe. Screeching horribly, the screen door swung back against his shoulder but he did not feel it. Silently, he watched, waiting for time to start again, to begin that inevitable spiral. And then, to his dismay, he saw a thin dust trail building from behind the spur and a few moments later the tiny golf cart crested the rise, paused for a moment, then began the winding descent to the paddocks and the waiting trucks.

The cart seems to inch down the slope as the dust billowing behind it was whipped away by the breeze. Through the haze he watched it draw nearer. Eventually, he recognised Samuel behind the wheel and Nettie next to him under the canopy, and he felt some relief that it wasn't her younger brother sitting there.

The golf buggy came to a halt twenty metres from the prospecting trucks and sat as the dust cloud thinned. An ominous stillness settled once more across the valley. The cart sat there, dwarfed by the hulks of the trucks. Harry felt anxiety grip his chest and his hand rose involuntarily to scratch his hollow cheek. He had half a mind to go inside, to escape the gruelling certainty of the meeting. He turned away but still he paused. Then abruptly his shoulders slumped, he turned back and slowly walked down the steps and out across the garden to the paddock.

Samuel and Nettie had left the cart and were standing off a little from the silent trucks. Knowing the prospectors would make them wait, Harry stopped a metre behind and off to one side of the father and daughter. Looking up at the dark windows above them, he felt the gaze of the truck's occupants on him. He knew their minds would be ticking over, wondering at his presence there, rechecking their list of possible stakeholders. He could almost hear them discussing alternative strategies to accommodate his unexpected presence. But, for a moment at least, the silence seemed to hold some short reprieve.

Maybe they recognised him. Maybe, he figured hopefully, his presence might carry some weight with them. Then came a puff of dust and the clunk of a heavy door seal being broken. The passenger door of the lead truck swung open and a pair of clean, tan leather boots felt for the first rung of the short ladder down to the hub of the huge front wheel. A man dressed in clean blue work trousers and a crisp blue shirt stepped down onto the dust and was followed by another. Both men wore large, dark protective sunscreens attached to the visors of their white hard hats, which hid the top half of their faces. The first one to descend strode forward and turned his head briefly in Harry's direction before turning his full attention to Samuel and Nettie.

'His being here won't change things for you,' the man tilted his head toward Harry before lifting his sunscreen. He was greying at the temples and his eyes, sunk in his flat, expressionless face, were hard like two shiny black pebbles.

Both Nettie and Samuel were caught off-guard and glanced at Harry for a moment. Samuel stepped forward and, in an attempt to regain some authority over the situation, he thrust out his hand.

'My name is Bishop ... Samuel Bishop. What is it you want here?' He stood stiffly, looking up at the two taller men. Harry could see him becoming more and more unnerved by the their stony silence, till finally the man with the hard eyes spoke.

'We know who you are, and you know why we are here.' He ignored Samuel's outstretched hand and raised his face towards the hidden valley beyond the spur. Opening a cardboard folder, he unclipped a piece of paper and feigned reading from the crisp white sheet for a moment before he spoke.

'This is Clearwater's Prospecting and Extraction Permit for this zone.' He thrust the paper towards Samuel. 'It's all in order. Your people have until midday tomorrow to get any valuables out and vacate the property before the extraction crews arrive.'

'What? You can't just ... ' Samuel stammered but the prospector ignored him.

'After that time, if you approach the cavern or the installation, you will be in breach and liable for a minimum five-year gaol sentence. Do you understand your obligations under the permit?' He waggled the letter in Samuel's reddening face.

Samuel gaped but reluctantly took the sheet. His face grew even redder, he licked his lips and stared unseeing at the paper before he spat. 'You have no right ... we ... we have been here for decades. This is our ... ' His voice cracked and failed.

'No, this is Government property, granted to us under Section 47b of the Federal Emergency Water

Procurement Act,' he smiled thinly at them both. He spoke as though he had repeated the same words a thousand times. 'Unfortunately, being here for however long does not denote any right to the property or the water by default. The Regulations are very clear on this.'

The man turned and looked Nettie slowly up and down, making Samuel bristle. But the man had softened his tone a little when he spoke again.

'Listen,' he sighed. 'Don't make this any harder–you have no rights here. We're licenced to take possession the easy way … or the hard way.' He shrugged then suddenly turned his broad shoulders to Harry and a slight smile formed at the corners of his mouth.

'Tell them, Sinclair. You know what's in play here. Do these people a favour, will you?'

The shocked silence was like a thunderclap between the two groups.

'What's he talking about?' Nettie's voice was slow and steely as she turned to face Harry. 'You know these men? You … is this your doing?'

The grey-haired prospector chuckled to himself before he spoke in mock disbelief. 'You honestly don't know who he is, do you? Well, in that case, let me introduce you.' He nodded at Harry, 'This is Harry Sinclair, one of the original billionaire watermen. Not now, of course,' he smirked at Harry. 'But back in the day, Sinclair here set up Clearwater. Before the first water boom, wasn't it, Harry?' He shook his head and looked to Samuel. 'You really didn't know?'

Harry saw the tidy trap they were setting. He knew the script well but it was too late to derail it. And right on cue, Samuel turned to Harry, his round face screwed into a tight red ball, 'You sold us out to them! You bastard, you sold us … ' He shook uncontrollably, rendered speechless by his outrage.

Harry lowered his head for a moment before looking again into Samuel's angry, bloodshot eyes. 'No, how could I? I didn't and … I wouldn't. That was all a long time ago … Tell them,' he pleaded to the prospector but the man only smiled at the mischief he was sowing.

It was too late. Samuel's anger had found meat, something of its own size to bite on. Harry had seen people–landowners and farmers–played this way many times. He had turned them against one another himself, time and time again, back when he worked these rigs, long before his rise to Clearwater's Board of Directors. This man was a slick operator to have picked up so quickly on the potential in Harry's surprise presence.

Harry turned away from Samuel's damning glare, back to the two prospectors. 'Look, I still have shares in Clearwater. I'll sign them over to you and your men, I'll pass them on for nothing … just leave these people … '

A soft laugh cut him off. The man's cold eyes held his. 'It's a bit late for that now, isn't it?' He glanced fleetingly at Samuel, assaying the effect of his insinuation, 'Anyway, Clearwater's shares aren't worth a pinch of shit these days. Any influence you had is well and truly gone on that score, Sinclair. If you won't tell them to make it easier for themselves, stay out if it.'

Dismissing Harry, he turned back to Samuel, 'Of course I can't reveal our sources in this. You can believe him or not, it makes little difference.' He raised his eyebrows and shrugged again, feigning disinterest in any further discussion.

Harry looked away, up at the tinted windows of the trucks and despondently said no more. His offer was his only card and a forlorn one at best. He had guessed it would have little tender, but it had leapt to him anyway in his desperation to save them and perhaps redeem himself in their eyes. He sighed inside. Things would follow their own inevitable course now, as he had known at his first sighting of the trucks. Silently, Harry hoped Samuel and the rest of them capitulated quickly—it would spare them much hardship.

Harry winced, grabbed his side and groaned as the pain under his ribs thumped up—and the people gathered in the paddock thought it was about defeat. He turned away, unable to look into their eyes. And leaving Samuel and Nettie to argue the ins and outs of it, he stumbled away. They watched him for a moment, the faces of the father and daughter twisted by anger and scorn for the thin, angular hunch of the man walking dejectedly back through the broken garden to the house.

Gaining the shade of the veranda, he reluctantly turned back once more. Sounds of renewed argument filtered faintly across to the house. He watched Samuel step forward and raise his fist in the prospector's face and the other company man, react so swiftly to step up and push Samuel back, flat on his arse in the dust. He watched Nettie, her tall frame suddenly quickening, bend to help her father. He heard her voice rise across the paddock, her words still muffled and unintelligible in the heat. He saw the two men standing before the vehicles, unmoving, satisfied at the ticking of another box. Violence had been triggered and that then, Harry knew, allowed them more freedom to manoeuvre within their rules of engagement.

Exhausted, Harry left the veranda, shuffled to the cot and rested against the wall and shut his eyes. He did not need to see to know what would follow.

* * *

Finn sat with him at the kitchen table, sent back to the house by Samuel to keep an eye on him and, Harry suspected, to keep the young man out of harm's way. The others, Samuel, Nettie and the people he had seen only in passing, were standing vigil at the Cistern.

The trucks had not moved that day and no one had climbed from the cabins after the first meeting. There was no need to talk again, not yet. They would wait things out in the air-conditioned vehicles. Harry knew they were well equipped in there. They had food and water, narrow fold-out bunk beds and high capacity internet communications via the restricted corporate satellites.

They would not come out until the allotted time had passed and they were permitted to move forward taking possession of the water. Things were done to well-defined and tested timetables, potential hiccups had been ironed out through years of experience with these altercations. The prospectors would leave nothing to chance.

Now, with the sun just on rising, Harry and Finn ate the cold canned soup from the night before in silence. Harry saw a cocktail of worry, fear and, maybe, a little supressed excitement in Finn's pale blue eyes. His face was flushed and he fidgeted with his spoon, laying it down as though finished, then quickly picking it up again to poke at his food. Tapping the spoon against the edge of his plate, Finn finally spoke.

'What will happen today, Harry?' his voice cracked.

Harry looked into Finn's eyes and shrugged. But it was enough and the young man glanced away.

'I didn't lead them here, Finn, you understand? I wouldn't do something like that.'

Finn looked to him, held his gaze and nodded.

A little later, Finn watched Harry wash his face in the sink. There were three drums on the kitchen bench next to him. One, already used for the kitchen, was half full. The other two were Harry's payment, brought by the younger man the evening before. Harry placed a hand against one and was reassured by the heavy bulge in the plastic wall. Then suddenly, through the thin walls of the house both men heard the deep growl of the vehicles starting up. Finn stood in excitement but Harry remained facing the sink and splashed the dirty, lukewarm water on his face again. He slowly dried his face and arms with a grubby towel and sat back at the table to put his shirt back on.

'Stay clear of it, Finn,' Harry spoke meticulously, one word deliberately placed after the other. 'Stay clear, eh? Don't waste yourself on heroics, huh?'

The young man merely hung his head, unable to look into Harry's eyes. It was almost unbearable, hearing the growl of the engines rise in pitch as the trucks climbed the ridge and still worse to hear them fade, as they passed beyond the boulder-strewn crest. In the hour that passed after the sound had died, Finn's face was carved stone. Dark bags now marred his face below his usually sparkling eyes. His face too had lost its healthy colour, replaced by an ashen pallor, his mop of wild blonde hair now looked limp and greasy.

An hour passed. Finn stood and sat and stood again and wandered about the room. He poured a tea but left it abandoned on the table as he stood before the yellowed picture of his family. Then suddenly he spun and fled down the darkened hallway. Harry heard the screen door shriek and heard him sit in one of the chairs and imagined the young man staring out across the paddocks to the trail over the ridge.

Then, softly at first, Harry heard a growing rumble begin. The sound grew for several seconds and then ceased abruptly and he heard Finn gasp and call out his name.

'Fuck,' cursing as he struggled to his feet, Harry hurried to the veranda. He found Finn leaning forward in the chair, his eyes wide, staring at the ridgeline opposite. Following his gaze, Harry's breath caught in his throat.

The deep tyre tracks of the trucks led up the ridge to join the narrow trail through the boulders. Beyond, where the tracks disappeared, a thin column of smoke was just beginning to rise from behind the ridge. Harry leaned against the wooden rail and watched as the black trickle grew in the sky. A soft sob came from the young man behind him and turning he saw Finn's eyes were wide and brimming with tears.

'What's happening? What has ... ' he swallowed. 'I have to go, Harry. I have to get back ... to help them. I can't stay sitting here.' Finn's voice grew stronger and his face more resolute as he stared up at the rising column of smoke.

'Finn ... ' But Harry could say nothing more. How could he stop him? Harry knew Finn would go over the range and see. And he hoped to himself that it was all over before he got there—before he could be drawn in and caught and hurt. Desperately, he hoped Finn would be too late.

Harry ached to flee, get away before the cruelty of the world crashed down on Finn. He started to speak again but for a moment he could force out no words—he could only stare at the young man's face. Then in a rush, he found the strength to speak.

'I'll go up there with you and see what has happened, Finn.' Immediately he regretted saying it, but Finn's eyes lit up, his face brightened a little and he nodded eagerly.

'Yes, yes ... thank you, Harry.'

* * *

The two of them stood looking down at the installation from the ridge above. A gasp escaped the young man's pale lips. Harry felt Finn shudder next to him with their first sight of the Centre.

Smoke hung in the valley but they could still make out a few of the buildings. The glass of several of the cool-houses was shattered but most of the housing and the workshop remained intact. Nearly all the damage seemed to be limited to a small building near the covered parking area. Smoke still rose from the smouldering shell and only the aluminium skeleton remained. Bent and leaning crazily, it looked as though an explosion had torn through the shed, a blast large enough to utterly destroy the shed but little more. Roofing iron was torn like paper and strewn willy-nilly in front of the three prospecting vehicles that jammed the narrow entrance to the Centre.

'It's the generator and battery shed,' Finn whispered.

Harry immediately saw the sense in targeting the generator and batteries. With their power source gone it made it all the more difficult for the residents to stay and mount a defence. Harry looked at Finn and put a hand on his shoulder.

'At least it doesn't look like anyone got hurt.'

Finn nodded and looked into Harry's eyes, thankful for the fleeting reassurance.

A breeze momentarily whipped away the smoke and what they saw made Harry gasp and the younger man whimper. The Centre's entire population of ten people stood before the cool-houses, facing off against the line of six surveyors, who stood thirty metres away in front of their trucks. The residents had erected a hurriedly built barricade of trailers, sheet iron and timber at the entrance to the Centre but Harry could see the flimsy structure would barely stand up to even the most half-hearted attack.

Harry quickly understood the real reason for the stand-off–the residents, fronted by Samuel and Nettie, were armed with a few rifles and several pistols. Harry realised the utter insanity of this for the Centre's inhabitants. Armed resistance would only give the surveyors more leeway to reciprocate with increased violence and make it possible to call in Clearwater's feared Security Division. He appreciated that the residents had little choice but the presence of weapons would only make it easier for Clearwater to bring full force to bear on them.

Harry saw all this at a glance and shivered. Finn, standing next to him, groaned and moved as though to begin the descent to the Centre, to join the others. But Harry put out a hand and held him back.

'Wait ... just for a few more minutes, huh?'

'Why? They need all the help they can get, Harry ... I ... '

'Just give it a little bit longer ... please, Finn.'

Finn shook his head but reluctantly stayed by Harry's side. And soon they saw one of the prospecting team, his torso bulky in a Kevlar vest, walk forward to stand in the middle ground and call out to the gathered residents.

They watched as Samuel crossed the open ground slowly to join him. After a minute or two, Samuel turned and walked back to the people clustered behind the barricade but his shoulders were slack and he looked dejected as he rejoined the group.

'They have given you extra time, till tomorrow morning I imagine, to consider your options. They do this to give themselves time to bring in the Security Division. The guns mean they will wait, but they have open slather now, with the way things have played out. It's like a bloody chess game to them, Finn—the extra time means nothing.'

'But can't we ... I don't know, wait them out?' Finn wiped his pallid face with his hands and then let them fall uselessly to his side.

'I don't know. I think ... ' Harry paused before he continued. 'Maybe, anything's possible, Finn ... '

They stood for a few moments more as the trucks' engines fired up again and the vehicles, one after the other, turned and withdrew a few hundred metres to halt near the mouth of the valley to wait out the new deadline.

'I have to go, Harry. I can't just stay up here. I have to talk to Samuel and Nettie.'

Harry nodded to the young man and patted him on the back. 'I know. I won't come with you–I don't think I'd be welcome somehow. I'll head back to the house, eh?'

'Sure. Yeah … ' Finn's voice was high and agitated and he chafed to go, but he paused to look nervously into Harry's eyes. 'I'll come over when I can, Harry.' With that he turned and sprang away down the slope, slipping and sliding towards the column of smoke below, finally leaving Harry alone.

Harry and Finn

Harry sat once again behind the dusty brown rump of the camel. The animal's short frayed tail flicked back and forth, ceaselessly shooing away the non-existent flies from its narrow, bony arse. The endless creak of the dray, as it rolled over the corrugated dirt of the road, was music to Harry–soft and familiar. The sound and rhythm soothed the echoes of the disturbance he knew still raged behind him.

Harry suddenly sighed, trying to shrug off the clamour of the past day and desperately sought the familiar hypnotic solace of the road. He sniffed the air. It burnt his nostrils but he drew it in anyway and savoured the smell of dust and dung that wafted back from the swaying beast.

Now, even as the heat again surged up like a great all-consuming wave, he felt the reassuring pleasure of being alone. It was good, he thought, to be alone in that stewing heat–good to be moving again. It was like opium, to sink into solitude and leave the nagging toothache of humanity further behind with each long stride of the camel.

His thoughts began to drift slowly again, set adrift by his plodding progress. Leaning back in the seat, he pulled his hat down over his eyes and let the reins slacken, and gave himself over to the familiar sensation of being swallowed by the broken land. And eventually, as he began to nod, he felt himself shrinking to become a tiny solitary insect, crawling across that vast red plain.

But he could not yet completely shed the thoughts of Finn and the Centre. He felt for Finn and Nettie and even Samuel, for all his gruff insensitivity. They were trapped now, in the falling dominoes of action and reaction. It was not pretty to think of the little oasis being torn apart. The Cistern would probably be drained to the last drop within a few weeks and Harry frowned under the shadow of his hat brim at the thought of it. Maybe water was liquid gold, but Harry saw the ridiculousness of it too–that the whole damn cavern was merely a drop in a vast ocean of humanity's unquenchable thirst.

Harry shook his head at the horrible inevitability of it all and then tried to force the thoughts down as the ripples of anxiety rocked his lethargy. But it held him. He felt a tinge of guilt at leaving them but, in the end, he knew his presence would not have postponed the inevitable for one more moment. His power over those men had waned years ago. But knowing it didn't really help somehow.

In his mind he saw Finn's face sliding into hopelessness. Harry had witnessed the same emotions play out in similar circumstances–other people snared in that same trap. Some stayed on to fight, as the people at the Centre were doing. The smarter ones left before it was too late. But now, seeing it all from the other side–knowing Finn and the rest of them–the thought of that desperate battle over the coming hours, dismayed him more than he would have guessed.

He sighed, sniffed the hot air and rested his chin on his chest. Closing his eyes, he let the world pass by unobserved, hoping that, by dozing, he would sever the unsettling threads linking him to that chaos. And, eventually, lulled by the repetition of movement, it did.

* * *

Finn caught him that evening as the heat bled out with dusk.

Late in the afternoon Harry had urged the camel off the road onto a rough track, which led into an eroded dry creek bed. The steep, crumbling rock banks of the gully were high enough to hide him and his campfire from the road and the flat sand of the dry bed was good for a camp.

Harry had revelled in the simple preparation of a fire to be lit later as darkness fell. He had fallen into the familiar process of hobbling the camel and releasing it to wander and browse. The renewed routine reassured him. He sat silently on a rock, his back resting against the bank and waited for the darkness and the cold to release him from the fog of the day.

Just as he had grown bored and his thoughts had drifted to lighting his fire, he heard the familiar clatter of the golf cart in the distance. Its distinct passage made his heart sink and he willed it to pass by his hidden camp. He held his breath, but as the noise reached a crescendo it stopped abruptly on the road near the track and silence fell. Harry cursed but stayed seated.

There was a small slide of sand and rock as Finn scrambled along the track. When the young man saw the camp, he stopped for a moment as though composing himself before he called out.

'Hey! Harry, I've found you!' His voice was high and forced as he walked a few more metres and stopped near the dray. Peering down at Harry, he pulled off his cap and his ridiculous flying goggles and held them loosely before him. Harry said nothing, preferring to stare at his own dusty boots crossed in front of him. Unfazed by the old man's silence, Finn propped himself against the dray and began talking rapidly.

'Lucky, really, finding you … I saw your wheel tracks leaving the road. Samuel said I would. But the cart is almost out of battery. I only had another half hour, that's it. Lucky, huh?'

He petered out, seeing no spark of interest in the sitting man, and nervously shuffled about. Then smiling again, his voice lifted as he resumed his rolling chatter.

'I brought water and food with me—for us, I mean. Should keep us going for a while.' He threw himself down in the sand of the creek bed a metre away and looked at the pile of twigs and branches that made the unlit fire.

'You going to start that fire?' He looked sideways at Harry where he slumped sulkily against the bank.

'Not now, later–when it's dark and the smoke won't be seen,' Harry continued to stare at his boots, his face hidden by the brim of his hat.

Finn grunted and sat for a moment longer, digging a hole in the sand with his boot heel. 'It would be easier to travel together, wouldn't it?' Running his hand through the sand he poured a handful slowly through his fingers. 'I mean, we could help each other, travel a bit safer maybe.'

'You've got it all figured out, huh?' Harry looked up for the first time. 'What if I said forget it? What if I don't want your company?'

Finn's mouth opened and closed silently. His face fell and he frowned and glanced away to hide the hurt in his eyes.

"They told me to catch you. Samuel and Nettie … they told me to leave. They said it was no use … me staying back there … ' his voice fell away.

Harry saw the fretted chewing of Finn's jaw, marking his turmoil at leaving the others. Cornered, Harry sat there staring at him, uncertain of what to do, wanting to cut at the young man for all his presumption, and the audacity of Nettie and Samuel too. He wanted to tell Finn to piss off but he knew the decision for him to stay was already made– made by the failing battery in the golf cart and the emotional blackmail perpetrated by the father and sister. They knew he would not let the younger man wander without a vehicle in this country. Samuel had gambled, perhaps with Finn's life, on Finn finding him but he had won his dangerous bet.

He sighed, cursed and then rose and wandered over to the dray and hunted for a tin of something for their dinner. Turning, he grunted to Finn and, as the young man looked up, Harry tossed a flint lighter to him and turned away again.

Finn smiled, watching the man's back for a few seconds more, and then began to remake the fire to his liking, carefully fluffing the collected leaves and gently stacking the smaller sticks above the kindling to allow for oxygen flow, before he leant over and squeezed the flint lighter and sparks flew to the tinder-dry leaves and grass.

* * *

They left the bones of the golf buggy in the gully, having first stripped its canopy and roughly attached it to the dray with some frayed dags of rope and wire that Harry had hoarded amongst his things for operations such as this.

The dray creaked more severely under the weight of the extra food and water as they pulled up the first hill beyond their camp. Finn settled himself in the seat next to Harry and pulled his faded baseball cap down over his eyes. When Harry had suggested that, given their slow pace, he might not need his comical goggles Finn had shrugged and left them hanging on a dead branch beside the road. Holding the reins loosely in his hand, Harry muttered to the camel to pick up its pace. The camel ignored the command and plodded on, slotting quickly into its preferred ambling rhythm.

They were quiet on that first day travelling together. Soft grunts and sighs in the heat were the only punctuation to the camel's soft footfalls and the rhythmic creak of the dray. The heat rose and rose, seemingly without end, and the heavy buzz of silence over the country rose with it. Both men felt the growing disquiet that always came with the building heat. The sun's blistering intensity brought a strange crawling irritation that, by the afternoon, would become almost psychotic.

The heat and blazing light made it almost impossible to think. Alone, Harry would have endured it all by mumbling a stream of curses or occasionally yelling abuse at the camel. With Finn as company, he resisted those outbursts. But without the release, the heat seemed even more unbearable.

Harry spoke for the first time at midday to break the buzzing of the heat.

'Where is it you think we are going?' he growled. He knew the answer, but felt irritated enough to ask it anyway.

'Well, I ... ' Harry held up a hand to silence Finn.

'I'll tell you now–there's no answer in the east. The coast is fucked!' The heat had driven him to display more anger than he had intended.

Finn slumped in the seat, saying nothing.

'You're wasting your time. It's chaos.' Harry sniped, but the young man refused to bite and the silence swallowed them again.

* * *

The broken rock outcrops of the hill country slowly disappeared over the next few days as the road fell and flattened to forge out across the southern mallee country.

Over millions of years the mallee forests had colonised the ancient dunes. Low and stunted, each tree produced a multitude of narrow spreading stems from a large, buried lignotuber. Each year their falling leaves and branches had helped to build a few more millimetres of impoverished soil. This thin crust helped to stabilise the shifting sand and, in turn, helped other plants like the spinifex to take hold and spread from beneath the trees' spindly frames.

Nearly two centuries before, great swathes of the forest's eastern and southern edges had been cleared to create huge wheat farms and fickle grazing country for cattle and sheep. Yet, despite this clearing, the mallee forests remained immense, surviving the uncertainty of the fluctuating climate and erratic rainfall. Thousands of years of tenacious persistence maintained sway on the ancient plain until The Failing had set its teeth in the land and the great unending drought had settled to permanence—the prolonged absence of rain slowly throttling most of the remaining forest.

Now, where an occasional clump of spinifex or mallee still survived, the dunes were held in place by their shallow roots. But the wind had dug in around many of the dead trees, exposing their gnarled lignotubers. The skeletal trees were left perched precariously above deep scours and gouges, their exposed roots raised above the sand like giant, mummified heads, crowned with a pincushion of brittle, leafless stems.

As Harry and Finn drew away from the hills, the vast woodland quickly swallowed them. Both men found the land of gaping scours and garish trees jarring and oppressive. There were no points of reference in that broad, rolling country. The road ironed out, running straight like an unfurled ribbon, kilometre after kilometre. The ancient decaying dunes did not rise high enough to give them a view of what had passed or what was to come. They simply plodded on, the day unbroken by changing landscapes. When they did occasionally speak, it was mostly in hushed whispers.

Each night they camped and sat silently by a small fire until the cold drove them to their beds, and eventually to shallow, shivering sleep. Each morning they woke as the first light filtered through the surrounding woodland of leafless tines. Out on the plain, the heat would soar quickly after that first glimmer—the long, thin shadows of the trees shortening rapidly as the two men hurriedly scoffed their left-over dinner and repacked the dray.

Then, four days on, the endless road brought them suddenly to a junction. A dirt track, running at right angles to the tar, met the road and ran dead straight through the decaying woodland until it disappeared over a nearby rise. And then, a quarter of an hour later, another track and then, at a similar interval, yet another crossed their path. At the next intersection a tilted post with a small metal arrow at its top stood pointing out into the dunes. A red A47 was stencilled there, the letters badly faded by sun and the sandblasting of the wind.

Harry grunted, the first sound he had made in hours, and Finn turned to look at him questioningly. Without speaking Harry slowed the camel and guided it off the tar and onto the soft dirt of the side road. The camel gurgled and protested at the detour but Harry urged it onward with a quiet sucking through his lips.

'Why are we leaving the road?' Finn's face creased in confusion.

'I know these grid roads. Thought I'd show you something,' Harry mumbled.

'What?'

'It probably won't be far. Wait and see,' he smiled grimly at the younger man.

The dray rolled up and over the first dune, slowing nearly to a stop at the crest and then increasing speed as they descended into the tangled swale on the other side. The camel stepped delicately over the thin fallen mallee branches that cluttered the track but the brittle wood shattered loudly as they went under the fat rubber tires. At the lowest point of the next swale, a second track crossed theirs, running exactly at right angles, disappearing quickly in the chaotic clutter of the mallee forest. A hundred metres more and they passed another track going off at right angles along the dune top, and yet another in the next hollow.

Puzzled by the grid of seemingly senseless sandy tracks criss-crossing the otherwise featureless mallee, Finn scowled but refused to ask again about their detour. But, as they ascended the next dune, a strange vista began to be revealed. A small white peak appeared over the dune's crest. At first only small, framed by the blue of the cloudless sky, the peak soon grew larger as the dray reached the crest. Harry pulled the camel to a stop on top of the dune and they gazed down on a large flattened basin of bare sand excavated from the rolling dunes and forest. The mallee forest at the clearing's edge had been buried by the spoil of sand and a tangle of uprooted trees pushed up by the flattening and clearing of the basin. But the strange artificial valley paled into insignificance as Finn's gaze was caught by what lay at the clearing's centre.

Blinding white in the full sun, like an ancient, pearl megalith, sat a great sparkling hill. Its exact dimensions were difficult for Finn to define. Maybe twenty of even thirty metres high, there seemed no mark or feature with which to judge its exact size against the low rolling mallee beyond the clearing. The glittering peak, its steep sides almost perfectly smooth, seemed to hover within his vision, as though the megalith was somehow detached from the country it inhabited. Squinting his eyes against the reflected light, Finn's mouth flapped open in astonishment.

'Salt,' Harry said in a self-satisfied tone.

'What... why?' Finn wrenched his gaze from the glittering mountain to look at the older man.

'The spoil from the gas—the road grid was to service the gas field ... the pipes are underground. The mining process drew salt water from deep underground, beneath the good water in what was then a vast underground aquifer. The gas companies added chemicals, cadmium and barium and the like, even uranium. They pumped it back down to fracture the rock below to release the gas and then pumped it out and left it to evaporate in these shallow ponds, leaving massive quantities of salt residue. The waste salt was just bulldozed into piles and left like this.'

He waved a hand at the sparkling hill, 'Poisoned the groundwater with the chemicals, and poisoned the land above with the salt ... all for twenty years of gas ... twenty years!' He scoffed, 'Made no difference in the end, pissing in the wind with peak-oil hitting. They had other options but ... ' he paused and looked sideways at the younger man. 'This, Finn, is a little monument to all that futility ... to maintain that madness you so desperately want to see ... Beautiful isn't it?' He chuckled a little maliciously and waited for a reply.

Finn said nothing and contemplated the towering salt cone. He had a headache and no energy for Harry's cryptic games.

Harry shrugged at the silence of his companion and the dray lurched forward as he flicked the reins.

'It's as good a place as any to camp. Eh?' He raised his eyebrows, 'Little weird, but kind of interesting.'

Finn watched the white mound loom upwards as they descended to the clearing. The dray's hard rubber tyres crunched noisily on the thin patches of salt that coated the clearing around the hill. Finn sensed Harry was toying with him, bringing him here to make some point. He snorted crabbily. He didn't really care for Harry's vague jibes but he was too engrossed in his newfound freedom to fret too much about the old man's obscure games.

* * *

They set up their camp off to the side of the salt hill. The camel stood facing away from the white cone, as though the beast refused to acknowledge the offensive monolith.

A slight breeze blew from the north as they ate their dinner sitting before the small fire and after a short while the two men's faces began to tingle and then sting, flayed by the fine grains of salt kicked up from the cone by the wind.

'Why camp here, Harry?' Disgruntled, Finn rubbed his stinging eyes.

Harry looked at Finn with a blank expression for a moment then shrugged but said nothing. Behind him, the light of the dying fire danced off the sparkling crystalline cone that loomed above their camp. They sat for a while before they crawled beneath their blankets early to escape the abrasive sting of the salt.

Late in the night, Finn awoke with a start. The fire had died hours before and the sprawl of stars overhead was the only light. He lay there shivering, staring up at the night sky framing the vague outline of the salt hill. The deep silence was suddenly broken by a soft groan from the man sleeping opposite. Another groan followed, a little louder, and the camel shifted its position and its bell tinkled. Finn rose at the third groan and under the dim light of the stars, went over to stand above Harry's sleeping figure.

The groans did not seem to emanate from a nightmare but from some kind of pain that whittled away at Harry's thin frame. Under the blankets the man's body was curled protectively. His hands, protruding from the blankets, were clenched into tight fists. He half coughed, half groaned again, then his body arched suddenly and Finn knelt beside him and gently touched his shoulder.

Rolling in his sleep, Harry's faced appeared from the shadows, a grimace had drawn his lips back from his teeth. Harry's eyes flew open and a long shuddering sigh escaped through his teeth. He coughed and sniffed loudly as he slowly recognised the silhouetted figure kneeling beside him.

'What?' he croaked.

'You were groaning and thrashing about ... I was just ... '

Harry grunted and rose to a sitting position. The pain of the movement made him clutch at his side and he hissed softly, like a cornered animal.

'What is it, Harry? What's wrong?'

Harry looked up at Finn. His eyes were wild with the pain. 'It's nothing to worry about. It comes and goes. I'll be fine in the morning.'

'Bullshit, Harry! Tell me what's wrong with you. Are you sick?' Finn's voice rose.

'It's all right ... forget it ... I'll be good tomorrow,' with that Harry carefully lay back and pulled the blankets up over his head. 'Go back to sleep.'

Chewing his lip, Finn knelt above him for a moment longer, then stood and circled the fire, returning to his own bedroll. He lay there for a long while, contemplating Harry's mysterious illness and later he began to fret on how it might hamper their journey to the coast. And doubt stole into his mind.

He had thrown his lot in with Harry not knowing much about him, their journey or his own ultimate aim. His rashness rushed in. Suddenly he thought of Samuel and Nettie and what was happening back there. He felt a sudden desire to return and see them but knew, guiltily, the feeling came mainly from this new uncertainty. And this sudden realisation chewed at him as he lay in his blanket staring up at the stars.

These rumblings kept him awake. Every now and then, from across the smouldering fire, Harry emitted a stifled groan and rolled in his blankets. After a while, unable to bear listening to him thrash and struggle any longer, Finn called out, knowing the older man was still awake.

'Why didn't they do something, Harry?' There was silence from the other man but his thrashing and groaning stopped abruptly. After a few seconds a reply came from beneath the tousled bedclothes.

'Who? Do what?'

"The people, back then ... before The Failing, I mean. I know why it happened—you know, the weather changes, the disrupted climate ... the rain stopping ... all that, but how did they not do something when they could have?"

Harry snorted and mumbled, 'I don't know, Finn. Once they could have changed things, I suppose, maybe twenty or thirty years before The Failing really began ... but that point came and went long ago ... that's The Failing, Finn—they let the chance slip through their fingers ... '

'I know they did. But how ... why did they let it happen? They knew the science even back then, didn't they?'

There was another prolonged pause beyond the fire before Harry answered. 'They just kept doing what they did ... It's hard to explain. It seems crazy, I know ... looking back on it ... but I guess, despite knowing it was coming, even when the shit really hit the fan, even then things just kept going.'

'But how was it possible to ignore those warnings, Harry? I mean, they still had time back then, didn't they? I just can't figure it. I mean ... just look around you at this ... this place ... it's ... '

'Fuck, Finn!' Harry cut him off angrily, 'You won't get any arguments from me!' Finn heard the strange vehemence choking Harry's voice.

'But they saw it, Harry. They saw it in time! How could ... '

Harry rubbed his face with his long bony hands and groaned impatiently. 'In hindsight, I know it's difficult to understand. I was only a kid back then, but ... I ... even seeing things getting worse every year ... it was ... I don't know ... easier to ignore somehow. The corporations pushed back hard against any move away from the old carbon economy. Despite the irrefutable evidence they still protected their short-term profits. The politicians took the corporate dollars—they were bought off ... ' he sighed deeply and shifted to look across at Finn.

'There were global agreements you know, but they were always half measures with little or no teeth. I guess, they all thought there was still time—some miracle of science or something would turn things around. Even growing up in the midst of it I still ... ' he scratched his head and rolled back to stare up at the stars but continued talking softly.

'They finally did act, fifty or sixty years ago, but it was already too late. It was the beginning of The Failing and the warming threshold that they had set first at two degrees was broken and they raised it to three, and then finally four-degrees, lifting the bar each time the agreements were ignored. Things really began to unravel then. Climate change and the oil crisis, coming together like they did, were just too much,' he paused thoughtfully.

'They did what they could, Finn, with the limited oil supplies they had. Over the next couple of decades, they fought hard, threw everything at finding new water supplies and building thousands of big wind and solar energy farms—you'll see them on the coast,' his voice grew softer. 'The last of that emergency money made me rich when I was in my thirties. But it was too late—they should've rolled out those projects fifty years early if they had wanted to stop all this.'

Harry groaned in pain again, sat up and hung his head for a moment before he spat. 'Ah, fuck it! You want the short answer, do you?' Finn's silence gave Harry leave to continue, his voice full of derision. 'The short answer is greed. It's simple really—all that bullshit is window dressing. Old-fashioned greed steam-rolled common sense ... sadly it really just comes down to that. They ... governments, corporations ... we fiddled while Rome fucking burned, Finn. That's the simple bloody truth of it!'

Finn lay silent in his blankets. But Harry, as though his outburst had somehow eased him of a little pain, took a more conciliatory tone as he spoke to the younger man through the darkness.

"There are no excuses really. I'm sorry... sorry I can't give you better, Finn, but I can't.'

Harry rolled over again to face away from the fire and stared up at the salt cone. He coughed and winced when he breathed in a little of the fine salt blowing around him.

Finn wanted to ask more, feeling Harry's disgruntled answers were somehow inadequate but, sensing the other did not want to speak more of it, he lay quiet. Mulling it over, from any direction, it seemed so ludicrous. To Finn, it was impossible to understand or, more pointedly, to absolve them from blame. His blasted world was a diabolical inheritance from the past. A gift that Harry and his forebears could have avoided sending.

But Finn couldn't find it in himself to hate them, he was not easily given to anger, and what would anger or hate achieve now, he thought. History was history, a done deal, and they now merely lived with the wanton mistakes of The Failing generation. Yet it was hard for Finn not to feel more than a little contempt for the grotesque weakness of his forebears.

He shook his head as the stars hung above him. At least Harry had the decency, Finn concluded just before falling into sleep, to be alive to bear witness to all the hell they had they left for his generation.

* * *

Finn woke to the sound of Harry repacking the dray. He lay for several minutes listening and soon heard Harry hiss sharply and curse softly to himself. Finn let him shuffle around the camp on his own, allowing Harry and his pain some privacy for a little longer before he emerged from the cocoon of blankets.

They joined the road again, the sun only inches from the flat eastern dunes of the mallee and immediately the camel set his habitual slow, plodding pace. Harry held the reins loosely as always, but today he leant forward rather than slumping on the wooden bench as he usually did. His body was knotted– Finn could see it. His elbows were drawn protectively into his sides and, from the corner of his eye, Finn saw him wince with each bump and slew of the dray on the broken road.

Harry said almost nothing all morning. He offered only an occasional grunt or gave a single word reply to any question, his jaw remaining clenched even as he spoke. By mid-morning Finn was desperately trying to ignore the muffled whimpers but Harry's pain was driving him mad. By noon the scorching heat bore down as they plodded through the silent endless woodland. It rapidly grew intolerable. Even under their new protective canopy, the thickening heat only adding to Harry's misery.

'Harry, what the hell is going on?' Finn's sudden question cut across a soft groan but the man did not reply for an excruciating minute. Finally, Finn sensed Harry's head swivel toward him and felt his grey eyes fix on his face. But he did not turn, letting the other have his time.

'You take the reins,' Harry grumbled, passing the leather to Finn.

He took them and immediately flicked the camel's dusty rump, the camel's burbling fart registered its displeasure at the new regime, but never the less, it picked up its pace a fraction.

'I'm dying, Finn,' Harry's words hung in the heated air as the dray crested another low dune.

Finn looked to Harry's long, pinched face, into those translucent, grey eyes, searching for a hint of some sour joke–for anything other than the literal meaning. But there was no hint of mockery in Harry's ashen features, only a horrible resignation.

'What … what do you mean? Why?' Finn's voice rose and cracked a little.

Harry snorted derisively and shrugged, delaying his reply. 'Stop. I want to get a drink.'

'What?'

'Stop the damn dray, I need some bloody water.'

'Oh. Right, right,' Finn tugged the rein gently and the camel halted and sagged in the traces. Grimacing and groaning Harry climbed over the back of the bench, avoiding the searing heat pouring down outside the shade of the canopy and, through a steady stream of curses, rummaged among their things for a cup. Finding one at last, he half filled it and gulped a long mouthful then offered the rest to Finn. Taking the cup, Finn watched the old man over the dented rim as he drank.

Climbing slowly back to his seat, Harry leaned forward with his elbows resting on his knees, looked at Finn and spoke in a deadpan tone.

'I've got cancer.'

Finn's face fell with the utterance of the word. 'What … really? How do you know? I mean, how long … how long have you had it? Where?' Finn's barrage of questions was wallpaper, an attempt to avoid the enormity that Harry had laid between them.

'Since before I came out here. Probably three years or more,' he paused, shrugging his shoulders.

'Harry! That's terrib … ' Harry held up his hand to cut him off.

'Forget it, I went through all that long ago. It's settled on me. The specialists back then said it was cancer of unknown primary,' he snorted. 'They found it first in my spleen and then in my liver … some lymph nodes here and there … they had no idea really, but they gave me six months to live anyway. That was three years ago. What the fuck would they know, eh?' he snorted and smiled crookedly at Finn's incredulous look.

Finn chewed his lip and said nothing.

Harry grimaced at the young man. 'Snap out of it, Finn, there's no need.'

'Oh … well, what did you do? I mean, did you get treatment?'

'No.'

'But … I thought they could … '

'Those doctors didn't know their arses from their faces. That circus would've killed me even quicker, and with more pain and less dignity. They told me the odds were stacked against me anyway. Giving into that desperation seemed … I don't know … worse somehow. I'm happy with that, Finn.' He looked at Finn's dour face, daring the younger man to challenge him.

In the pause Finn made a vigorous attempt to force the sympathetic look from his eyes and shrugged. 'Well, I guess it was your decision, huh?'

'Yes, and I'm glad of that at least,' and he chuckled half-heartedly. 'These bouts of pain come and go. Like I said, I'll be right in a day, maybe two. Don't worry … or at least don't worry at me, OK?'

'Right-o, Harry, I get it.' It was Finn's turn to break out a weak smile and then he turned to the camel and softly urged it back into motion. But for the rest of that day, Harry's new tore at him as he sat ridged on the wooden seat, lurching back and forth in a stunned silence.

* * *

They meandered a week more through the mallee forest and slowly Harry improved, pulling free of the bout of pain. Then one afternoon, like a razor cut, the fish bone prison of the trees abruptly vanished. In the blink of an eye, the land changed from the seemingly endless woodland to a vast expanse of naked, red-soiled farming country.

Relieved at first to be free of the monotony of the mallee, the two men quickly grew sullen again, crushed by the tumultuous scarification of the open country. Once a great food bowl, the gigantic, now defunct, wheat farms, Harry explained, had quickly turned to barren sand with their abandonment to the great drought.

Only a few scattered clumps of mallee trees broke the vast rolling lands that now engulfed them. In many places the wind had torn into the skeletal sandy soils, exposing bedrock at the bottom of deep open scours, into which fences ran and toppled, forming suspended tangles of wood and wire. The landscape was flayed with these tears and gouges, there was no grass anywhere to hold the soils against the searing winds from the west.

The raw paddocks seemed to move and shift before their eyes as waves of moving sand skittered across the road before them, carried by a soft, syrupy breeze. Back in the woodlands, the dead roots of the mallee trees had, to some extent, held the teeth of the relentless wind at bay, but out here, in the abandoned farming country, the full force of drought was ravaging the ancient dunes. Without the intervention of the farmer, the country was slowly being devoured by the searing westerly winds, bearing open the raw bones of the bedrock beneath.

A few days into the old wheat belt, they passed through a small abandoned town of subsiding weatherboard houses. Plodding along the deserted main street of collapsing shop awnings they saw cloud, low but building, in the southeast. They stopped to scrounge through a small corner shop and found some rusty food tins hidden in a storeroom. As they gathered the cans they both paused, hearing a soft rumble in the distance.

'Thunder,' Harry said softly in response to Finn's questioning look.

They hurried outside to watch the sky. The cloudbank was dark and had come above them, rushing in behind a slightly cooler, southerly wind. Both men bent their faces to the wind, enjoying the brief respite from the superheated air. The camel shifted in its traces as a large raindrop hit Finn's upturned face and another patted heavily into the dust at his feet. Finn turned to Harry and smiled hugely.

'Rain,' he said, his voice hushed with his excitement.

'Rain ... yep,' and Harry smiled back and squeezed Finn's shoulder.

Slowly at first, then quickening its tempo, the rain began to patter about them in large fat drops that hit with force, rattling the rusted tin of the shop awnings and kicking up puffs of dust around their feet. And, as they stood, the rain grew harder, enough to begin to gather in thin runnels down the weatherboards and roofing iron and to wash the dust from the shards of broken glass that lay in the dirt of the street.

Finn, holding out his arms, palms upward, turned his face to the sky and let the big drops fall on his dirty face. 'How long has it been, Harry?' he shouted. 'How long since you've seen rain?'

Harry smiled again, rolling up one corner of his mouth, 'Maybe three years, I'm not sure.'

'More for me ... more for me, I think,' Finn opened his mouth and caught a few drops on his tongue and laughed. 'Should we put out the tarp, to catch some in the drums?'

Harry could barely hear him above the clatter of rain on the iron awnings. But, as though Finn saying it pronounced its death, the rain spluttered–there was a sudden final flurry of drops and then the storm was finished. The pale grey clouds behind the dark advancing anvil passed over quickly. The shredding clouds split and broke, revealing the fierce eye of the sun, and the heat at once began to beat away the brief flutter of cooler air. And suddenly Harry and Finn felt the humidity surge as the fallen water began to rapidly evaporate.

Finn's frame slumped. The young man's face took on a look of appalling disappointment. Harry heard the camel grumble behind them. Harry felt the defeat and disappointment too but he was not surprised. It was a wicked thing, to tease them like that. Cruel, to dangle that carrot then whip it away. But, as always, the storms were weak out here, leaving little but the rapidly fading sweet smell of wet earth and a memory that would thrash at them for weeks.

Finn huffed and returned to the decaying shop to collect their scavenged cans. Boots dragging, he carried the booty slowly down from the veranda, prolonging the return to the broiling sun as long as possible. Walking stiffly to the dray he stowed the cans, climbed up to sit and hung his head, silently waiting for Harry.

* * *

Over the next few weeks, moving south and eastwards, Harry had remained free of his pain as they left the decrepit wheat country behind. The wind-stripped sandy soils had been gradually replaced by a rising country of much deeper, darker loams. The odd giant dead stringybark tree began appearing among the shrinking paddocks, which still remained bare of all but a few patches of grey lifeless grass. Their road rolled through more abandoned towns, where they picked through the slowly collapsing houses and shops, and they passed an increasing number of smaller farms, all deserted and silent but for the rattling of loose roofing tin in the wind.

The road began to rise and wind to and fro through the undulating paddocks and Finn began to see an occasional clump of green among the grey. The living plants–grasses mainly, but the odd stunted shrub too– could be seen under the sheltering shade of a fallen tree trunk, or hunkered down in the lee of a fence-line woven with a protective screen of dead vegetation, hung there by the wind. Finn pointed out these patches of living vegetation to Harry and Harry nodded with increasing interest, repeatedly assuring Finn they would see growing signs of life as they drew farther south and east. One day they even came upon three ravens scavenging on a long dead horse carcass, the scrawny black birds halted their probing and pulling to watch the dray pass before returning to their half-hearted investigations.

But soon Finn's continued excitement was met with only grunts and shrugs again as another bout of pain swept through Harry. For days Harry let Finn have the reins and at night when they camped Harry managed only the bare essentials of setting up their camp. Throwing down his bedroll and pulling the cooking things from the dray, he would retire to sit quietly, his head hanging and breathing in slow heavy gasps, leaving Finn to unharness and hobble the camel, collect wood for the fire and open the tins and heat their meagre meals over the flames.

Their conversations again grew few and far between, Harry lacking enthusiasm even for his usual caustic sarcasms. When Finn tried to draw the hunched man out of his brooding anguish more forcefully, Harry would quickly hold up a palm to halt the younger man's words.

Finn had been certain they would see other travellers as they grew closer to the coast, but the land remained deserted but for them. The two men foraged in deserted farmhouses for food and water. Most were barren, stripped years earlier of anything edible or useful, but some still bore fruit. Many of the homesteads were falling down, almost torn apart by the wrenching of the fierce heat of The Failing's endless summer. Occasionally they found a homestead with an underground water tank that still held a little water and Harry showed Finn the trick of pulling the water pipes from the walls and from the baking ground to find small quantities of water that hadn't evaporated away and they gained a few litres here and there to replenish their supplies.

One afternoon a long disused rail line appeared next to the road and the rails followed their path for a while. At one point they came upon a derailed train, its carriages– eight or ten water cars–were overturned in a chaotic zigzag beside the line and, at its head, next to the rusted steel wheels of the overturned engine, the tracks were torn up and scattered about in the dead grass. Harry explained the wreck was probably caused by farmers and landholders sabotaging the lines to stop the train taking the water pumped from their old leases to the cities in the east.

It had happened more and more often as The Failing drew on, as the pipes ran dry and the drought had progressed to permanence. The farmers, becoming frantic, had derailed trains like this one, hijacked water trucks or severed pipelines, to stop the theft of the remaining water from their lands. It had been more anger than a fight for survival, Harry told him–futile really, the land was already sentenced to death by the great drought. But the last hangers-on had not let the water corporations off scot-free. Some had fought till the bitter end, spilling blood sometimes and spilling the precious water too, in acts like the derailment, rather than hand it over to add to the booming profits of the companies.

Finn looked back at the overturned train as the dray dropped behind a rise. He tried to picture those desperate men and women and those embattled times, but he could only see blurred ghosts now, incongruous echoes against the deserted fields and the fallen homesteads.

*   *   *

'How much farther to the coast?' Finn asked.

Harry paused, scowling at the question, and then mumbled, 'A few weeks still I think. We haven't crossed the Divide yet.'

'Shouldn't there be more people by now? You know, we're getting closer to the coast. Things are better here aren't they, it not being so dry?'

Harry frowned, 'I expected it too, Finn. But it seems the exodus has crept closer to the coast as the desert moves east. Maybe, as we near the mountains or on the eastern side, we'll start to come across more people.' He shrugged but his sallow face, beneath its coating of dust, was wrinkled with concern at the continued desertion of the land.

At noon, another week along their slow journey, the road topped a high point in the country and they saw, through the ribbons of heat, a faint black line on the horizon. And, as the day drew on, the narrow line before them grew to the width of a thumb and then a hand.

'The Divide I think,' Harry muttered quietly.

Woken from his nodding, Finn raised a hand to shade out the glare. 'Really?' He sat up straight. His eyes followed the line of mountains, first south until it disappeared below the horizon, then north too, till again the range was lost in the haze.

'How far do the mountains go?'

'For thousands of kilometres, Finn,' and Harry grew animated then, as though he spoke of some magnificent, freshly-discovered fossil. His eyes shone through the dust of his dirty face and his spidery hands swept in an arc from one horizon to the other excitedly.

'The Great Dividing Range separates the plains out here from the coast. It's a great winding spine, Finn–the backbone of the continent–running north to south along the east coast. It starves the country out here of the coastal rains. Even before the great drought, before The Failing, the Divide was a barrier to the storms coming off the sea. Some storms and rains made it then–the big weather systems–but not now. The storm fronts are much too weak now, they break up on the Divide's eastern flanks, well before they reach the western plains or, if they do make it, they only have a few drops left in them by the time they get here.' Harry sniffed, 'Over the ranges, maybe, the country will still be alive. People still grow things out in the open back there–or they did at least.'

Harry sat gazing at the mountains, his face slowly draining of colour, the brief tide of enthusiasm had rapidly ebbed, leaving him sitting again in his underlying exhaustion. Sitting alongside him, Finn suddenly daydreamed of the lands he had never seen, of the great cities and the hubbub of people and their comings and goings, of the green fields he would see and of the cool winds sweeping in off the ocean. He sat there lost, still smiling, as Harry finally tapped the camel into motion.

At dusk the road they had followed for weeks ended abruptly at a t-intersection. Beyond it, the range loomed large in the failing light. The new road ran across their route in either direction, hugging the western flanks of the range. Facing them on the opposite shoulder of the road, framed by the mountains behind, stood a large twisted road sign. Harry and Finn climbed down and crossed the road, their legs creaking with sitting, to better read the sign in the fading light. The sign's left side was faded beyond recognition, the right, pointing to the south, still held a hint of its original lettering. The first word, once printed in large white letters, was unreadable apart from an A and an f, but the second word was just discernible and reading it made Harry pause.

'Dam,' he chewed the word over and sucked his teeth, hesitant about its implication and its inherent potential for disappointment.

'Dam,' Finn too read the word out loud, his voice hushed with repressed excitement.

'Don't get too excited–they were the first things to fail.'

'Yeah, but ... we should look, huh? I mean, in case there's ... we're down to one full drum now,' Finn's voice petered out as Harry turned to stare at him through the gloom before replying.

'We'll camp here tonight, off in the scrub, and decide tomorrow, eh? No point in going on now anyway, it'll be dark in a few minutes and there's no moon tonight.'

Harry returned to the dray and led the camel off the road and into the dead scrub and trees of the verge. Finn watched, standing next to the sign until the dray had disappeared, and then hurried after them into the shelter of the trees.

* * *

They woke well before the pale glimmer of dawn had silhouetted the range. Hurriedly packing their camp, the two men quickly harnessed the camel and, leading the animal back to the road, they climbed up to the seat and Harry gently flicked the rein against the beast's dusty side. Unusually enthusiastic, the camel instantly took up the strain and strode out along their new road towards the south.

'You're right ... about the dam ... it's worth a look,' but Harry spoke without much enthusiasm.

Their new route ran over gentle undulations in the cleared foothills for a few kilometres, before at last turning towards the mountains. The cleared land around them became increasingly peppered with gnarled eucalypt trees and the grey fields began to sprout granite boulders covered in peeling lichens and powdery clumps of dried moss. The isolated boulders soon became great jumbled castles between the dead trees as the land rose to meet the range. The road began to climb, winding this way and that among the increasingly steep paddocks. Soon they left the farming land behind, the steeper slopes carrying dense but still desiccated forest and the granite outcrops joined to become great shelves and steps of rock that jutted from the valley's flanks.

Higher up, the road had been cut into the rock of the narrowing gorge and they encountered occasional landslides of scree, which had been flattened and cleared a little by the passage of previous travellers. Following the snaking of a dry riverbed far below, the road became shaded from the sun as huge slab cliffs rose above them. The vegetation quickly thinned to a few pitiful shrubs and stunted trees, hanging precariously from the ledges and cracks in the walls.

In the growing shadows the two men fell silent, the creak and groan of the dray echoing in the cooler air of the gorge. The camel snorted and grumbled as it struggled with the increasing grade. Sitting on the seat closest to the road's edge, Harry felt vertigo claw at him at each turn as they slowly drew upwards and the river dropped farther and farther below the road. Then, turning his face away from the precipice, suddenly Harry was forced to cover his eyes against the sun's fierce light as the gorge broke out into a new valley, nestled high amongst the steep, tree-clad slopes of the surrounding mountains.

Just above them, the concrete dam wall cut across the valley narrows as the road swung upwards in a final pinch to cross the colossal wall. On the far side of the great curve of the dam, perched the spillway. But sadly, the two men saw there was no shine to its blackened gullet–the chute ran dry to the silent cascades of the river far below. Finn felt his heart sink, but it was no surprise to Harry. The dry riverbed had told him as much on their ascent. Harry had known that it would have been unimaginable that the dam could contain enough water to feed the overflow and the river below through such a drought.

Harry stopped the dray and they sat. Through slitted eyes the two men stared out across the expanse of the valley that now spread before them. Steep and narrow, the valley wove through the fingers of repeated interlocking ridges, cutting back to the distant higher mountains of the main range. Across the shimmering landscape, ridge after ridge, a thick heavy stillness wrapped the country. Nothing, no bird nor animal, seemed to stir in the dense air that filled the elongated basin. Even here, high above the baking plains, the relentless heat and silence seemed to pin the country down in its immovable grip.

It was a small dam, by dam standards, but that was the way in the desperate days when the giant wall had been built. There were still rains then. Desperate for water and continued profit, the water corporations, fed by generous government subsidies, had tried anything, even damming small isolated valleys hidden in the higher rainfall zones, to feed the cities on the coast. However, with the rain failing, there was little run-off from the catchments to replenish the dams and, when the infrequent rain did come, the steep slopes covered with mostly dead and dying vegetation did not capture or hold the water and, eroding rapidly, the sediment quickly fouled the reservoirs.

Any water that did collect, quickly evaporated in the rising temperatures. There had been little choice but to try, Harry understood that, but these isolated dams had, in the end, amounted to little–just another fruitless engineering fix, only serving to prolong by a few years the water crash and The Failing. Still, thought Harry, fighting off his pessimism, perhaps there would still be a little water hidden behind the giant concrete dam wall. And, with that frail hope, he urged the camel up the final pinch.

The road rose to cross the gorge. Once at the top, they saw a small concrete cube of a building sitting beside the dam wall. The building had two small windows on the side facing them–both were blackened and covered in a thin layer of dust. Drawing closer they saw that a large dog had been tied to the building and had died there, the carcass, almost covered by drifting dirt. Well and truly mummified, its bones poked through its parchment skin and long straggly fur. The dead dog's one exposed empty eye socket seemed to glare at them as they approached.

Looking down from the dray, Finn scowled. The carcass filled the place with a foul air. The road curved past the building to cross the dam wall but, as they were about to pass on, they noticed fresh tyre tracks in the fine powdery dust leading to the building's rear. Harry pulled the camel up again and sat there for a moment. Finn looked at him, chewing his lip, unsure of their next move.

'Wait here.' Harry climbed down but Finn, ignoring the curt command, followed and, looking back, Harry shook his head in dismay but said nothing.

Circling the carcass, they crossed to the building and, cautiously peering around the corner, they saw two things that stopped them dead in their tracks.

The first was a white utility parked against the rear of the building and to their relief the cab was empty. The second was the arresting vista that rolled out beyond the utility. Below them, over the edge of the dam, lay the vast expanse of the reservoir itself. That first glimpse made them forget the vehicle momentarily.

Before them lay a vision born of an apocalypse. The huge basin, warped by the ribbons of haze, was a vast, baking hell. The valley floor, once drowned under a hundred metres of water, was now a raw waste of sun-blasted sediments. The deep, sun-hardened mud had cracked and split in long fissures, which snaked back and forth across the reservoir's bed–some of the cracks seemed wide and deep enough to swallow a man. Blocks of sediment, some the size of a small car had been pushed up into a chaotic chessboard by the years of expansion and contraction, driven by the rise and fall of the sun. At the edges of the lakebed, a great multitude of dead trees, once inundated by the flooding of the valley, circled below the old shoreline. Disappearing off into the distance, stark white against the dusty brown mud, the skeletons of the trees seemed like great dead corals, crowding the edge of the vast, tortured wasteland.

They stared silently at the desolation for a long moment before Harry tutted, 'Dry as a bone, huh?'

Finn looked at him and shrugged, made speechless by the cataclysmic vista.

Harry turned away, bending his attention to the vehicle. He looked in the back at the clutter of shovels, smaller tools and fuel drums. There were several empty plastic water containers, a tangled steel cable and a hand-operated winch, an axe and a large padlocked trunk pushed against the rear of the cab. He recognised the utility then, as the one that had visited the gorge before him weeks ago, before he had been attacked, the one owned by the same Aboriginal men who had given him the bottle of water and told him of the Bishop's farm. But before he could relay this to Finn the younger man spoke excitedly.

'It's Dun and Clifford.'

'Who?' Harry turned and stared blankly at Finn.

'Duncan and Clifford—they visit the Centre sometimes. They ... '

'You know them?'

"Sure, sure Harry ... they have visited us on and off as far back as I can remember. Not often, but they dropped in sometimes, when they were passing. They even helped us fix things sometimes.'

Harry quickly scanned the cliffs and road on the other side of the dam, searching for the men but could see no sign of them. They wandered across from the vehicle and found the entrance to the building on the far side. The painted steel door, fading and rusted, stood half open but Harry could discern nothing farther inside.

Harry stood indecisively for a moment. His immediate instinct was to turn and leave the men to whatever business they had up here. It was best, in his experience, to leave people be, unless you were desperate. But then again, he thought, these men had helped him once and had seemed friendly, at least in a gruff kind of way, so they might know something of water nearby or on the road ahead.

As Harry procrastinated, Finn pushed past and stuck his head through the open doorway then disappeared inside. Too late, Harry raised a hand in caution, but a moment later Finn's young freckled face appeared again grinning.

'Come on, I can hear voices down there somewhere.' He motioned with his hand for Harry to follow him into the building and disappeared back inside. And, somewhat reluctantly, Harry followed.

Through the doorway an empty concrete box-like room greeted Harry. There was no daylight except what came through the half-open door as the windows were coated with dust and dirt. The room was empty of furniture but a steel trapdoor, lying open in the middle of the floor led below to the bowels of the dam. A faint light bled from the open trapdoor and, as they stood letting their eyes adjust to the dim light, Harry heard voices filtering up from the hole.

Both men leant over and looked down. A steel ladder, attached to the concrete wall, led down a five or six metre shaft to the floor below, where a passageway disappeared in the direction of the dam wall. The voices were louder now as they leaned over, but the words were still mostly inaudible mumblings and the odd smattering of soft laughter. Suddenly, before Harry could stop him, Finn shouted down the hole.

'Hey, Dun, Clifford … It's me, Finn.' Amid the cacophony of echoes, the men's voices immediately fell silent.

The light flickered below and the scuff of footfalls echoed, first on the steel rungs of another ladder, then approaching on a concrete floor before a face appeared at the bottom of the shaft, its features cloaked in shadow. The face stared up at them for few seconds then a grunt came and a voice quietly drifted up to them.

'Who's that with you, Finny?'

'Harry Sinclair, a friend, I'm travelling east with him,' Finn's voice was hushed but excited.

A sigh answered him and then the man called softly up to them, 'Come down then.' And he disappeared back along the passageway.

Looking sideways at Harry, Finn shrugged his shoulders and grinned as he began climbing down to the floor below. Harry followed more slowly, carefully placing his boots on each rung as he descended. They followed the voices down a low passage to the head of another ladder and, as they descended, the light grew brighter and the voices louder still. Harry could hear the men below clearly now, speaking rapidly in their own language.

Harry reached the foot of the ladder and felt the chilled air in the depths of the dam—a chill Harry had not felt since his time at the Cistern. The room, like the one above, was a simple concrete box, low ceilinged and bare walled. Ten feet away, on the opposite side to the ladder, the floor fell away to the blackness of some kind of pit. The two Aboriginal men sat on an old mattress in the middle of the floor, the dark fissure at their backs, with a small oil lantern set before them that emitted a soft light and a trickle of dark oily smoke. A tiny portable stove set beside them held a small pot that gave off wisps of steam. The two men, tin cups held between their palms, sat watching the newcomers as they stood uncomfortably at the foot of the ladder.

After a little while, the older of the two, sporting a bushy grey beard and with wild grey hair circling his dark face, set his cup down on the floor and gestured to them to come over to the light and sit on the battered mattress lying next to theirs.

'Hey, Clifford, how's things?' Finn smiled shyly at the men as he sat down clumsily. The older man scratched his bearded cheek as though having to contemplate a detailed response.

'What are you doing here, Finn? What's happened?' The old man spoke slowly, his voice low and considered.

Finn paused and looked down between his knees to the sagging mattress. 'I ... there was trouble, Clifford. Water prospectors turned up at the Centre ... they were going to kick us off. Samuel ... Samuel and the others were going to try and stop them but ... I ...' he took a breath and glance quickly at each of them, 'They told me to go ... they said I wouldn't be much use there.' His words stumbled and he fell into silence.

The two men stared at him, then at Harry, who shrugged and nodded confirming Finn's story.

'What about your dad and sister? What happened to them?'

'I don't know, Clifford. The batteries and generator were all smashed. They gave us more time to go, but ... there was going to be a fight ... I know it. Samuel ... he ... ' Finn stalled again as he struggled with the memory.

Clifford raised a hand to stop Finn and grunted, speaking in language to the other man sitting at his side and a rapid conversation ensued. At one point both men turned and glanced at Harry, then continued their dialogue for another few seconds before the younger man spoke for the first time.

'What're you doing with this fella, Finny?'

Finn paused, taken by surprise by the question. 'He ... Harry was at the Centre, staying with us, fixing the pump. He did a good job too. But the prospectors and security turned up ... we're heading east ... he's taking me to the coast.'

Both men raised their eyebrows and spoke in unison. 'East?'

They both turned to Harry and Clifford leaned forward and stared into Harry's face. 'Why the hell are you taking him to the coast?'

Harry shrugged, 'I'm not taking him. I'm heading back that way, that's all. Don't ask me why he wants to go ... that's his business. I told him it's gone to hell but... '

'Wait a minute!' Finn started up. 'You can't just write it off like that. I want the chance to see it too, for myself. Those cities, the people ... the sea–I've always wanted to ... even before Mum left.' His voice faltered but his gaze passed to each face in turn. 'I ... There's more to life than all this isolation, this ... this desolation.' He paused again and drew a breath and straighten his shoulders, 'There's nothing out here for me now, anyway.'

Dun snorted softly. Clifford, his eyes staring into the flame of the lamp, put a hand on his knee but Dun, ignoring the older man, continued on harshly. 'A shit-load more people is all that's waiting for you on the coast, Finny. Believe me, we were there not that long ago. Its no better on the coast–just more of the same crap.' His face closed in and his eyes grew bright under his thick eyebrows. He raised his arm and pointed angrily in a vague easterly direction. 'Those people are greedy, pure and simple! Tearing at each other, stealing from each other ... It's a terrible thing to see ... people like that, they've sucked every last drop of blood from this country ... '

'But ... ' Finn shook his head, trying to shake off Dun's words.

Clifford held up his wrinkled hand to cut them both off, then suddenly chuckled good-naturedly, 'Duncan's seen too much. Go, see it, Finn. Everyone should see it for themselves, once–it's the only way.' He considered Finn for a moment. 'But listen here, Finn. It's not easy over on the coast. It's tougher than here in many ways–believe me. I wouldn't trust just anyone you meet, but there are some good people too.' He smiled, but his eyes were clouded with worry as he leaned over and patted Finn on his shoulder, 'If you're careful, you should be right.'

Harry sat silently, staring at the floor. His face had grown hot in reaction to Dun's tirade, but he also agreed with the man's grim assessment. He knew it was chaos–he had seen the worst of The Failing back there. But still, knowing all that, the ferocious critique had touched a long-dormant protective nerve in him. And Finn was right, he thought in a confusion of conflicting emotions, what was there out here for him now. There was no going back for Finn, but the city would serve up no panacea for him either. Harry sighed with exhaustion but then spoke up softly.

'Finn's right, in his own way, what's left out here for him ... or for me or you, for that matter?' Harry stared at the flickering flame. 'Why stay out here ... the country's a wreck now, isn't it? It won't recover, not now ... This far into The Failing there's even less hope here than on the coast, it seems to me anyway.'

The two men said nothing for a long while. Harry fidgeted in the silence. Finn hung his head and huffed sulkily. Clifford quietly produced a tobacco pouch from the pocket of his dirty suit jacket and deftly rolled a cigarette with his long, gnarled, but surprisingly nimble, fingers. Dun reached out, raised his cup and, slurping his tea, watched Harry from under his brows until finally he spoke.

'It's our country. Our people have been out here for hundreds of generations. We farmed this land long before you lot rolled up. We had huge villages out there on the plains. Our people built vast stone fish-traps and stone houses long before the Egyptians even thought about sticking one rock atop another.' He sat erect, his large hands resting on his knees and glared at Harry, his mouth set and proud. 'We traded across this country when the first whites came through—not that they admitted to that—to them we were just savages and wanderers. But we know this country like no one else.' He smiled, his eyes sparkling in the dim light.

'We've waited a long time—watched you lot trash the place, but now most of you are gone—got your reward for all that blundering about. And now we've got the country back. We waited you lot out.' He stared at Harry, as though challenging him to dispute his words. 'It'd be better if things were different, if the climate wasn't fucked up, but... ' he shrugged, his face expressionless.

'It's a sorry history. I know it ... but that still doesn't change things. Why stay, when it's all dead?' Harry kept his voice low, not wanting to antagonise the younger man.

Dun's soft, rasping laugh filled the tiny box of a room. 'Dead, you say? I don't know ... maybe.' And he looked to Clifford.

'But ... there's no water, no food.' Harry shook his head. 'There's not much time left, is there?'

Clifford, lighting his cigarette off the lamp, carefully replaced its glass cover and leaned back, his eyes holding Harry's as he drew on the cigarette and blew a cloud of acrid smoke slowly into the air above them.

'There's water here in the country—you know it. You followed our tracks, didn't you? You saw the gorge? There's water, if you're smart enough to find it.' He nodded to the dark gap behind him. 'There's always water—bits and pieces, here and there—enough for us anyway.' He smiled again, showing his teeth this time. 'Enough if you're not too greedy, not busting to make a god-damn profit off of it,' he snorted again.

'But the companies are out here–they won't stop looking,' Harry interrupted him.

'The water boom days are long gone,' Clifford replied slowly. 'The companies are dying, and good riddance to 'em. Did nothing but rape this country, all just to feed that frenzy back then,' He scowled to himself before his face softened again. 'But there's enough water–if you know the country, you can find it. Word of it is passed around. We leave markings for those that know them. There's still enough out here for a few, if you're smart–for a while at least.'

'But what will you do then? I mean, it's all going to run out pretty soon, you must know that.'

The two men shrugged in unison. Dun looked to Clifford and then spoke again.

'Maybe.' He smiled crookedly, 'But it's far too fucking late to worry about all that, isn't it? Worrying is a waste of time–the change is here–no one can stop it now. The country'll be empty soon–even the damn prospectors'll finally bugger off. We've got water that the prospectors can never find or don't want, so … ' he stopped abruptly, as though bored of telling it. And shrugging again, he slurped his tea loudly.

There was silence for a long while as the four men chewed over the conversation until, finally, Clifford broke the silence, 'You two want a cup of tea?'

Harry and Finn nodded and Dun stood and strode to the edge of the hole in the floor. Reaching down he picked up a plastic bucket tied to a coil of thin, weathered nylon rope and dropped the bucket into the blackness and a deep resounding splash filled the room. He waited a moment then began pulling the bucket up. Finn and Harry listened to the slosh of water far below as Dun retrieved the rope until the full bucket reappeared.

'See there's water, if you know where to look,' Clifford smiled broadly again and chuckled good-naturedly.

'It's the residue in the pipes–the stuff that was left when they decommissioned the dam ... in the low points and corners.' He drew on his cigarette. 'No interest to the prospectors, not enough carbon-credits here, but there's enough for one or two, or a few, if you're careful.'

He dipped the pan into the bucket Dun had brought to him. He stuck a twig into the lamp's flame and, using it as a match, he relit the stove, carefully placed the pan on it to boil and rummaged around in a small bag he had pulled from under his leg producing a packet of tea, 'No sugar unfortunately.'

* * *

They bedded down with Clifford and Dun after seeing to the camel and retrieving their bedding from the dray. The company of the others had drawn both Finn and Harry to stay and the conversation had soon strayed away from the uncertainties of The Failing and the cities, to the sightings of wildlife and people along the roads east. Harry queried the two men on the best route across the mountains and on any particular places to avoid on the way to the coast.

Another week or ten days following the road that crossed the dam should see them on the coastal plain, the two men told them. Another few days to a largish town and from there they shrugged, telling them it depended on how safe the roads were as they grew closer to the cities. Harry listened and nodded at each direction but Finn, listening to the talk, grew excited again at the prospect of crossing the mountains and their descent to the coast. His mind wandered and he began to nod on the gutted mattress.

But Finn had only slept for a few hours when Dun shook him.

'What's up with your mate?'

Grunting, Finn rolled onto his side and looked across at Harry as the old man let out a stifled groan and his body thrashed in his sleep.

'He's sick,' Finn replied softly.

'Sick? What's wrong with him?' Dun frowned.

'Cancer. Had it for years he reckons … but it's got worse in the last few weeks.'

Clifford and Dun both leant in closer to observe Harry in the dim light of the lamp and tutted to themselves.

'Poor bastard,' Clifford scratched his head thoughtfully. 'If he's this sick, you'd better hurry up and get him to the coast, there's no help for him out here.' And Harry, as though confirming their prognosis, groaned again and curled into a tight ball under the blankets.

'It's nearly light outside—we're off soon,' Clifford told Finn.

Harry slept on as the two men packed their things and said goodbye to Finn—telling him in low, serious tones to be careful on the coast. And, after shaking his hand earnestly, they disappeared up the ladder. In the silence, Finn rolled up his blankets and climbed the ladder to retrieve their empty water drums from the dray. He filled them from the well at the back of the room and, using the rope, he pulled them up the ladders to the surface and stored them with the rest of their things under the tarp. Harry woke as he returned but stayed huddled in his blankets as Finn, squatting beside him, filled him in on Clifford and Dun's departure and his replenishment of their water supplies.

Harry lay for a moment longer, his narrow face turned to the ceiling, until he spoke in a rasping voice, 'Thanks, Finn, thanks for doing it all.'

Finn paused. Harry's eyes were shadowed with pain. His body seemed tightly knotted with the illness that his body fought within him. The skin of his sunken cheeks looked grey and lifeless and even his lank grey hair, Finn noted, seemed more sparse than it had.

"It's OK, Harry. No worries, huh? Rest up a bit more if you like–there's no hurry.'

Grunting, Harry struggled to his feet. Huffing and sucking breath, his movements guarded and hesitant, he rolled up his blanket and thin mattress and tied them with the piece of string he saved each night in his pocket for that purpose. He shuffled about the small room and stared down the hole into the blackness for a long while, as though desperate to postpone their departure.

'Do we have enough water, d'you think?' he asked Finn.

'Sure, two more drums will keep us going for a while.'

'The camel all right?' Harry looked upwards.

'Sure, he's OK. There's more food for him here,' Finn scratched his head and, holding their own lantern, he waited by the ladder and, at last, Harry tentatively slung his bedroll over his shoulder and moved to leave.

'You want me to take your bedroll? It'd be no trouble.'

Harry only grunted and gestured grumpily for the younger man to climb first.

At the surface, in the semi-darkness of the small room, Finn waited at the top of the ladder for Harry to appear. He heard him shuffling and groaning quietly to himself below before his face appeared out of the gloom of the shaft. Breathing heavily, he took a break between each rung and, with each new step, a soft whimper broke from his lips.

Finally he reached the top and Finn held out a hand to help him up. Harry waved him away defiantly and stayed on his knees, gasping for breath. At last he climbed slowly to his feet and staggered out the door. Stumbling to the dray, he climbed slowly up and slumped there, his head hanging, and waited for Finn to join him.

* * *

The road they followed crossed the dam and wound back through the mountains, at first running alongside the moonscape of the reservoir with its pincushion fringe of skeletal trees then, leaving the dam behind, the narrowing road sprang upward in short surges along the steeper forested slopes of the mountains proper.

They climbed relentlessly for two days through rugged granite country, the tall dying forest turning gradually to stunted woodland with the higher altitude. The hardier stunted trees grew thick and, more frequently, were alive among the great confusion of granite boulders, and the rank grasses and shrubs held an occasional wash of green. The two men even noticed the odd flash of a yellow acacia flower among the tangled undergrowth and for the first time they began to see insects, flies and small butterflies and even mountain grasshoppers in the foliage beside the road. They passed thickets of short sturdy tree ferns, which still retained the odd living frond or two, sheltering in the shade of the boulders in the deeper gullies.

Their road climbed higher still. During the day they began seeing small flocks of ravens and a few solitary pied currawongs flitting among the trees. There were even a few smaller birds too—yellow robins and scrub wrens and a lone cuckoo-shrike—darting across the gaps between the shrubs of the high woodland. The birds scrutinised their passage suspiciously or, sitting in trees above them, watched the men eat their food in the dying light of the evenings. Occasionally Finn woke in the night to the sounds of small animals, bush rats probably, or a larger bandicoot, scurrying about the camp. And once they even saw the dark shape of a wallaby disappearing into the undergrowth as the road meandered through a sheltered gully.

These small sightings of life enthralled Finn and, occasionally, they even managed to draw Harry out from behind the veil of suffering that mostly shrouded him in silence. Finn saw him follow the flight of a bird through the branches with renewed interest or he would seem mesmerized by a fly landing on the back of his hand. And sometimes Harry even found the energy to grab excitedly at Finn's arm, alerting him to a movement off in the bush.

But the nights were still bad for Harry. Tossing and turning, he was wracked by stabbing pains in his abdomen and ill-fitted aches and weakness in his arms and legs. Worryingly, Finn saw him begin to use his left arm less and less, as though he had lost strength in it. Exhausted, Harry left most of the camp doings to Finn, helping when he felt he could but often he was too weak to do more than stack the plates and bowls beside the fire after they had eaten before he rolled out his mattress and blankets to sleep.

* * *

'We'll find help for you soon, Harry,' Finn touched Harry's arm and the older man flinched and grunted and roused himself from his doze. Following Finn's gaze, he considered the country before them.

For the first time in a week, the road ran straight and flat for a kilometre or two across the shallow depression of patchy alpine heathland. Beyond the treeless depression, a line of rocky crags hid what Harry knew must be their first sighting of the coastal plains and perhaps a glimpse of the far-off sea. The country that surrounded them—spiny heath and knee-high scrub—was a sign that they had reached the high point of the mountainous divide. The stunted alpine plants, Harry knew, occurred nowhere else but on these high, treeless plateaus.

Their road had turned from tar to dirt two days before as they had passed a broken steel gate, the boundary of some old, long-forgotten National Park. And then yesterday, the track had devolved into two wheel ruts among the greying tussocks as the peaks around them abruptly lost their tree cover, revealing their raw granite teeth to the cloudless sky.

Looking now at the once boggy heathland, the dark peat bogs were dry and shrunken between mounds of dead button grass. The once spongy sphagnum mosses and lichens were dried to round, crusty chancres of powdery earth. Even here, at the highest point above the plains, more exposed to the moister coastal weather, there was a devastating dearth of water.

Harry turned away. Through glazed eyes, he looked back, out to the west. Below, beyond the mountains, lay the western plains. The vast plains lay beneath the huge ball of the sun. Low on the horizon, fiery and shimmering in the haze and dust, the orb seemed to devour the plains before Harry's weary eyes. The sky, clearing to that watercolour blue of infinity, bore down on him. All those years under that blue endless sky rushed in. The sight of it now, the memories of the dry, breaking hardship, the huge thirst of the plains, drew in on him, bringing a sudden gasp and Harry teetered in the seat and Finn threw out an arm to stop him from falling.

Harry's relief at parting from that desolation was tempered with anxiety. He heaved a sigh, turning again to look to the east, to the country beyond the last row of peaks. In his mind he pictured the coast and the people, and its spiralling chaos. But it wasn't the chaos that frightened him. Its dangers were already known. Crossing the mountains spawned his anxiety. The crossing, he knew, would somehow, one way or another, herald an abrupt end to his drifting.

The landscape made no difference, he knew that, but still the coast seemed to herald a kind of reckoning. Somehow, crossing the Divide would rip away the tissued veil of aimless wandering. And, suddenly, in his mind, the road before them now seemed steeper and more precarious. He saw it, tilting crazily, falling before him, as though it carried him inexorably eastwards in some unstoppable avalanche.

Harry shook off the image and smiled weakly at Finn and the young man smiled broadly in return. 'We'll find you help,' Finn said again, with as much fortitude as he could muster.

Harry snorted good-naturedly, took the reins from him and called to the camel. 'Hup, hup, come on you decrepit dust bag.' And the camel raised its head up, sniffed at the air and turned a baleful eye back to them before taking up the strain.

And, in a few minutes, drawing over the final crest of the mountain pass, the track again became a well-formed dirt road. At the highest point of the road, Harry pulled the camel up and both he and Finn sat in silence looking east. There, spreading out almost beneath their feet, was the great eastern fall. Beyond the high granite crags, the land rapidly fell away, the towering escarpment forests clung to the slopes and the lower hills of the ranges, and then, spilling out beyond the forest fringes, maybe twenty kilometres away, a narrow brown band of farming land rolled into the huge arc of a coastal bay. Surprising Harry, the bay could not have been more than thirty or forty kilometres away, but beyond that, through the haze, there was nothing but the great, deep turquoise of the sea.

Finn gasped at his first sight of the coast and the ocean. 'It's huge!' he whispered and stared out at the gulf before them, his eyes slitted against the immensity of the vista.

'Hm … it is big.' Harry looked at Finn and smiled, savouring the look of awe on the young man's face. 'Ready?'

Finn nodded once in agreement as they began the long descent to the coast.

* * *

Through the first day of their descent through the mountains, they watched as the country slowly began to come alive. As their road wound back and forth down steep ridgelines and through pinched gullies, the forest grew in stature and closed in above them. Harry saw small swarms of insects dancing in the dappled shafts of light that spilled down from the gaps in the canopy and his mood began to lift a little. Silently, he gazed out at the jumble of huge tree trunks and crowded tree ferns and tall shrubs that dominated the floor of the escarpment forest. To both men, the air was luxuriantly moist here and the trees and shrubs seemed to crowd their vision with a rich green Finn had never experienced and Harry had not seen for years.

The trees, some with girths as wide as the dray, towered upwards from the dense confusion of the forest floor, their enormous mottled white trunks ran smooth and free of branches until they reached the canopy high above the road. In awe, Finn craned his neck and stared upwards at the great ribbons of peeling bark that hung from their branches. Mounds of bark and sticks piled up around the trees' broad buttressed bases and hung from the tree ferns and shrubs of the forest floor. And the smell of vegetation and rot and earth clogged Finn's nostrils. All around him, he was swamped by a profusion of green and growth.

'The smell, Harry!' Finn kept repeating in hushed tones.

Many of these giant trees had still not succumbed to the great drought, their canopies helping to hold off the searing sun from the soils beneath their feet. But even here they could see the grey stags of dead trees spearing up through the living canopy when they looked down on the land below, as the road occasionally broke free of the trees. In the dark, sheltered gullies the trees seemed to survive reasonably well, but out on the drier, more exposed spurs, the dead crowns dominated the tall forest.

Buoyed by the new signs of life through that first day, their conversations became unusually long and sometimes even cheerful till dusk overtook them–the sun disappearing early behind the range that towered at their backs. However, as they moved out from their camp on the second day, Finn noticed Harry had again slipped into a silent knot on the seat beside him. The old man flinched and hissed when the dray passed over potholes and the broken rock of the road and he leaned out to his left, all hunched and bent, protecting his side. Finn tried on occasion to draw him out, asking him what the unfamiliar birds or animals they saw were called. But Harry only shrugged or grunted in reply, hugging his arms about himself.

In the afternoon, Finn watched Harry as he moved tentatively off into the fringe of shrubs to shit and saw him return, white as a ghost. The older man's clothes now hung from his tall, bony frame like old bed sheets. His faded shirt seemed only to touch his coat-hanger shoulders, as though there was little solid flesh below that. He had pulled his belt to its tightest notch, and his dirty, grey suit trousers hung from his hips and bunched around his worn leather boots. Even his boots, when he pulled them off to sleep, seemed to fall from his feet. His hands too had grown more narrow and elongated, his fingers becoming spidery twigs in Finn's mind's eye. His once haggard features under his lank fringe of grey hair had now become sallow and jaundiced, his eyes sunken pools, making him seem more than a little ghoulish. All this made Finn fret. He desperately wanted to speak up–to ask Harry what they should do–but could not bring himself to talk of the future, seeing Harry as he was.

That night, camped beneath the towering trees, Harry lay awake as Finn slept on the other side of the fire. Staring wide-eyed up at the tree canopy high overhead, Harry shivered despite the warmer night air of the coast, his mind wrestling with tomorrow and the days to follow. With his teeth clenched tightly he tried to stifle the groans and whimpers that threatened to escape his lips when waves of pain and nausea coursed through his body. Once he crawled from his blanket to the fringe of the forest and vomited. His bones ached abominably—no change in position would ease his ill-fitted limbs. Finally, when he could lie still no longer, he rolled over and sat with the blanket over his head as the morning drew near. Exhausted, he could barely summon the energy to rise from his blankets and climb to the seat of the dray.

At midday, his bones jarred to shattering by the jolting of the dray, he climbed down and unrolled his blankets in the back between the water drums and camping gear.

'You take the reins again,' he said haltingly to Finn. 'I need rest today … and the fucking seat is killing my arse.' Wheezing, he hoisted himself up, covered himself with the blanket and lay shivering and cursing as the dray rattled on through the shadows of the trees. At one point, Finn heard Harry's teeth chattering and the sound, in that heat, drove the spear of worry even deeper into his gut.

That night Harry needed help to clamber from the dray. Finn took him under his armpits, easing him to the ground, and was shocked at how little the old man now weighed. He was like a child in his arms—Finn could have carried him quite easily. Staggering to their camp, Harry sat hunched over in silence. He did not eat before he slept. And the next day he lay all day in the back of the dray, only moving to lean out and retch and spit into the road as nausea swamped him.

The days had been a little cooler since leaving the western plains but now another long hot spell had hit from the west. The temperature under the dray's fringed canopy soared–the throbbing heat suffocating the two men as it crept ever higher. And, to make matter worse, during the afternoon they broke free of the forest into steep, cleared farming land and the sun beat down unhindered once again.

They passed a broken-down farmhouse as the sun was setting behind the mountains and Finn made camp behind the tangle of timber and roofing iron, out of sight of the road, making a small fire of the crumbling building's weatherboards. Again, he almost carried Harry from the dray and propped him up by the fire as he laid out his blankets and made them dinner. The bowl of soup lay untouched at Harry's feet, the old man staring vacantly into the darkness beyond the fire, his head wobbling ever so slightly on his scrawny neck, until Finn helped him to his bed.

Sitting beside the fire, Finn felt more alone than he had ever felt before. Harry's sickness had put fear into him. Their long journey had abruptly shifted from a strange meandering dream to the stark light of day. The road ahead seemed suddenly much more treacherous without Harry's guidance and gruff companionship. Fretting, Finn ran his hands through his thick mop of hair and rubbed his neck. Harry might not make it and what would he do then? His lack of a plan set on him as the flames of the fire flickered and spluttered, the darkness seemed to ooze and shift behind the twisted silhouettes of the abandoned homestead's drooping peppercorn trees.

* * *

For most of their long journey from the west, time had seemed to roll on with little impediment. But now Finn counted each passing hour. Each kilometre, crossing the undulating farming lands toward the coast, seemed to toll in

Finn's ears and his agitation became almost unbearable. Looking back occasionally at Harry's inert form curled up under the blanket, he desperately sought Harry's guidance but nothing coherent was forthcoming.

At first he let the camel slowly plod toward the sea, now lost beyond the rolling hills. His anxiety tasted like aluminium in his mouth and he squirmed and fidgeted uncomfortably in his seat and, as their dirt track met a wider tarred road, he turned northeast without consideration and flicked the reins to urge the camel into a weary shuffle over the smoother surface.

In the paddocks around the road large patches of greener grass appeared and disappeared as the dray rolled on. Then, as the road made a long curve east again toward the bay, Finn saw a cow standing on a balding grassy knoll. The angular beast slowly raised its big head and ambled off as it spotted the dray. Finn watched it disappear, heartened by seeing life among the stricken fields. He saw another pair of bony cattle off in the distance as the road rose up a hill and he saw too that the tarred highway had finally brought them close to the vast curve of the bay.

At the sight of the sea, so close, Finn slowed the camel back to its normal ambling pace and for the first time heard far-off waves crashing on a distant beach. And, although he had never heard it before, the surging crash set his heart racing. A warm wind had kicked up off the white-capped waters of the bay and Finn sniffed the air and smelled the scent of seaweed and salt. Unlike in the west, here the air seemed as clear as glass. The breeze came off the ocean and, free of the dust that coated everything back beyond the Divide, the coastal world seemed vivid and crisp to Finn's wondering eyes.

The road turned and ran parallel to the bay and Finn lost sight of the sea for a few minutes before they crested another hill in the rolling farmland and the horizon appeared again. Closer now, maybe only half a kilometre away, the ocean sounds and smells sparked an intense urge in him to get closer to that vast volume of water. He could taste the salt in his mouth and he yearned to touch what he had dreamed of for many years.

A narrow dirt track presented itself off to the right, running towards the beach and, without hesitation, Finn turned the camel off the tar and followed the track through the fields. Weaving its way through tall tussock and stringy grass between the bare sandy patches, the track eventually breasted a final low dune before petering out as it met the beach. Finn stopped the camel on the fringe of the sand and stood in the dray to better see and hear the roar of the waves. And the sea's raw scent, so strong now, struck him forcefully. The warm breeze ruffled his unruly mop of hair and, washed by the cacophony of sound, a broad grin leapt to his lips–the first for many days–and he called out excitedly to Harry.

'Harry, it's the sea!' But there was no respond from the old man.

So Finn jumped from the seat and wandered out across the beach alone to where the whitewash surged across the sand and hurriedly threw off his boots. Expecting a rush of chilly water as the first wave washed across his bony feet, he was surprised by the warmth of the ocean surge. Standing, the water washing around his ankles, he watched the waves build and break fifty metres out. With excitement and a little trepidation he saw tendrils of loose kelp floating in the turquoise faces of the rising waves. He watched hypnotised as the waves built until they broke to foaming white and surged up the sand to his feet. A lone seagull called mournfully as it crossed his view, gliding a few inches above the water in the calm between two breakers, then flitted up and over the incoming surge and away, soaring out across the bay.

The water and the waves and the clarity of the air exhilarated him. Finn looked over his shoulder at the dray, tucked in the gap in the dune and desperately wanted Harry to be standing there with him, revived, perhaps, by the sound and smells of the ocean. But the camel, nonchalantly chewing on a tussock, was the sole watcher of his adventure. Walking a little way back from the water's edge, Finn paused for a second before undressing. Leaving a pile of clothes next to his boots, he walked slowly back into the water and waded hesitantly out towards the breakers.

The first wave surged up his thighs and around his balls and he jumped and laughed. He waded out, pushing through the surging foam and weed, up to his belly, but went no deeper. He was not a strong swimmer and the unfamiliar surge and pull of the waves dragging at his legs made him nervous. And a moment later a second wave swamped him and rolled him and, as he went under, the boom of the ocean faded and there was a silence. Then a low roar filled his ears and he stopped his struggling and floated among the foam and stirred-up sand, letting the noise of the ocean and the coarseness of the salt water caress him till his lungs screamed for air.

Letting himself be tugged and pulled by the waves, he felt his skin soak up the saltwater as the dust of the west was washed away, and he felt his anxiety slip back a little under the roaring in his ears. Then, finding his feet he burst from the water and gulped in the ocean air. Standing again, his eyes stinging from the salt, he gazed out to the bay and his sense of adventure came flooding back to him—cogs seemed to shift a little and realign to a better fit in his mind. Snorting water from his nose, he closed his eyes for a second, felt the pull of the tide against his tingling skin and he soaked it all up greedily. Then, letting fly with a great yell , he turned and strode back to the beach.

His eyes closed, he lay naked on the sand and let the fierce heat dry him. Again the sound of the breakers surged up and the warm wind lulled him and he felt the tug of sleep. He floated in that limbo for minutes or hours, he could not tell, until he was woken suddenly by a voice above him.

150

'It's dangerous to swim, you know.'

Startled, Finn rolled away and sat up, his body covered in fine white sand. Shading his eyes against the glare, he made out a small form silhouetted against the sun.

'What?' Finn looked out at the ocean and something he had read years ago leapt to mind. 'Oh, sharks you mean?'

'Sharks? There's not many of them left. No, algae– the blooms are poisonous–didn't you know?' Finn saw now that the voice belonged to a small, dark-haired boy, maybe ten, maybe twelve years old. Standing, unafraid above him, dressed in faded ill-fitting jeans rolled up to just below his knees and a thin, oversized, sleeveless shirt, the boy's hands were stuffed deep in the pockets of his jeans. A baseball cap, battered and faded almost to white, sat tilted above his round cheerful face.

'Algae?' Finn rolled the word around in his mouth. 'Really?'

'Yup … You take some of that in and you're a goner. New strain or something … caused by the warmer, more acidic water, Claire says.' The boy spoke emphatically and continued before Finn could reply, 'Is that man back there … is he sick?'

The boy twisted his bare feet in the sand, widening his stance, and stared down at Finn.

'Well, yes, I guess … yes, he is,' Finn looked guiltily back to the dray and the camel. 'I was just washing … '

'Don't worry, I checked–he seems OK … just sleeping.'

The boy's youthful earnestness made Finn want to smile but he stifled it. 'He is very sick actually.'

There was a long pause as the boy digested the news and the two assessed each other and then, noticing his own nakedness, Finn clambered up and struggled into his clothes before turning back to face the boy.

'My name is Mortlock but everyone at The Bay calls me Morty,' the boy spoke rapidly. 'What's yours?'

'Oh, umm, Finn.' The boy nodded sagely, his lips silently repeating Finn's name. Finn would have laughed if a hundred questions weren't whirring in his brain.

'What's up with him?' the boy tilted his head toward the dray. 'I mean, you know, is it catching?'

'No, no … it's … well, he has cancer. It's not contagious.'

'I know,' Morty stood there looking Finn up and down for a moment. 'I need to have a better look before …' and he jogged off toward the dray, his bare feet kicking up the sand. Finn, brushing the sand off his knees, hurried after him.

The boy stopped short, gave the chewing camel a wide berth as he approached the dray and peeked over the side of the tray at the bundle of blankets hiding Harry's sleeping form.

'Don't wake him,' Finn whispered and the boy shook his head, his eyes full of worry as he lifted the blankets and inspected Harry's narrow face. Morty placed his small hand gently on Harry's forehead, checking the sleeping man's temperature before inspecting his neck and hands like a doctor examining a patient. He tutted and scratched his head thoughtfully, before tucking the blanket carefully around Harry's shoulders and turned to Finn.

'Do you need help?'

'Help? Well … we have plenty of water and … '

'No, no, I mean with him,' Morty indicated the sleeping Harry. 'Does he need a doctor?'

Finn turned sharply to look at the boy, 'A doctor … yes, he does. I'm … I'm not sure what I should do.'

Morty nodded, 'Wait here, I'll be back in half an hour, maybe less.' With that the boy took off, sprinting away north along a narrow track and disappeared over the dunes leaving Finn, his hand gripping the wooden side of the dray, staring open mouthed after the disappearing form.

* * *

'He's been getting worse for the past few weeks—now he can barely stand.' Finn stared over the man's shoulder as he leant in, holding Harry's wrist, taking his pulse.

The man had arrived a few minutes before—the boy Morty jogging at his side—and, without a word to Finn, immediately began examining Harry. Morty stood back and began inspecting the camel from a safe distance. After eyeing the boy momentarily, the camel ignored him completely, its attention directed at the coarse tussock grass growing on the bank of the dune. The man, short, thin and business like, had said nothing for several minutes before he had turned to question Finn.

'He's weak, all right. Cancer you said?' The man turned to him and when Finn hesitated, raised his eyebrows questioningly, 'Cancer?'

'Yes, yes … sorry. He said it was in his stomach … umm … it started as a cancer of unknown origin or something but … he's had it for a years, he said.' Finn looked into the man's face searching for some sign that he knew what to do.

'Unknown origin,' a deep frown now crossed his round, red face as he stared up at Finn. 'That's not good. Diagnosed years ago, you said?'

'Yes, two or three years ago I think he said,' it was all Finn could muster. Slipping back into silence he chewed his lip as the man nodded, pushed back a stray strand of dark hair plastered across his sweaty forehead and began a second, more thorough, examination. Harry groaned in his sleep as the man's hands felt about under his shirt. Seemingly satisfied, the newcomer carefully tucked the blanket back around him again.

'Sorry, but I had to be sure he wasn't infectious. He has several large lumps in his abdomen and his … ' he paused and frowned, showing the wrinkles of age around his eyes and narrow mouth. Wiping his hands on his stained t-shirt he spoke rapidly.

'My name is Collis. I'm a nurse … well, a mid-wife really. Where have you come from?'

Finn had taken an instant liking to the man, with his rather gentle brown eyes that turned down at the outer corners. Although Collis's manner was brusque and business-like, to Finn he seemed a caring sort of person, a man who was easily moved to help others. 'From the west,' he said finally, looking back toward the far-off range. 'From the plains–back there, over the ranges. I'm Finn and his name is Harry. I … '

'The West! You mean there are people still out there?' Collis raised his eyebrows, obviously impressed. 'Well you can tell me about all that later, eh? Finn, was it? It's important now to get your friend to The Bay, where we can get some fluids into him and see if we can make him comfortable. The heat and his sweating is making things worse, but … ' he paused and, despite his strangely measured calmness, the deep concern in his eyes caused anxiety to flare again in Finn.

'Thank you … Thank you so much. Harry would … ' Finn stammered but Collis raised a brown, calloused hand to cut him off.

'We always help if we can,' he smiled and turned to the boy standing silently beside the camel, speaking softly to him. 'Morty, can you go on ahead and ask Claire to have a bed made up in sickbay? Quick as you can, eh?'

Morty nodded and, without a word, ran off back along the track again, his shirttail flapping behind him.

Finn and Collis followed in the dray more slowly so as not to add to Harry's discomfort.

* * *

"We'll do what we can for Harry … but I'm not sure … ' Collis's voice trailed off as he saw Finn's face drop. After a long silence, Collis touched Finn on the shoulder.

'Try not to worry too much, eh? In his condition– having the cancer this long–he must know his time will be running short. He would know there's not much to be done–not these days anyway.' He paused and looked into Finn's eyes. 'I won't lie to you, Finn, the next few days or weeks won't be easy but … the knowing of it is sometimes better, huh?' Finn nodded, finding Collis's directness somehow reassuring.

'You came all that way in this?' Collis nodded at the camel and then looked behind at the dusty wooden dray and their battered gear that surrounded Harry.

'Yeah,' Finn spoke softly, trying to dig his way out of the dejection that had begun to envelop him again during Harry's examination. 'The dray and the camel are Harry's really, I'm just along for the ride I guess.' He shrugged and smiled half-heartedly.

'What's his name?'

'Who … oh, the camel you mean? I don't think he has one. Harry found him long before I met him and … well … he's never called him anything–not in my hearing anyway.'

'Really? Fair enough I suppose,' and Collis chuckled softly looking at the beast's swaggering bony arse.

Collis's soft laughter cheered Finn a little and he got to talking with him, abandoning himself to the telling of their journey and the trouble at the Centre and even touched on his stifled fears about what had happened to his father and sister and what he would do now that Harry was so sick. Collis listened, nodding and murmuring occasionally, but saying little himself. And after a while an easy silence descended as they followed the track through the tussocks on the low hills that hugged the coast.

They rounded a bend and suddenly came upon a broad, grassy flat nestled in the dunes and low hills just behind the beach. A large iron shed, its roof packed with a mismatched collection of solar panels, and three long, low glasshouses stood at the centre of the flat and, on the far side, four identical dilapidated weatherboard shacks huddled against the surrounding dunes. Perched high on the flanks of the flat, overlooking the buildings, sat a strange array of reflective solar panels, pipes and several large steel tanks. Along the beachfront, where the surrounding hills and dunes opened to the beach below, Finn saw a high concrete and rubble wall, built, he presumed, to keep the rising sea and storm surges at bay.

However, the thing that struck Finn most about the small, secluded basin was the greenness of the grass. There were several garden beds here, open to the elements, that were bulging with vegetables and he saw fruit trees too, green and healthy looking in rows near the garden beds. The flats around the buildings seemed almost luminous, much greener than the dry, brown tussocks of the surrounding dunes. There were very few bare patches of sand that Finn could see, as though the little valley miraculously possessed its own sheltered microclimate protecting it from the ravages of the drought that hung on the surrounding lands.

'What is this place?' Finn asked quietly.

'Way back, before my parents bought the place and set up our community, it was called Clementine Bay. It was a holiday camp for underprivileged kids run by one of the old worker's unions, which, for one reason or another, was abandoned a few decades before The Failing,' Collis's voice grew reflective as his eyes roamed over the cluster of buildings. 'Most of the original people who started our community ... they're dead now, my parents among them, but we've kept it going. We just call it The Bay these days.' Collis climbed down and opened the makeshift livestock gate where the track crossed the fence line and continued down to the flat.

Flagging Finn through and pulling the gate to behind him, Collis climbed back on the dray and smiled at Finn, 'Don't worry, it's safe. Harry will be comfortable here.'

They crossed the flat to the large iron shed as a small group of maybe twenty adults and seven or perhaps eight children, including the boy Morty, came out to meet them. A short, slightly plump woman with short, roughly-cut grey hair, her hand on Morty's shoulder, stepped out with the boy to stand a few paces in front of the group as the dray drew near.

Calling out to the woman Collis, jumped down before the dray had come to a halt. 'He's in the back, Claire. Can someone fetch a stretcher ... Oh, here it is, thanks.'

Another man and a woman had come forward carrying a collapsible stretcher between them. Collis guided them to the rear of the dray and, with Finn's help, they gently hoisted Harry's sleeping form down onto the stretcher and the two stretcher-bearers carried him towards one of the buildings.

Collis turned to Finn. 'You can go with him, Finn, it's fine,' and he guided him by his arm to follow the stretcher.

* * *

Harry opened his eyes to a cracked white ceiling. He blinked slowly and instantly wonder where he was. Long, tortured dreams that had seemed to roll on for years still gripped him. Visions of being submerged in a bath of burning sand–a sarcophagus of choking heat encasing his face and body. Then he had dreamed the touch of hands searching for him and momentary relief as the hands pulled him free of the bath. But their touch too scalded his skin, their grip becoming a horrid burning. And, when the hands finally dragged him free of the sand, there had been no salvation from the searing heat. In the bright, scorching air above, more pain, and the abject terror of an all-consuming feeling of impending doom.

The memory left a sickly pall on his already wasted body. He floated weakly between sleep and waking. But, even as his dream faded, reality slowly began its creep upwards and the pain flowed in with it. He felt the stifling heat of the room and the damp sweatiness of the sheet that lay over him, and the jangling bells of panic rang as his predicament fluttered back to roost. He coughed and the sudden movement wrung a soft cry from his lips.

'Take it easy, Harry. You're safe.' The sound of Finn's voice reassured him a little. Gulping air, he turned and looked to the young man sitting in a chair next to the bed.

'What happened?'

'You passed out as we came down the escarpment, Harry. You've been out of it for days.'

'Really?' Harry stewed on this for a long while. 'Where are we though? Did we make the coast?'

Harry lifted his head and surveyed the sparsely furnished room. Beside the single cot where he lay, stood a small bedside table and a thin steel IV drip-stand holding a clear, half-empty bag of fluid, its line wandering across the sheets to beneath a bandage wrapped around his forearm. A narrow table, covered with a clean, white sheet, was pushed up against the wall near the solid-looking wooden door. Directly opposite the bed, a small timber and glass bookshelf held an assortment of packets, bottles and plastic pill containers. The only window, behind Finn's chair, showed a bright, clear blue sky outside but little of anything else.

'Can you hear the waves, Harry–can you? The coast … it's amazing, eh?' Finn spoke excitedly. In the pause after his question, he and Harry listened and caught the gentle crash of the surf not far off. Harry smiled and lay his head back down on the firm foam pillow.

'You are in the sickbay of this … this sort of community,' Finn scratched his head, trying to figure out where to begin. 'When we first got here, I went for a swim … I met a boy … well, he sort of found me, really … on the beach not far from here. He brought us to his home, this place. It's kind of … an eco-community thing.'

Harry raised his eyebrows but Finn continued on, 'I haven't looked around much since we got here yesterday. But there's a nurse, Collis, who seems OK. They can help you I think, Harry.' Finn leant in over the bed and hesitantly patted Harry's shoulder.

'It's not … you know, like one of those commune-type places, full of … well, you know … ' Harry's voice petered out.

'I don't know, they don't seem weird … if that's what you mean?' Finn was a little hurt at Harry's questioning. 'They gave you some of their morphine … you know, to ease the pain … I don't think they have much to spare either.'

'Oh,' Harry paused and changed tack. 'Good on you, you know, for getting us this far, eh?'

'That's OK, Harry, I'm just glad you're awake. You feeling any better?'

Harry grunted equivocally and they both fell into the familiar silence that had accompanied them on much of their journey. The shadows inched across the room and the two men chewed on their own particular thoughts in the heat. Eventually Harry began to doze in the smoky warmth of the morphine, until the soft scrape of Finn's chair woke him from his drifting.

'It must be nearly lunchtime. Shall I go across to the Hall and see if I can get you some food ... if you're hungry?' Harry nodded and waited for the door to close before he rolled onto his side, wincing with the fresh stab of pain. He felt under the sheets, his fingers gently prodding at his bare torso and soon found the firmness of the enlarged growths. He winced again as his mind shied from the tenderness there and an ugly panic tugged at him again. Puffing out his cheeks, he huffed and screwed his eyes against the horror of it all, and a soft, half-stifled moan escaped from him.

Harry lay there, frantically trying to dodge thinking about the gruesome inevitability of his illness, but he could not avoid it. It crept over him and made him gasp and gulp for air.

His mind baulked like a frightened beast, knowing, at last, it had been cornered, that flight was now futile. Finally, he thought, finally after all this time, it has caught me. He fought a shuddering sob. His mind reeled and he felt tears build. Desperate not to be overwhelmed, he breathed out slowly, and the flood of anxiety settled a little with his escaping breath. He recalled a practice he had learnt many years ago at some corporate retreat, a calming meditation used to reduce stress. Back then he had used it occasionally but had not applied it for years. Now, despairing and seeking some relief, he directed his mind to wander around his body.

He felt the heat of the day wrapping him, touching him everywhere. Touching his scalp, his mind's eye felt the slicks of sweat trickling down his forehead and around his left eye. Moving on, he felt the heat in his shrunken cheeks and the parched skin of his cracked lips. He focused next on the sunburnt skin of his neck and throat, felt the rawness there, then moved on again. The rise and fall of his chest fought against the heat of the room and his breath, running from his lungs, caught prematurely. And lower, tentatively he felt at the pain, like clenched fists inside him, tangled around the tumours, twisting his organs. Following the tendrils of pain, which rode out along his jangling nerves, he saw the pain surge and spread and then contract again, back to those fierce, hungry knots. He touched the pain and rolled it over in his mind, examining its edges, its grain and listened intently to its biting song.

Then Harry moved his mind onwards, abandoning the pain, passing downward to his buttocks and then his thighs. He found an itch, niggling at the patches of dryness on his skin, examined it momentarily and moved on again, down his aching calves, eventually to his feet, touching the arch, the tops of his feet and, finally, his toes. The search for and finding of feelings in his extremities, the painstaking examination, drew him away from his aversion and anxiety, and the pain in his abdomen receded a little more.

The battle to creating some objectivity brought a degree of balance to his trembling mind. Packaging the pain and fear as known quantities made it easier to hold them within himself. Lying perfectly still, he repeated the process twice more, until another soft click of the door reverberated through the stillness of his meditations.

'Hello,' a quiet voice spoke and Harry raised his head from the pillow and looked towards the door. He saw a woman's round face poking through the opening. 'Am I disturbing you? Can I come in?'

'Sure,' his voice seemed a little stronger now.

The stocky, grey-haired woman wearing a patched summer dress entered and bustling across the room, settled her short frame on the edge of the chair by the bed.

'I'm Claire. I'm doing a shift as the community spokesperson, so I've come to sort of introduce ourselves I guess.' She laughed little self-consciously. 'How're you feeling?'

'Um ... OK, I guess.' He replied quietly, waiting to find his footing with the woman.

'I thought I might have a chat with you, before Finn comes back with your lunch. Promise it won't take too long.' She smiled warmly and Harry was grateful not to see too much pity in her eyes.

'I'm not that hungry, really.'

'That's probably understandable in your condition. The morphine won't help your appetite either,' she paused, opening her lips but frowned before continuing. 'Um ... well ... '

Pausing again, she cleared her throat, 'Look, Harry, we try to be rationalists here, we try to speak plainly as much as we can, so I won't beat around the bush with you— no time for all that guff, eh?'

Harry nodded.

'You must know your condition is terminal? Collis, our nurse, isn't an expert by any means but he thinks you may only have a few weeks, maybe a month or so, at best before you ... well, before you die.'

The saying of it—so matter-of-factly—gave Harry pause. His breath caught but he dug out the required words, 'I know.' And it was a relief to say it. The woman next to him inclined her head acknowledging the weight of it.

'Well, Harry, there's no access to technical treatments, not here anyway, and Collis doubts it would help you anyway. We could get you to the city to get more help maybe ... or we can do some things for you here. We have a little morphine, to ease the pain over your remaining time or ... '

'No, no, that's not necessary, well, not yet at least, keep it for someone else, for the future.'

She raised her eyebrows, 'If it's what you want then sure, but you need to know it's there for you, you know, if you need it.'

Harry nodded. And then he rushed a question in.

'How long will you have us here—how long can Finn and I stay?' He glanced across at her and waited for the bad news he knew must come. But she sat back in the chair looking a little perplexed. Then she placed her hands on the arms of the chair and smiled reassuringly.

'Well, till the end, if that's what you want.'

'What?' Relief washed over him. 'But what about your water and food supplies, won't we put pressure on you?'

She waved a hand, 'We don't have much, but we have enough to help the odd visitor! It hasn't got that bad yet. Well … not here, at any rate. Don't worry, Harry, we're not that ruthless here, we'll help you and Finn—we won't throw you to the wolves.' She chuckled softy and her light-hearted warmth cut him to the quick.

He lay back and stared at the ceiling again. A shuddering sigh escaped his lips and Claire saw a tear well up in his eye and watched it roll down the deeply-carved lines of his pale cheek and onto the pillow.

'I … ' his voice caught in his throat.

'Forget it, Harry,' she spoke softly to him. 'We wouldn't boot you out, not even if things were different.' She shook his arm reassuringly, 'You might regret staying, mind you, when young Morty, Collis's son, gets hold of you. He loves a chat and he's already chewed Finn's ear off.'

He turned to her, his washed-out eyes still brimming but he smiled, 'Thank you.'

A grin crossed her round, cheerful face, 'I'll explain how things work at The Bay later, when you're a bit stronger, eh?' And she quietly got up and left the room.

A few minutes later Finn returned with a bowl of vegetable soup and some sort of crumbly cornbread and a cup of lemon water. Finn sat and watched Harry eat and, over the afternoon, he filled him in on the rest of their travels from the Divide to the sea.

* * *

They sat in the shade of the sickbay, the sun dropping till it almost touched the mountaintops in the west. Harry and Claire sat side by side in two rusted foldout chairs and Finn, on the grass next to them, leaned against the peeling weatherboards of the hut. Harry had recovered a little of his strength overnight. Looking less like he was about to keel over after a day or more on the saline drip, nonetheless it had been a slow teetering walk from his sickbay bed to sit outside in the fresher air.

Harry sipped from a tin cup of water and he and Finn listened while Claire told them of the workings of The Bay. She spoke slowly, but with barely supressed enthusiasm, of how the community had been started by Collis's and her parents sixty years before. It had been started as a refuge against the coming upheavals that were then only just beginning to fracture the larger cities of the coast.

She explained how the original twenty or so people had pooled their money and bought the abandoned holiday camp from what remained of the Allied Workers Union. She went into great detail about how they had spent many months writing a constitution for The Bay and how they had based it on a model of sufficiency and human rights, principles that still remained at the heart of their existence here, and how they had researched and then set up the solar and water systems that sustained the community to the present day.

The original community, she said, had built the system when things were relatively stable, before climate destabilization and oil scarcity had crippled the big economies and shattered global trade—while the machinery and equipment were still affordable for people like them. They had used an idea, she told them, a technology that had been still in its infancy, and thrown the last of their combined money into building the system that drew seawater from the bay and used it for the small solar-thermal turbine that powered the community.

'You see ... ' she smiled proudly. 'It's beautifully efficient. We produce electricity and create fresh water in one system. Our setup here powers The Bay by using solar reflectors, those panels on the bank up there, to boil water and create steam that drives a small turbine and generator. Creating the steam also desalinates the seawater to provide fresh water for The Bay. We recycle our wastewater too, but our solar-thermal setup provides most of our needs. This is how we have managed to survive through the drought. We ... '

'But, if it works so well, why wouldn't the government give this technology to everyone? I mean, with The Failing coming and all?' Finn interrupted her, his brow wrinkled in confusion.

'I don't know, Finn, perhaps they could have once but they never just gave things away back then, all had things were based on a profit, and, but ... ' she shrugged again. 'There's no simple answer, Finn, but let me try and explain. The focus during the years running up to the beginning of The Failing was mostly on funding the corporations and their big technological fixes—carbon cleaning of the power stations, weather modification, atmospheric scrubbing—there wasn't much interest in simple little systems like this.' She laughed, but there was little humour in her eyes when she continued.

'Governments put all their eggs in one economic baskets so to speak, and, unfortunately, it was the wrong basket. Maybe it was just easier or something, but most people kept their faith in a system that was failing them.

Don't ask me why, because I don't know,' she sighed, rubbed her eyes with her fingers and looked to Finn.

'Anyway, to cut a long story short, the big corporations refused to rollout small systems that gave them no on-going profits–why would they when they were only there to make money? By the time governments tried to roll out emergency measures and forced the companies to change–the tipping point had already been breached–The Failing was in full-swing and sadly, unstoppable by then. The United Nations eventually ploughed trillions into wind and solar farms, wave energy and geothermal power–but it was all just too late. And then ... bang!' She suddenly clapped her hands, snapping Finn and Harry out of their reverie. 'Suddenly peak-oil and the ensuing fuel crisis hit them too.'

Claire leaned forward in her chair. 'Oil was getting scarce ... and astronomically expensive, the changing climate was wrecking food production across vast areas, pesticides and herbicides, being mostly oil-based, were unavailable, the global economy was in the early throes of collapse and, well ... the rest is history I suppose.' Claire raised her eyebrows at the young man, 'To answer your question, Finn, by the time they even thought about rolling out these small, stand-alone systems to communities for free, governments simply couldn't afford to help–they were all broke!'

'Claire's right, it was a massive mistake!' Harry's voice was weak but his eyes sparkled, as he was carried away by the terrible history that he hadn't discussed in years. 'The profits on systems like this were far too small for the big companies to be interested in. The economic system just kept ... '

'Exactly, Harry! Exactly!' Claire patted him on his bony shoulder. 'Small was no good to the companies and conglomerates–for them, big profit was the only god. And, till the very end, they pushed back against any action that threatened their profits. And in the end ... they were swamped, like the rest of humanity, by a tidal wave they had ignored for too long. Harry, of all people, would know about that.'

Harry swiveled to look at her, a frown flashing across his pallid face. But Claire laughed, brushing his grim look off.

'You think we don't know who you are, Harry Sinclair? Do you think we don't know you're the ex-CEO of Clearwater?' She turned to Finn, a broad grin playing across her round, rosy face. 'This man, Finn, this man was one of the big players in the last great water rush, but ... ' Finn nodded, but she glanced at Harry conspiratorially. 'But, he was also one of the few to betray the corporations. He jumped ship—and not many do, even now. It was almost unheard of for a conglomerate director to abandon their company, wasn't it, Harry?'

Harry sat for a long moment, gazing at his feet, until finally he spoke softly, 'I was one of the few, I suppose. But I was still part of that machine ... propping up the chaos back then.'

Claire snorted at his comment, 'For whatever reason, while the rest of the corporate elites hung in there or scurried off to the new Company enclaves in Antarctica and Greenland or New Alaska, you, Harry, chucked it all in, and ... puff ... disappeared!' She sat back, pleased with herself. 'You might be surprised to learn, your disappearance made you a kind of folk-hero to some back here on the coast.'

'What? Why the hell would they ... ' It was Harry's turn to snort with derision.

'It's funny, but your leaving ... ' Claire smiled wryly. 'It triggered a sort of final crisis of confidence in Clearwater. That Mérida fellow denied the company was going under, of course, but the damage was done.'

She paused and watched Harry's face as he digested the news. 'Maybe you haven't heard about it, but there was a rout on Clearwater shares and a domino effect more broadly through the other major conglomerates. Like it or not, Harry, it was partly down to you!' She chuckled again at the look of incredulity spreading across Harry's face.

'Ptttrt!' Harry snorted. 'I left because I was ... I was sick, not for any other reason. Certainly not as some sort of ... '

'But it's funny though, isn't it ... ' her eyes twinkled. 'How rumours fly ... the nervous nellies at the exchanges, already jumpy, panic even more. The more that stuffed suit Mérida denied that there was a crisis, the more people believed there was one,' she chuckled softly. 'It was the start of the last huge tumble–the worst yet I believe. The global markets were already at breaking point. They're even more fragmented now.'

'But the chaos ... The Failing ... it must be even more terrible now. How can you be so ... ' Harry shook his head.

'Yes, it is ... it's horrendous, but it was inevitable sooner or later wasn't it? After the catastrophic failures back before the Failing our path to this juncture was inevitable really. Is anyone surprised? Climate disruption has caused hundred of millions of deaths, probaly billions ... we'll never really know. The massive refugee migrations are all still playing out.' She paused, her voice growing somber. 'Two or three years is a long time to be away, Harry. The collapse is pretty much global now. We hear bits and pieces ... snippets ... but it is beyond anything humanity has seen before–far beyond the horrors of the two world wars. It was all predicted of course but still, it's not till you actually see ... ' She stopped and stared out to the bay, and then turned to them both, her face more dour than either had seen it in the short time they had been at The Bay.

'But what can anyone do now? The time for fixing this was a century ago.' She shook her head. 'There was still time then–they could've made things so much easier for us,' she sighed. 'But that, Harry ... that's the past ... and we can't change that now, can we?'

Harry saw what she said was ultimately the truth but, as always, he groped instinctively for a simple answer– some solution to all the devastation–an answer that they had somehow overlooked. They had all believed it back then, that something would come, a miraculous solution, just in time. He grasped for that solution now, hidden just behind the jumble that filled his brain. But depressingly, he knew the answer was not there. That great opportunity had slipped through a generation's fingers, long before his time.

'But there must be something left ... something to do?' It was Finn's voice that broke the silence, sounding small and willowy. 'Can't they ... I don't know ... repair things ... even a little ... over time? Won't things get better?' He looked to them, but they both refused to look at him.

'Repair? Well maybe, Finn,' but there was little enthusiasm in Claire's voice. 'At The Bay we believe we can help build things again. We must adapt as best we can and help others set up small communities like this, build something better, based on the sufficiency model rather than growth at all costs. The lesson from all this, if we survive, is that we cannot live beyond the planets means,' she paused for a moment and the smallest smile played across her lips, 'Others are building solar-thermal systems from scavenged parts we scrounge from the cities, there are small factories being set up to build and share these things There is hope ... but the climate is like this now ... the damage is beyond our ability to repair, I think. And things will never be like they were ... '

'But how ... how have you survived so well here, in all the chaos, I mean?' Harry was desperate, shying away from all that hopelessness.

And Claire looked at him, the numbness in her face slowly draining. She stood slowly and walked out across the grass into the fierce afternoon light, and stood looking out to sea for a moment before she turned back to them, her face stark in the bright orange glare of the sinking sun.

'Like I said, we are a deeply ethical community here—we believe unity, a common purpose, that society should be based on ethical principles, on the intrinsic human rights of all. We don't hold much store in that survival of the fittest rubbish they peddled way back then, before The Failing. We believe there is a strength in looking after each other—in a truly equal society.'

Wiping her sweaty face with a scarf as she spoke, she paced back and forth across the grass in front of them. 'You're right, Harry, it is surprising we have survived. Many people said we'd be devoured by those strong enough to take what we have here. And that may still happen, who knows ... but it hasn't happened yet.' Her face grew defiant. 'And we would be utterly compromised if we let that fear rule us—now more than ever this is true. We need to hold onto those basic principles that were lost before The Failing.' She looked to each of them in turn, 'We must take our responsibilities seriously if we are to build something better from the ruins, and not just repeat the mistakes of before.'

She came and sat next to Harry and Finn again, waiting eagerly for them to ask a question but none came.

'Our survival here—it's simple really. The idea at The Bay has always been to live within our means—to only grow and use what we actually need—it's called the Sufficiency Principle. Any surpluses, and there aren't many, we give away or trade with the other communities up and down the coast. We have some comforts here but none that put at risk our, or others', survival. This has dominated what we grow and what we use and, in the end, meant The Bay has stayed very small. Our production capacity has always been tied closely to our real needs, in a way.' She frowned thoughtfully for a moment. 'I ... '

'But what has this got to do with people coming here and stealing what you have?' Harry challenged her and she stared at him for a moment, examining him as if he were some unfamiliar bird or exotic plant, before she replied.

'I'm getting to that Harry, just stay with me,' she smiled at him. 'Maybe try thinking of it like this. You see, communities like us, we are like the early mammals hundreds of millions of years ago—they were only rat-sized things then, tiny and insignificant. The corporations on the other hand, were like dinosaurs—big and hungry and forever lumbering about. Being small, the mammals scurried around unnoticed by the dinosaurs for millennia ... then boom ... a meteor struck. In our time—it's The Failing and the planet has warmed, but it's kind of the same result really—the climate is out of control. The dinosaurs started dying off, as the companies and mega-corporations are doing now—they simply can't survive without a lot of water and resources like oil. They can't survive without continuous growth and they ate the planet trying to do it back then. They have almost died out and we, like those little rodents scampering around in the undergrowth, we have lived on. You see, like the prehistoric mammals, our model is far better adapted to a hot, water- and resource-poor world. Now, Harry, now small is good all of a sudden!' Pleased with her analogy, she chuckled, seeing the look of disbelief stitched on both their faces.

'But, that's not answering my question. What if someone comes and tries to take all this?' Harry asked, gesturing around him.

'Well, Harry, I just told you—because we are small,' she held his eyes for a second and saw that his face was still full of doubt. 'Look, it's simple really. We've had people come demanding this and that. We let them look and they see we don't have huge caches of food or water. We give them as much as we can—enough for a few days or a week, perhaps two ... and they move on.' Claire shrugged. 'We just wait for the solar-thermal system to desalinate more water, and ration our water and food if we need to. We always get by. Our sewerage water is recycled, we use it on the paddock and gardens, it's no use to anyone else.' She smiled again and placed her hands on her knees. 'Some who come have stayed, a few over the years, replacing older members who pass on, but most leave us alone. Their minds seem too fixed on the big cities or on getting to the enclaves, I guess.'

Finn sat listening to her but did not look up. He did not want to find her looking at him.

'But what if someone comes who wants to take over? How could you stop them?' Harry pushed her, looking for some chink in her argument.

'What if, what if!' She was growing a little frustrated with him. 'Should we build a fortress for all those what ifs? How high is high enough for a wall, Harry? How long could we hide behind it? And, anyway, like I told you, we don't want to live in a fortress ... living like that, soaked in that fear, is a slippery slope ... we like it the way it is here. We have enough for us ... and the odd visitor,' she squeezed his arm affectionately.

'But ... '

'Don't try to dissect it, Harry, just try to remember, it's how we live, not how long we last ... not any more. No disrespect, Harry, but your mind is still fixed in dinosaur mode, try thinking like a mammal!' she chuckled cheerfully and patted his arm.

'But it can't be that ... '

'Enough, Harry, enough! Believe me or not, it matters little ... it is how we are,' she laughed again. 'You need to rest. Collis will string me up if you take a turn for the worse again. We can talk again later ... as much as you like. Everyone here loves a good debate. Tomorrow at dinner, if you're strong enough come to the Hall and test us!'

* * *

Harry did go and eat dinner and argue with the people of The Bay. He sat at the long table in the Hall among their cheerful chatter and laughter. But, in all the discussion, he could not shoot holes in their optimism. Despite all the chaos around them, their belief in the ethos of The Bay seemed unshakable. He tried to poke holes in their crazy, false sense of security, in their theories, and in their quiet confidence in the fundamental goodness of humanity. He pointed out the risks of their naïve optimism, to one after another but, to Harry's utter frustration, they freely admitted them. And all, even Morty, shrugged and fled to the fatalism of the times in which they lived.

It would do them no good, they smilingly told him, to fret about all that now. They would survive for a week or a year, or even decades, it didn't matter. They could not change that anyhow—what mattered to them was how they lived and looked after each other. And Harry saw it all in its altruistic simplicity, but still he couldn't shake the feeling that somehow it was all just a little suicidal.

Late one afternoon, Morty visited Harry in the sickbay. Harry was alone—Finn was out in the gardens helping with some harvesting. Morty had finished his gardening shift and his lessons and, a little bored, had come to see him, worried because Harry had been unable to get out of bed that day.

They sat in silence for a while, Morty in the chair beside Harry's bed, swinging his dirty bare feet and sucking his teeth, until Harry asked him a question that had been niggling at him for a day or two.

'Do you ever wonder what its like outside The Bay, Morty?'

Morty stared at him for a second, holding Harry's gaze with his large clear brown eyes. 'Outside? You mean in the cities?'

'Well ... yes, in the cities if you like, but you know, out in the world in general.'

'I know what it's like ... ' he paused thoughtfully. 'I read in our library and we still get the Internet sometimes. But I guess I do sometimes wonder what's happening out there ... but not so that I'd want to go and look.'

'But Finn wants to go to the city to look ... to see what it's like.'

Morty shrugged and looked as though he might lose interest.

'Don't you want to see it too, one day?' He felt a little guilty at his mischievous probing but he couldn't help himself.

'But what's there to see? People come past sometimes and tell us about what they see in the cities ... no one says much good about it,' he kept looking at Harry and Harry, under his unblinking gaze, tried to think of something that might tempt the boy's curiosity. He told him of the great high-rise towers, the sparkling mirrors of the buildings, the broad streets, the cars, the things you could still buy there—3-D games and micro-TVs and the like— thinking to spark his curiosity. But none of it seemed enough of a bauble to snare the boy's interest.

'It's all falling down, isn't it? All those things ... they are why the world is so crazy, aren't they?' The boy's face held neither irony nor fear. He had told a truth as he saw it, and Harry could not answer. He fell silent for a long while and the boy grew restless and wriggled in his seat until eventually Harry turned to him.

'You know, Morty, you're right—there is nothing for you in all that. It's all just smoke and mirrors—you know, a silly magic trick,' he smiled and Morty smiled back. 'Go fishing or something if you like. I think I'll have a sleep.' He smiled crookedly as the boy scuttled from the room, closing the door quietly behind him.

* * *

In the days after Harry and Morty's conversation, Harry remained quiet and contemplative. Finn could get little out of him except for a few small light-hearted conversations as they sat outside the hut and watched the sun slowly cross the sky, anticipating the diminishing heat of dusk.

Harry seemed somehow more settled in himself to Finn. He did not talk of his cancer or his rapidly shortening future. He spoke to Collis about those things, and seemed satisfied just to be sitting, or sleeping, as he grew weaker day by day. To Finn he seemed somehow to be fighting it less and, despite his increasing weakness, the pain seemed somehow diminished and his disposition was much more cheery than Finn had seen over the past months. This change bewildered Finn as he watched Harry slowly fade.

Finn had taken a vacant bed in one of the weatherboard huts shared by the other younger people at The Bay and he enjoyed their company after the long days travelling with only Harry and his stilted conversations. The young people talked of the gardens and the sea, of the philosophy and principles of The Bay, of sailing on the bay and walking along the trails of the coast and often, to Finn's surprise, of visiting other small communities up and down the coast—of friends there, and sometimes lovers, too.

To Finn their world seemed reasonably comfortable—there were shortages and they did without when they could not trade with the other communities for what they did not have, but the young people seemed happier, or at least less fearful, than he remembered Samuel and Nettie being—and the other men and women he had grown up with in the west. Yet Finn found their humility and contentment in some strange way hard to take and he sometimes caught himself scoffing inwardly at their rather simple expectations.

The young people seemed to hold a gentle fatalism about the future, not unaware of the risks from the outside, but disconcertingly accepting of the chaos that might come to them one day. This acceptance was hard for Finn to grasp. It hurt his head when he tried to release his own grip on the threats and fears posed by the outside world. Perhaps because he had seen something of them, he thought, and they had not. They met and talked to visitors who came and went, bringing news of the troubles in the cities, but they still seemed immune to being overtaken by the fear of those troubles   .

It was confusing to Finn, but he didn't worry at it, not for too long at least. He let his mind wander to the towers of the cities—all those things he had read about on the Internet when he had been able to or seen on the old DVDs back at the Centre. All the talk of the chaos and troubles did not deterred him too much. Listening to Harry and Claire talk, and the discussions of the others, had sown some seeds of doubt but not nearly enough to corrode his dreams of the people and the vibrancy of the cities. But, even with his mind whirring constantly with these visions, he still remained hesitant about continuing alone.

Like Morty, the younger people at The Bay held little desire to go to the cities—to venture out with him when he had suggested the possibility. They seemed more curious about why he desired to go, than to have any real desire to go themselves. Trying to explain, he talked of the adventures, the hustle and bustle, the new people they would meet, but they always fell to weighing up the problems—ticking off on their fingers any possible benefits their visit to the city might bring to their community, which seemed paltry when compared against the many potential risks they would encounter, and the additional work the others at The Bay would need to do to make up for their absence. They simply looked bemused at his excited talk, indifferent to his thirst for adventure. And, confronted by their blank faces, he quickly grew bored of trying to tempt them and kept his dreams to himself as much as he could.

* * *

Harry grew weaker and Finn sat with him as much as he could on his breaks from the gardens or from his shifts helping in the teaching of the younger children of the Bay. They would sit, stewing in the heat of the afternoon, in the shade of the buildings or he would watch over Harry as he lay sleeping in the sickbay. Finn watched the pain criss-cross Harry's features as he lay there resting and he worried for him. But then, occasionally, he would see Harry's face slowly relax and fall, as though the pain had faded for a time. Finn felt relief at the softening of those gaunt, grey features. The smoothing of the lines that carved Harry's forehead and the surrounds of his eyes and mouth, brought forth a younger version of the man—a man alive long before Finn had met him.

At these times a peace seemed to settle on the bones and angular protrusions beneath the white sheets, and when Harry opened his eyes they were free, for a while at least, of the shades of pain. He would talk then with Finn of the cities, and he didn't scoff at the young man's excited musings. He didn't even try to badger him with the dangers. Harry listened and nodded and spoke quietly of his time long ago in the cities, of times, he assured Finn, that were long gone now. But still he told him.

A week or so after their arrival Harry spent a morning ensconced in the sickbay with Collis and Claire. Finn visited but was told to come back after lunch and he went away with a deeper worry eating at him.

When he returned Harry was sitting again in the chair outside the hut in his shirt and trousers, his long, narrow feet stretched out before him, poking out into the sunshine. Engrossed in watching the camel chewing a mouthful of grass as it stood by the abandoned dray, Harry looked up as he heard Finn approach and smiled at the sight of the young man's sunburnt face.

'You know, it's funny, but I don't seem to notice the heat so much now,' Harry squinted against the intense light, his face covered in a thin layer of sweat as he looked at Finn's face.

Finn chuckled and settled on the grass next to him, 'Yeah, right.' Even in the shade, the heat was stifling. But then the young man's face grew serious. 'What happened this morning, Harry? What's going on?'

'My meeting with Collis and Claire you mean? We were just doing some planning, that's all,' Harry coughed and Finn saw his head wobble weakly on his stringy neck. Harry raised a hand, so thin now the veins and muscle stood out beneath his blotched, translucent skin, and wiped at his mouth weakly.

'What planning?'

'Me going, Finn ... what else?' Harry glanced up and caught Finn's eye.

'How can you plan ... ' Finn stammered to a halt and looked at Harry hard. 'What do you mean?'

'Collis is going to help me, Finn,' Harry smiled wanly. 'They'll help me go a bit more comfortably—with the morphine.'

'What! Harry, no ... I mean, you've got plenty of time yet ... '

Harry raised an eyebrow and Finn fell silent. 'Come on, Finn, we both know that's bullshit.'

Neither man spoke for a time, Harry let his head fall back, lifted his face to the sky and closed his eyes and Finn, agitated, worried at a cuff of his shirt and shiftted uncomfortably on the ground next to him.

'Can't they prolong things for you?' Finn's thin voice cracked.

'I wouldn't want them to, Finn. And it would do no good anyway. It's inevitable now and, well … I don't want to wither away like some carcass in the desert.' He shuddered at the memory of the mummified body of the camel's original owner lying all shrivelled in the dust of the homestead. 'I can choose, Finn. They have given me a great gift, Collis and Claire.'

'But … ' Finn paused, fretting over what he wanted to say. 'But what will I do? Once you're gone, I mean.'

Harry laughed softly, 'Do what you want, Finn. Stay here if you want. Go to the city, I know you want to … Do what you want.' He smiled at Finn but then he winced as a stab of pain wracked him and his features clouded again, his eyes closing for a moment.

'When? When are you … when is this going to happen?'

'In a day or two … when I can get my head around it all. Don't worry, I'll let you know.'

Turmoil shook Finn. For the rest of that day and the next he couldn't concentrate or hold conversations for long with the others. He didn't go to see Harry again that day. He could not imagine what they would say, what they would talk of, with this terrible pall hanging over them. And Finn did not trust himself to be able to control his own conflicting feelings in front of Harry.

The following day Finn was caught by Collis in the garden and given the message that Harry wanted to talk with him after lunch. And, after prolonging his shift and procrastinating well past the lunch hour, with great foreboding Finn crossed the flat to the sickbay late in the afternoon.

Finn found Harry sitting in his chair next to the hut. There was a slight breeze off the bay that day, helping cool the afternoon a little. Finn was surprised at how well Harry looked. His face seemed to have filled out a little and his long, thin hair looked thicker somehow. As Finn approached, Harry tilted his head up to him slowly, as though even simple movements were draining what little energy he had left. He sleepily half opened his eyes to look up at him.

'Hello, Finn, where have you been?' The old man spoke so softly Finn could hardly hear him. 'I missed you yesterday,' And Harry smiled almost shyly at the young man standing above him. 'Sit down for a tick, eh?'

'Sorry, Harry, I got caught up yesterday ... with the gardens and things.'

Harry, with the barest movement of his hand, waved his apology away. 'You like working in the gardens, huh?' Finn nodded. 'Then why not stay, Finn? The young people here ... ' but he stopped himself. Sighing softly, he breathed deeply through his nose to relax himself.

'I do like it here, it's ... but I can come back if I want, Claire said so.'

Harry nodded, 'Remember that, eh?'

There was more silence and Finn grew nervous, guessing at the discussion that was to come. But Harry surprised him when he spoke again.

'Can I tell you something, Finn? I'll tell you once more and won't mention it again, OK? What you're looking for, in the cities, it's all just a mirage, Finn–a disease the world is slowly ridding itself of. All that stuff is broken. You'll find the gloss long worn off by the upheavals and cataclysms of the Failing. Claire is right–people like me, things like those great cities–it's all fading Finn, it's all from the age of the dinosaurs. We were too dumb to change ... '

'No, Harry ... '

Harry waved his hand weakly to silence Finn's objection. 'We are, Finn, but that might be a good thing,' and he chuckled weakly. 'Once you see those tattered cities, you will know it. It's places like this, the simplicity of their lives here, that hold hope for you, Finn.'

He closed his eyes and sighed again before continuing in a softer voice. 'And now, back to me, Finn. I'm going to finish things in two days. It's all set. But we have a little time yet, eh?'

'Why, Harry? You look better today than you have in weeks. Why not give yourself more …'

'Why? Why wait, Finn? What's left to wait for exce … ' he winced again. 'It's torture, Finn.'

'I know all that but … what will I do Harry, without you?' He put his head in his hands and he felt Harry pat him weakly on the back.

'Same as you would do in a week or a month, Finn, nothing will change, eh? Even if I weren't sick, I wouldn't go back,' he drew a tired breath. 'Do what you feel is right. Go to the city, or go back and find Nettie and Samuel—it's your choice. But let me choose too, eh? I'm frightened too, so help me feel better about it, will you?'

Finn gnawed on Harry's words for a long while until he spoke with difficulty, 'I'm sorry, Harry, I'll try.'

* * *

The next day and the one after took an aching eternity and yet, at the same time, the hours seemed to slip from Finn's grasp more quickly than any he could ever remember. He was excused from his gardening and teaching shifts and spent his time sitting with Harry.

Harry asked him to leave the camel with the people at The Bay. The city was no place for the big shaggy beast he told him and Finn nodded in agreement. The camel seemed to have settled in at The Bay, spending its time eating sedges and grasses down by the banks of the dry creek or standing, gazing from under its long lashes at the community's slightly aloof herd of five dairy goats.

In the afternoon Harry produced a yellowed slip of paper with a line of numbers scribbled in pencil on it.

'These are my bank account access codes, Finn. I'm not sure what's left of the account but some of my dividends from Clearwater might be still in there, if the bank's still operating. Take what you need, Finn, if it's still worth anything that is, and if you come back bring the rest here to The Bay will you?'

'Sure, sure, I will, Harry. Thanks for this,' Finn did not look up, instead playing with the slip of paper between his fingers.

They talked on into the evening. Talking again of the city and what Finn might find there. Harry told him of friends he had known there, wrote their addresses down and told Finn to seek them out if ever he needed help. Harry spoke sleepily, telling him of the quieter, richer enclave suburbs that might have remained less affected by the upheavals wracking the cities, and of places that still might give out food or clothing. He told him of these places even though neither Claire nor Collis had had any news that things like this still existed. But it was all Harry could think to give him.

* * *

And, with a lethargic certainty, the final morning came. Finn woke early with a dread on him like nothing he had ever felt before. Almost immediately, as he slipped quietly out of bed and crept from the hut, he felt the anxiety rising in his guts and limbs. His legs felt shaky as he crossed the grass to the sickbay, the sun's falling across the bay.

Collis answered Finn's soft knock and waved him into the dimly-lit room. Harry's form drew Finn's eyes like a magnet. He lay motionless under the bed sheet and Finn, his feet glued to the floor, studied him from across the room. Harry's head seemed over-large, lying on the yellowing pillow, and his eyes were huge and black in the sunken flesh of his face. The old man's face was so grey and his leathery skin so tight across his raised cheekbones, it shook Finn to his core. Harry's breathing, soft and shallow, was now agonisingly slow. His arms, lying outside the sheets, looked so thin Finn feared he would be too frightened to touch him when finally he went to him.

Harry turned his head and smiled at him and raised a hand motioning him over. Finn crossed woodenly to the chair by the bed. Collis and Claire stood quietly on the other side and Finn saw that Collis had set up the saline drip again and had reinserted the cannula in the rope-like vein on Harry's forearm. Finn looked to the drip and then to Collis and Claire, but they both looked impassively at Harry.

The air suddenly felt cloying and the silence clawed at Finn, bringing a sudden urge to flee the darkened room. A strange vertigo threatened to overwhelm him but, steadying himself, he swallowed it down and spoke, his tongue feeling as dry as rice paper.

'Are you OK, Harry?'

A long shaking sigh came before Harry spoke. His voice was thin and wavered a little, 'I don't know Finn. I ... I can't seem get my head around it all. I've known it was coming for so many years but ... it's ... ' he swallowed loudly. 'Now it's here ... it's too big to see. I ... I'm scared.'

Finn touched Harry's arm and it felt as flimsy as an old, dry leaf, tears welled up in Finn's eyes and the anxiety rose again and gripped his heart. He tried to speak but his words were trapped behind his swollen tongue and, when he finally got them out, they were nothing like the things he had wanted to say.

'Harry, you don't have to ... ' he halted, remembering Harry's words two days before, but he could not help but say it. 'I ... You can still change your mind if you want.'

Harry shuddered and shook his head, 'I'm frightened, Finn. It's ... I ... ' he paused and took a few rapid breaths. The old man felt a tear fall on his arm and he looked up and saw the fear and the uncertainty in the young man's fallen face, and a little of the weight lifted from Harry and he smiled then, 'You'll be right, Finn.'

Seeing that fear in Finn's eyes had suddenly eased the terrible turmoil in Harry's own mind. He saw something then—only he could ease this for Finn. He could give Finn a parting gift. He could soothe the absolute horror of his own end that Harry saw reflected in Finn's eyes.

'I'm scared Finn, but ... I'm more frightened of going on.' He smiled softly and touched Finn's arm, 'Am I supposed to give you some advice or something at this point? I really have no idea how this all goes, Finn.'

Harry chuckled, the sound of his own gurgling laughter lifting a little more of the weight from him.

But Finn could not look up. His lips trembled and his hands fell to his lap. The thought of looking Harry in the face made him tremble—he could not cast himself into those eyes.

'I ... I don't know, Harry,' Finn sniffed up the snot that threatened to dribble from his nose.

'Ha! Finn, that's all bullshit ... what could I tell you? I'm just a bloody dinosaur. You know what you need to know, huh? It's all yours already, Finn.'

Finn looked up quickly to see if there was mockery in Harry's face but found none. He only saw Harry's eyes, wide with the intimacy of the end, resting like polished grey marbles in that narrow, ravaged face, and Harry's smile, bright but weak, in the increasing light from the window. He squeezed Harry's cold hand hard but still he found it difficult to speak, 'Harry, I … '

'Go on, eh? Go and sit outside.' Harry squeezed his hand. 'You don't need to stay, I'm fine with it, Finn, really I am. Claire and Collis will be here to finish things, huh?' Harry laid his other hand on Finn's and they stayed like this for a while until Finn final spoke softly to Harry.

'I … I don't know what to say, Harry. I … '

Harry shook his head and closed his eyes briefly before he spoke, 'It was good to travel with you, eh? Having you along … at first I thought you'd be a pain in the arse … but it helped me. More than you know.' He smiled broadly at the young man sitting, hunched up next to him, 'What can either of us say, really?'

Standing, Finn paused for a moment longer as though to speak, but he only nodded to the older man, a fragile smile finally creasing his face. He looked into Harry's faded grey eyes and held them, 'Goodbye, Harry—you have been good to me.' And he turned and hurried out into the morning.

* * *

Finn sat on the grass outside as the sun climbed above the breakwall and the heat began to rise with it. His eyes stung, his lips felt thick and blubbery, but no tears ran down his face.

At last he heard movements in the sickbay and soft, indiscernible voices before another elongated silence caused his mind to whirl, guessing at what was taking place inside. He breathed deeply and thought of his and Harry's long journey here—that plodding passage across the blasted plains and up over those mountains seemed an eternity ago now. That long journey, to end like this, he thought. He shuddered then and looked upwards at the cloudless, brightening sky and exhaled, feeling utterly exhausted.

The door of the hut finally opened but he dared not look. Claire and Collis stepped down onto the grass and came over to sit beside him and Claire put an arm around his shoulders.

'It's over,' she whispered. 'He's gone, Finn. It went well for him.'

With her words he felt a sudden vacuum suck the air from his chest. The vacuum, the vacancy where Harry had once been, seemed to expand, and a great spectre seemed to coalesce in the air above him. But, just as the spectre seemed about to overwhelm him, the apparition burst and Harry's shadow shrank back and settled again to something fitting the human scale. Finn saw something else freed up by that vacancy–there was a hint of gentle relief, not for himself, but for Harry and the cessation of his pain. Finn hung his head between his knees for a moment before he looked first to Collis and then to Claire.

'Thank you. Thank you, both, I ... I couldn't have done that.'

Claire looked at him, her face close to his, and squeezed his shoulder hard. 'It's not easy, Finn. It is never easy, but in the end, the end was owned by Harry. He was the one who made the decision–anything else would have been a cruelty, wouldn't it?'

He nodded weakly. The three of them sat on the grass and watched the bay brighten to full day. Finn lay back on the still cool grass. Even with them both by his side, he felt the unnerving chill of loneliness, as though he were a boat that had suddenly slipped its moorings and was being drawn outwards, to the sea.

Finn

The battered mini-bus had dropped Finn, and two others who had come in from the country, on the city fringe. Carrying his heavy pack and his bedroll, it took Finn the entire day to reach the outskirts of the city proper as he followed the highway as it cut through the suburbs. He had company for the first couple of hours but the other two men had peeled off into the suburbs to scavenge for their communities and Finn had continued on alone. Occasionally he saw people in ones and twos on the streets walking, driving battered cars or riding bicycles but none stopped when he tried calling to them.

For most of the day the streets were lined with dilapidated, single-storey brick houses, all silent, even where he saw evidence of recent habitation. Decaying gardens lay in front of each house, dried and long dead through lack of watering and littered with piles of old furniture and broken household items. On the main roads there were abandoned cars, some still being stripped by wary men and women who, most times, refused to even acknowledge him, let alone answer his requests for directions or, if they did reply, they were sullen and vague and quickly turned away.

Throughout the day he saw distant columns of smoke out in the suburbs, above the tiled roofs of the houses and, once or twice, he came upon a still-burning house, but he never heard the wail of sirens. Even with the infrequent sightings of people, the streets remained uncannily quiet. Finn's footsteps seemed loud in his ears and the far-away yapping of dogs echoed in the eerie relinquishment of the streets. Once, off in the distance, he saw a pack of rangy-looking dogs trotting along a street and saw their heads rise and swivel in his direction as he drew near and then, as one, they turned and slunk away through a broken fence at the rear of a house.

He walked on in the silence. The footpaths were buckled and cracked, dead weeds clogged the gutters and by midday he started to come upon the first mounds of rotting rubbish in the gutters, and then collections of tattered garbage bags, deposited in great piles on the street corners. The stink from these mounds of decay, as he hurried past, made him gag and hold his breath. Eventually, as the piles became more frequent, he was forced to tie a t-shirt around his mouth and nose to hold off some of the stench.

At each major street intersection there was a large billboard, put up by the area's water supply company. Each sign told of the hours and days each week when water would be available through the mains and the restricted amount each household was allowed and, in large, bold lettering, the fines for using more than each household's allotted allocation. Many of the signs were burnt out or vandalised with roughly painted, angry anti-water rationing slogans.

Sitting in the gutter resting, Finn heard the roar of a vehicle winding its way through the streets toward him and, as he gawked, a utility passed him. A slogan on its door read Conglomerate Farming Employment Services. It slowed to pass a mound of rubbish and he saw in the metal cage on its tray a crowd of islander men and women, their dark fearful faces staring back at him as the utility disappeared toward the suburban fringes.

He walked on through this desolation as the sun slowly sank behind the roofs. Then in the growing darkness, as the houses began to crowd closer to the road, becoming lines of decaying terraces and shop fronts, he climbed over a broken wire fence and crept into the back of an abandoned shop to sleep.

He awoke when first light began filtering through cracks in the boarded-up windows of the shop. Lying in his bedroll, he surveyed the graffiti-covered walls and ceiling of the room in the dim light. The floor where he lay was covered in a thick blanket of dust. The wooden doorframes and window architraves had been stripped and, in one corner, the floorboards had been burnt through and the walls were blackened with the smoke of an old fire. In the light of morning, the decay seemed even more unsettling.

As he unwrapped the parcel of cooked vegetables and a small potato they had given him as he left The Bay, Finn heard a commotion filtering in from the street. Curious, he abandoned his breakfast and cautiously left the shop to investigate. The voices rose as he circled to the road and, climbing over the fence, he saw a large group of people had gathered around a badly dented, covered truck parked up on the footpath. Approaching cautiously, he watched the driver and another man, hefting a rifle, climb down from the cab and walk to the rear of the truck and unlock the roller door.

The crowd pushed forward as the door clattered upwards and Finn heard the man carrying the rifle curse and shout above the noise of the crowd, waving the gun above their heads.

'Hey! Back up! There'll be enough for most. If you get pushy, we're off.'

Reluctantly, the crowd backed off to form a disorderly line while the driver of the truck climbed in and flung a short thick hose out onto the ground. Beyond the man, several large plastic water tanks were lined up along one side of the truck's interior. With swift, economical movements the man bent and attached the hose to the first tank while the other stood watch, his rifle barrel still pointing above the heads of the crowd.

'Right, who's up first?' the armed man nodded to a woman with a small boy at her side, and they came forward and put down a large, battered, plastic water container at the man's feet. The man scowled at the woman and she produced a few grimy notes from her pocket and begrudgingly handed them over.

Finn had come up to standing at the rear of the group, beside a gaunt, roughly-shaven man carrying small containers tucked under each arm. The man looked Finn up and down suspiciously.

'Where's your water drum?'

'I don't need any water, I have my own,' Finn replied, nervously putting on a smile.

'Then what the fuck are you doing here?' The man glowered at him for a moment before turning and moving off a few paces, but Finn followed him.

'Why are you lining up to get water?' Finn asked.

'What? Where the hell are you from?' The man looked at Finn as though he were a gibbering fool. 'The rations are never enough. They cut them again last week. If you need more you have to buy it off the Leggers.'

'Leggers? Oh … right, I see,' Finn smiled again. 'I'm from out west.' And he shrugged.

Showing no interest the man moved off again, leaving Finn to watch as the woman and the boy hurried off with their heavy container and the line slowly inched forwards. After half an hour, the man doling out the water shouted out above the noise of the crowd.

"That's it … water's finished, tanks are empty. We're back Tuesday.' And, amid grumblings and curses, the dejected crowd began to trickle away into the nearby houses and off along the side roads, disappearing into the surrounding suburbs.

Finn stayed and watched as the two men packed up the hose and began to shut the roller door but, as they were getting ready to leave, a thought came to him and he hurried forward.

'Are you heading into the city centre?'

The man with the rifle considered him for a moment, 'Nup.'

Finn's face fell, 'Not even close?'

The man stared again into Finn's face and snorted, 'Hey, Russ, this fella wants a lift to the centre. What you think?'

'What?' A muffled laugh came from the second man as he climbed up into the cab. 'The centre ... Really?' There was a pause, 'He goes in the back–we'll drop him on the M10 ring and he can walk in from there. I'm not going closer than that.'

Finn asked them to wait and rushed back to the abandoned shop to hurriedly pack his bedroll and belongings. The man stood frowning by the truck's roller-door and grinned maliciously when Finn staggered up with his bag, his mouth crammed with food. Motioning him up into the back with the rifle barrel, he heaved the roller door closed behind him and Finn was plunged into darkness. Sitting heavily against the empty tanks, he grasped his bag and bedroll tightly between his knees as the truck pulled away, swerving this way and that through the streets.

* * *

The truck braked suddenly and stopped. A moment later the roller door was flung upwards with a deafening clatter. Blinded momentarily by the fierce light of the morning and covered in sweat from being in the stuffy back of the truck, Finn clambered down with his things. Happy to be free of the rattling and slewing of the truck, he closed his eyes for a moment before he gazed around at his surroundings.

On every side, huge buildings towered above the roadway. The driver had stopped on a weed-strewn, raised freeway that curved amid the mirrored towers at the edge of the city's centre. A monolithic forest of glass and stainless steel flashed and sparkled in the sunlight. Each building echoed the reflections of the others around it, bamboozling Finn's widening eyes. He gasped in awe and his mouth dropped open at his first real glimpse of the city proper.

He turned to the man leaning against the truck, 'It's amazing, huh?'

The man shrugged and shook his head at Finn's excitement. 'There's a staircase down, along that way a hundred metres or so.'

Finn thanked him for the lift, eliciting another disinterested shrug, and gathered his stuff to leave. But, as he began walking, the man called out to him.

'It's not pretty down there.'

Finn turned, looked back and caught the man smiling wryly, 'I'm just saying, that's all.' The driver turned, climbed back into the cab and the truck roared away through the rubbish and weeds of the freeway.

The raw concrete staircase from the freeway led Finn down to the streets below the forest of glittering towers. As he struggled down it with his backpack and bedroll, he saw the city crowd into the dreary grid of a large intersection. The harsh shafts of broken light streaming down from above lit on a scene that shattered Finn's initial awe at the sight of the high rises. On the street, long lines of cars, left by their owners when they were unable to escape whatever chaos had caused the colossal traffic jam, stood covered in thick grey dust. As he descended, a history of wracked upheaval crowded around Finn.

Trucks and buses were parked haphazardly on footpaths or poked their snouts into the lines of cars, caught in the gridlocked traffic. Opposite his vantage point on the stairs was a long broad boulevard running east towards the coast. It was almost completely blocked by piles of tyres, furniture, timber and burnt-out cars and trucks, and the massive jumble seemed to Finn to have been constructed to create a clumsy blockade across the boulevard that led off into the city centre.

Stumbling from the stairs he lowered his things to the road and stood gawking. Walking to the middle of the wide t-intersection he slowly turned in a circle. The lower floors of the buildings around the intersection were gutted. Streetlights and power poles had been brought down among the abandoned vehicles and, like the giant vines of a rainforest, fallen power lines looped and snaked across the street and up to the buildings. Shattered glass and pulverised concrete covered the footpaths and scorch marks scarred many of the shopfronts. Everywhere windows and doors were shattered or clouded with dust and soot. Their dark openings stared vacantly at him. Furniture hung from many windows above him, teetering above the cluttered footpaths, where more chairs and tables had been thrown, as if the buildings had been ransacked in a fury of wanton destruction.

Finn felt his anxiety rising as he searched nervously through the shattered windows for signs of life and saw none. He squinted, ducking to see inside the broken windscreens of the abandoned vehicles around him, but saw no signs of life there either. There was only a frozen stillness in all that chaos. A brittle silence reigned here—a silence vastly different from the thick, hugging quiet of the country of the west. It was a silence that to Finn seemed as fragile as tinfoil. He stood frozen for a long while, lest he disturb the clutter of metal and debris littering the tar around him and wake some hidden, brooding beast.

Shaking off his paralysis, he retrieved his pack and bedroll and began tentatively picking his way across the intersection. Finding a way through the cluttered blockade, he began snaking his way through more abandoned cars and smashed office furniture, following the wide boulevard east, towards the ocean.

* * *

An hour later, hungry and exhausted, Finn rounded a corner as a great whooshing roar and the sound of shattering glass filled the air. Fifty metres down the street a building was being devoured by flames. The five or six storey building had once housed a bank—a broken sign on its concrete façade and a raw, gaping hole where an automatic teller had been torn from the wall told of the building's past. Long tongues of flame spewed from the ground-floor windows and black, oily smoke billowed from its broken front doors. Finn stopped to watch as a large window shattered somewhere above and glass rained down to the street below.

Suddenly, through the oily smoke, three figures burst from the bank's doors. Staggering away from the burning building, the figures collapsed on the footpath opposite and lay there coughing and choking. After taking a few steps towards them, Finn paused again, realising their coughing had turned into convulsive spasms of laughter. Puzzled, Finn backed up into the shadows of a doorway to watch and listen.

The three were close to Finn's age, perhaps a little younger. They were all clad in an odd assortment of light, ill-fitting, summer clothing and their hair was long and oily and wild about their dusty, sun-tanned faces. One of them, Finn saw, was a young woman. She was short and stocky, and wore not much more than a pair of black lace-up boots, cut-off jeans and a t-shirt trimmed to just below her breasts, exposing her flat, tanned stomach. The two men wore cut-off army cargo pants, one a light singlet, the other, the taller and broader of the two, sported a loud Hawaiian shirt and a bandana tied around his neck. Their laughter subsiding, they stood, brushing the fresh dust and ash from their filthy clothes, and watched as the flames leapt to the higher floors of the building. Then the young woman shouted above the roar of the inferno.

'Did ya see that freaking pile of furniture in the elevator shaft go up, Cain? Did ya? It was a fucking fire storm in there!' She coughed and lay back on the bonnet of a parked car.

The shorter of the two men, the bottom of his face covered in a thin ragged beard, smiled broadly, revealing a missing front tooth.

'Shit, we were lucky to get outta there alive!' And then he snorted and fell into another fit of uncontrollable laughter.

'I told you, Kat, I told you … don't make the freaking pile so big, but you cracked fuckers never listen!' The third man, in the Hawaiian shirt, seemed to be taking their narrow escape more seriously, till he turned his narrow sun-baked face to the woman sitting on the bonnet, his grin clearly visible, and gave her a huge bear hug. 'Peep, that was fucking adrenal!'

'We had plenty of time, Sam, plenty of time,' the woman's rosy-pink, cheerful face remained serious for a moment longer before, unable to contain herself, she broke into a huge grin.

Giggling, the three turned their faces to the building just as the flames blew out another huge window and glass rained down on the abandoned cars across the street. Amid the sparkling hail of glass, the three let out yells and whoops of delight and, in unison, closed their eyes and silently raised their right arms and held up a middle finger in a raw salute to the building's fiery destruction. After a second or two the three turned away and, picking up a tattered backpack each, began walking towards the doorway where Finn was hiding.

So as not to startle them, Finn stepped from the shadows before they reached him but the three still jumped, startled by his sudden appearance.

'Fucking mayhem! Where did you pop up from?' the shorter man, Cain, eyed him suspiciously.

'Sorry, I … I was watching … I didn't want to jump out and scare you.' Finn spoke softly, growing uncomfortable under their gaze.

The woman, Kat, snorted with derision, 'You didn't scare us, ya dupe. But you'd better watch it—creeping around—some of the peeps round here would log ya off for a stunt like that.'

The four of them stood uncomfortably for a few seconds before Cain spoke in a more friendly tone, 'You're not from here right? Where're you from?'

'Um … from out west, from the plains,' Finn saw their faces blanch in disbelief for a moment before the three covered their shock with knowing nods.

'Out west … you've come a hell of a long way, huh? It's a cauldron out there they say!' From behind her fringe of sun-bleached, matted hair, Kat stared at him with a building respect. She sniffed and wiped her nose on the dirty sleeve of her cut off t-shirt. 'What ya loggin' onto in the city?'

Finn's confused look made her laugh and she repeated her question, 'What are you doing here, ya dupe?'

'Oh … well … nothing really … I came in … well, you know, to see what's happening … ' He found it difficult to explain himself under their gaze, but thankfully another roaring gout of flame saved him from further interrogation, as the three looked nervously over their shoulders at the fire now consuming the upper floors of building across the street.

'What-eva dupe.' Loosing interest in Finn, Sam looked back and forth, scanning the street. 'This Riser is gunna come down any freakin' minute. Drones'll be over—so we're fucking off.' And he pulled the bandana up over his nose and mouth.

'Oh, right,' Finn stood there mutely and the three stared at him blankly before Kat shrugged.

'Come on. Ya had food today? We're off to the Bus to get some lunch, come if ya want … or not … either way, it's no skin off us.' She smiled and raised her eyebrows and stepped around him, her two friends following.

'Oh … OK, guess I could … I'm starving.' Finn straightened his pack and slung his bedroll back over his shoulder and struck out after them as another shower of glass and falling masonry crashed thunderously to the street.

* * *

The Bus turned out to be a battered public bus that had been turned into a food charity kitchen. Completely covered in graffiti, it was parked alongside the broken gates of a large city park. Its wheels gone, the bus stood precariously on four assorted piles of concrete and bricks. Its windows, covered with heavy steel grilles, were secured with padlocks and metal bracing.

Finn could see the park behind the high iron fence was filled with humpies and shacks of scavenged timber and steel and there were ragged tents and tarpaulins stretched between the dead trees and steel lamp posts. Figures moved to and fro between the shacks and humpies and, as he watched, people began moving along the paths toward the gates and the Bus, as two or three men busied themselves pushing up the bus's steel shutters, setting up for the midday meal.

The intersection slowly filled with rag-tag groups of people from the park and many more who slowly filtered in from the surrounding streets. Finn stood gawking at the dishevelled assortment of city folk—he had never seen so many people in one place. Some were old and some were obviously sick, but there were families too in the crowd, the young children pressed to their parents' legs. All were clad in loose summer clothing, fighting the heat and sweltering humidity. Some men and women came and sat, dressed only in sarongs or their underwear and sandals or thongs. Hanging back, the families and the older people looked about nervously at the groups young people, like Kat and her friends, shouting and scuffling with each other for a position closer to the Bus.

While they waited Finn asked Kat why the three had set fire to the building. She stared at him thoughtfully before replying.

'To see the fucker burn, peep,' she stared at him and her eyes, looking up into his, glowed with a pale fire. 'Why not? They're fucking useless now ... they've been stripped ... no one wants them. No one was living in that one.' She shrugged again, 'Pushes our buttons, you know, to see those risers burn ... Bringing 'em down's kinda ... I don't know ... fun, isn't it?' She grinned and punched his arm, 'Ya big dupe, this is the time–the time to watch things tumble.'

Finn looked at her quizzically and Kat rolled her eyes at his bumpkin ignorance. 'City's crumbling, Finn. The world's collapsing around our freaking ears–we're just speeding things up!' She grinned fiercely and laughed, clapped her hands and for a second danced a bizarre twitching jig in front of him. 'This part of the city is ours now ... we fuckin' own it. The police, the companies–they're gone–fuckin' holed up in the centre blocks, skulking behind the barricades. Sure the drones come over but we're not freakin' scared–what can they do to us now?' She spoke with bravado but her eyes darted from Finn's, searching out Sam and Cain standing close by.

She gestured at the derelict buildings that towered over the dilapidated shanties of the park, 'This is our playground now ... the Company has given it up. The street peeps own these blocks and we can trash them whenever we damn well please!'

'But ... what's the point to it?'

'Ha! Finn, you dupe … that's exactly it … ' she smiled broadly at him. 'The freakin' point, peep … is that there is no freakin' point. The only truth is in crash and burn. Crash and fucking burn!' She smiled a snarling smile and looked into his bemused face.

'Don't ya get it? This is it, Finn, there's nothing left for us now. The companies have abandoned us dumb dupes. All those rich bastards have gone to the Last Refuges. Some thought they'd protect us, take us with em maybe, but we knew they would sell us out. Sun keeps burning, Finn,' the words shot out. 'This dried up husk … this is their parting gift for us … our playground.' Kat gazed up at the buildings and then spat on the concrete between her feet.

He looked around at the buildings, the debris and piles of garbage and wrecked cars, the scattered tarpaulins and timber humpies, trying desperately to get his head around all that hopelessness in her words. 'But what will you do? What will you do in the future? I mean … where will you go … in the end?'

She shrugged and frowned, 'Where is there left to go? Humanity is loggin' itself off–there's nowhere to fuckin' go. That's solid carbon truth.' She threw up her hands and grin as though she had told him a huge joke and was waiting for him to laugh.

'Well, what about outside the city … out there?' he swept his hand around.

'Out there … what's out there, Finn? Hope? Why did you come here, Finn, if it's so freakin' cool out there? Everyone's crowding in, coming here. It's the end game, Finn, and you've come to us … to play!' She stared into his face and broke again into a cackle of forced laughter.

To silence her, Finn almost told her of The Bay but something held him back.

'What about Antarctica or Alaska? I've heard that's where there's still some rain, still some hope.'

'Hope!' The stiff smile faded from her face and she turned to Sam and shouted above the noise of the crowd, 'Finn here, he want's to know why we don't go to the enclaves. There's hope there he's telling me.'

Sam swivelled to look at Finn, and a sneer crept across his face. 'The enclaves are in flames. There's no hope there. The war is making the refuges into one big freaking sewer. The Brazilians, the Chinese, the fucking Indians ... they're tearing Antarctica apart–they're fighting each other and the god-damn Predator Corps for last blood ... Alaska and Greenland are even worse they say. Full of refugees fighting for land, the Companies fighting for the last scraps of oil and water. It's freakin' carnage!' He laughed scornfully, 'There's hope all right, dupe–get a gun and join the fuckin' army! Only a total hick, fried outa their mind, would go down there now!'

Finn felt humiliated by Sam's scorn but, as Sam turned his broad frame away, Kat patted Finn's arm, 'Sam only got back from an Antarctic mercenary tour a couple of months back–fighting for the Chinese ... or a Patagonian Coal Corp ... one of 'em, anyway. He says it's one big blast zone down there–depleted uranium munitions and GM bacterial landmines–all the latest shit. He's still a bit fried from the gaming down there. Don't take his shit too seriously.' Her face saddened but she shrugged it off and moved up as the food line shuffled along.

* * *

They ate their meal of boiled potatoes and a small palm-sized portion of rice and watery lentils from worn plastic bowls, sitting in small groups, squashed in across the concrete entrance to the park. Finn was happy to listen while Kat and her friends spoke rapidly, discussing the events of the city with others nearby, most of which Finn followed only vaguely. Then, finally, as the sun disappeared behind the taller buildings, the three stood and picked up their packs and made ready to leave. Kat stared down at Finn where he still sat.

'We're off across the city. There's a rumour another block has been abandoned after the barricades were moved back—might find some copper there—old wires and pipes—to sell for c-credits. Come and help us for a cut, if you got nothin' better to do,' she smiled down at him and her twinkling gaze made Finn glow a little.

'Sure, OK,' he stammered.

Cutting through laneways tangled with piles of rubbish and wrecked furniture they moved towards the city's centre. At one intersection they passed a group watching a burning mound of debris. As they drew near Finn saw the bodies of dogs, hundreds of them, in the flames, and he recoiled, asking Kat what was happening.

'Dog cull,' she replied matter-of-factly. 'Every few months we have to hunt 'em out or they get out of control and start attacking people while they sleep.'

They hurriedly crossed the city, following Sam's lead, until they were abruptly brought to a halt by a flooded street. The water, full of foul smelling scum and debris, covered the entire roadway and footpath and had flowed into the surrounding buildings, blocking their route.

'Fuck!' Sam cursed loudly. 'Forgot it was coming up to high tide. We have to go round by the foot bridge, over the old rail lines.' And they doubled back for a few blocks before crossing the raised walkway to gain higher ground.

As they drew near the centre, the buildings showed less sign of destruction. The broader streets were soon free of abandoned cars and there was evidence of people living in the floors above them. People appeared from the alleys and doorways along the road but quickly turned and hurried about their business, avoiding looking into each other's faces as they passed.

The four of them popped out from a narrow alley into the brightness of a long broad avenue. In the distance a tall, grey steel barricade cut across the street and Finn could see the small figures of what looked like soldiers patrolling its high ramparts. On the side streets leading up to the barricade, there were massive piles of garbage piled up, almost two storeys high, as though these streets had now been transformed into the rubbish dumps of the city within the barriers.

They stopped and Kat and Sam studied a wrinkled map laid out on the dusty bonnet of a car, glancing up nervously every now and then at the distant fortifications. Finn's nose wrinkled at the stench that oozed from the garbage-filled alleys and Cain, catching his grimace, laughed.

'Not nice, huh? You'll get used to it, eh?' patting his arm he turned his gaze back to the map.

After a brief discussion they headed out again, zigzagging through the streets, seemingly skirting the fortified centre, until eventually they stood before a tall, relatively untouched office building. Finn gazed upwards at the unbroken windows and the reflections of the solar panels high up on its flanks.

'Fuck, Kat, there's still some panels up there! Peeps, we've hit a lode here!' Sam's voice was high with the excitement of their find.

But, standing there, they heard clanging and crashing coming from within the building and Cain cursed softly, 'Some peeps've beat us to it.'

'Ah, come on there'll be enough left for us,' Kat grabbed and tugged at Cain's sleeve. But, just as they were about to cross the street, a group staggered from the building carrying rolls of electrical wire and bent lengths of thin copper water pipe. When they emerged into the daylight, the group glanced nervously about and stopped, catching sight of Finn and the others. The two men and a woman were Asian. Maybe only eighteen or twenty at most, their dark eyes stared at them nervously and their faces grew uncertain.

'What the fu– You thieving bastards!' Finn jumped as Sam roared at the group across the street.

Kat turned to Finn, 'Climate boaties ... Chinese illegals most likely ... these bastards come across cause their countries are screwed. They steal anything they can get their freakin' dirty hands on. Watch on, peep ... Sam hates the fuckin' illegals!'

At Sam's shout the Asian group tensed and looked up and down the street, searching for an escape. Finn followed as Kat, Sam and Cain stalked slowly forward, closing in on the frightened group, shouting abuse and screaming at them to drop the pipes and wire.

Finn flinched as Kat screamed next to him, 'You boaties can fuck off! We own these blocks. There's nothin' for ya here ... hear me!'

Fear welled up in Finn but, not knowing what else to do, he walked forward with the others. As they drew closer, the three refugees suddenly dropped their spoils and sprinted off along the street, disappearing into a narrow alley. Finn felt a flash of relief but it quickly shrivelled as Sam and Cain sprang off after them, shouting to Kat and Finn to cut them off before the three emerged around the corner, at the other end of the alley. Kat sprang away and Finn reluctantly followed her.

Panting, he caught her as she stopped at the other entrance to the alley and looking in, Finn saw that Sam and Cain had cornered the youths between two upturned garbage hoppers at a turn in the alley. One of Asian boys was lying on the ground as Sam and Cain kicked and beat him. Finn's breathing caught and his skin crawled as he heard the soft, sickening thuds of the blows. Then the one on the ground began to cry out weakly, pleading in broken English, but the blows continued to rain down unabated.

Finn flinched and his bile rose as he heard the gleeful laughter of Sam and Cain as they stood over the inert form. Finn's heart shrank at the naked hatred he saw building in the two with each blow that they inflicted.

Finn stood rooted to the spot, watching on as the two men continued to beat the youth on the ground. So intent were Sam and Cain they failed to notice the other young man and the woman edge between the bins and sprint off towards the alley's mouth, where Finn and Kat stood.

Kat grabbed his arm, 'Find something—a weapon!'

Stooping quickly, she snatched up a length of steel bracing lying in the gutter. In a daze, Finn looked about but did not move as the two bore down on them. As they closed in, the fleeing couple slowed, realising their path was cut off, and Finn saw the wide-eyed fear etched on their sweating faces. In the stifling heat and stink of the alley the woman's brown eyes held Finn's for a fraction of a second before she screwed them shut and, followed closely by her companion, ran on, picking up pace as they closed on Finn and Kat.

Kat let out a huge, blood-curdling whoop and raised the length of steel to strike the fleeing boy as he tried to pass them. At the last minute, without thought, Finn turned and, with a lowered shoulder, shunted Kat into the gutter and, sidestepping him, the two refugees flew past, broke out into the street and were gone.

Finn stood there panting. Kat struggled to her feet and raised the steel weapon but the two refugees were long gone. Then she swung on Finn and spat at him.

'What the ... What'd you do that for, you fucking dupe!' Her eyes smoldered with her growing fury.

'I ... I couldn't ... ' his shoulders sank. He looked to the ground, as the full potential of his betrayal flooded through him, his arms and legs felt weak and about to fail as he backed away from her.

Finn failed to see Sam's blow coming as the heavy-set man stalked in from behind. Sam's fist struck Finn's cheek and he saw stars and staggered sideways. Sam's angry face loomed large in his swirling vision. He screamed at Finn–the spit and froth of rage flecked on his cracked lips.

'You stupid country fuck! You let those boatie bastards go!'

Finn recoiled at the venom in the other's words, 'But what did they do to you? I ... those people ... they're in the same hole as us ... can't you ... ' Finn's face burned and his voice sounded weak and far away.

'What did they do? You dumb dupe, they're here to steal our fucking fruit–our c-credits! This city is ours, not some damn climate boaties'. We were fucking born in this hellhole. We've earned the spoils. They can't just come here and take what's ours. I don't care how screwed their freakin' country is. Fuck them and fuck you!'

Finn stood there, his head hanging, unable to look into Sam's furious face. His eyes suddenly stung with the salt of building tears. 'I ... '

'You freak! You'd give it all away, ya weak bastard!' Kat's rage and scorn rained down on him. She stepped up and shoved him hard in the chest and he sprawled backwards to lie in the dust of the road, his pack and bedroll in the dirt beside him.

'I'm sorry ... I ... ' he mumbled through the snot, fighting back his tears.

'You're lucky we don't log you off!' Cain bent over him, his fists clenched. 'Fuck off back to the hell you came from–go starve out there ya boatie-lovin' dupe!'

Finn covered his face to ward off the blows he knew must follow.

'Come on. Leave this useless freak. Grab the wire and pipe and we'll leg it to the Trader before it gets dark,'

Kat spat on the ground beside Finn, stepped over his body and strode off. Finn flinched as Sam feigned a kick at him and sneered down at him as the two men followed Kat, grabbed the pipes and wire and set off along the street. None of them looked back as Finn watched them go.

Finn sat up. His face throbbed, dust and dirt clung to the streaks of tears and snot on his face and he shuddered with the jarring cocktail of humiliation and falling adrenalin. His mind whirled. He wiped his face and sniffed and shook his head dejectedly. He was alone in the chaos of the city again. After only a day his dreams seemed shattered beyond repair. The pent-up fury he had seen in Kat and the others frightened Finn and made him shiver uncontrollably despite the heat radiating from the tar. He hung his head between his knees for a moment and then, hearing a sound, he glanced up and saw through his bleary eyes, the two young refugees returning to help their beaten companion.

They looked at him coldly, but he tried to smile to reassure them before they disappeared into the alley, to return a few moments later supporting their hobbling friend. All three glowered at him. He struggled to his feet and, as he stood there, they spat into the dirt of the footpath and turned away, paying him no further heed.

Tears welled up again in his eyes. Exhaustion filled him as he looked about the streets. In the failing light he saw people at a distance, flitting in and out of alleys and doorways, going about their business. He stared off down through the canyons of the semi-deserted buildings and cluttered streets. It all seemed so desolate and grey to him then. The greyness fell on him. The shiny skin of the city had been utterly burnt away. The faces of the people he had met here flickered across his mind and all seemed cold or angry now. The rage in them ate at him. Finn felt then, the bitterness of disappointment overwhelm him. But he now knew in that instant, somewhere among the stew of bitterness and humiliation, what he would do.

Finn and Morty

Finn trudged slowly from the road along the two-rut track toward the sea. The smell of salt and the raw sting of seaweed and fish filled his nostrils and he paused. And, closing his eyes, he listened to the waves breaking out on the beach beyond the dunes and he smiled.

The bruise on his cheek had started to yellow and the pain in his jaw had faded a little in the last few days, but the sting of the fight, the humiliation, and the anger of that place, still stained his thoughts. Cutting through his melancholy, the roar of the breakers lifted him a little and his shoulders straightened as he walked on toward the beach.

Cresting the final dune, the warm breeze off the bay brushed his face and lifted the blanket of heat a little. Looking down on the beach he saw the small waves rushing in to push up the tidemarks on the sloping sand, and there, bizarrely, only a hundred metres away, stood the camel and the dray. The camel stood chewing and slowly lifted its huge head. Looking up to where Finn stood, it belched loudly in greeting and Finn smiled and yelled out in return.

Two hundred metres farther down the beach, in the shelter of the fore dune, a small figure looked up at Finn's cry, waved and began dragging a large piece of driftwood down the low cliff of sand and along the beach toward the dray. Finn clambered down the dune to the wetter sand and walked toward the camel. Finn smiled broadly as the figure drew closer, recognising Morty as the young boy yanked and tugged the timber down the beach. Surprised, his spirits rose at the sight of the boy and he felt a strange heat in his chest. He quickened his pace a little and reached the dray well ahead of Morty and stood waiting. The camel gazed at him and snorted, its huge questioning eye berating him. Slapping the beast's shaggy neck he rested his face against its side, feeling the beast's chest heave and slowly fill with air as the camel inhaled.

Morty arrived and without comment Finn helped him lift the heavy length of driftwood into the back and settle it with the others piled there.

Dusting off his hands, Morty looked up shyly, 'Hey. Finn, you're back huh?'

Finn smiled broadly, bent and gave the boy a huge hug, 'Yep, I'm back Morty.' And he felt the boy's thin, wiry arms about his waist tighten in return. Morty mumbled into Finn's chest, 'The others will be happy. We were worried about you.'

Finn said nothing to that. His throat was too thick to speak. He turned and walked out toward the surging waves and stood looking out at the bay, his boots sinking in the soft wet sand. Morty watched him silently for a long while before he grew impatient and shouted out to him.

'Come on, Finn, give me a hand to collect a few more pieces and we'll get back for lunch.'

* * *

They followed the same track that had brought Harry, Finn and the camel to The Bay only a couple of weeks earlier. That now seemed like an eternity ago to Finn and he suddenly missed Harry enormously. A sharp pang of loss swept him and he saw Harry's long face lying on the pillow the day he had gone and suddenly he wanted to speak to him and tell him of his trip to the city. Then he thought of Samuel and Nettie and wondered desperately what was happening with them—wondered if they too were coming east.

'It was awful. The city is hell, you know,' he turned and looked down at Morty.

'Really? I thought it might be.'

'The young people, they burn buildings for no reason … just for fun. I … they're so angry, Morty. They don't seem to care about anything more than getting what they can–scrounging and fighting. There are people from Asia–climate refugees, desperate people–but the city people hate them … It's not the refugees fault, Morty, no more than anyone else's. But the city people, they can't see it. Their anger, it's so … I don't know … aimless … or hopeless … or something.'

Morty looked at him and his brow furrowed, 'Does it make any difference–the fighting, I mean? Why don't they just help each other?'

'Well, I suppose they do in a way,' he scratched his head. 'They have gangs, they pick sides fighting each other, I guess. But there's not much love for each other–not that I saw anyway.'

'Why?'

Finn grew suddenly confused. 'I don't know, Morty. It's … it's like they can't help it … like they're just doing … reacting without thinking. They're too busy fighting each other for scraps. It's like they're too busy surviving to see anything other than what's coming in the next minute or hour. It felt like we were in some kind of hell, but none of them could see beyond it … '

'But they can leave, can't they?'

Finn paused and thought, his brow furrowed in concentration, and scratched his head again, 'Well … they could but … ' he paused again, his mind trying to rope it all into one thought. 'I guess people find security even in hell, if it's all they know.'

Beside him Morty fell silent and chewed his lip for a while as the dray lurched along the uneven track, the load of wood creaking and shifting as they drew closer to The Bay. Finally Morty looked up, smiled at Finn and spoke in his lilting, carefree way. 'Well, if they do leave, and they come here we'd help them, eh? That's what counts, huh?'

And Finn laughed then and shook Morty's shoulder with a surge of affection. He looked up as the dray crested the final rise and they could see the sun-bleached, white, weatherboard buildings and Finn saw three or four figures walking across the grass toward the growing houses. A sudden shyness fell on him and Finn felt a desperate need to be alone for a while.

Turning to Morty he smiled at the boy, 'I think I might sit up here for a bit, I'll come down when they ring the bell for lunch, eh?'

Morty frowned but shrugged, 'OK. Don't be late though, it's soup today.'

'Right-o.'

Finn clambered from the slow-moving dray and watched as the camel and boy wound their way down the slope. The boy climbed down to open the wire gate and lead the camel into the gavel yard in front of the buildings.

Finn climbed a little higher and sat among the dry tussocks, breathing in the air, enjoying the view of the tiny community below and the vast shimmering bay beyond. The sight warmed him and he smiled and rubbed his face with his hands.

Far-off he heard Morty shout to the others, excitedly telling them of Finn's return.

* * *